Poor Lazarus

Maurice Leitch was born in County
Antrim and educated in Belfast. His
first novel, *The Liberty Lad*, was published
in 1965, followed by *Poor Lazarus*, winner
of the 1969 Guardian Fiction Prize. *Silver's
City* won the Whitbread Prize for Fiction in
1981. His most recent novel, *Gilchrist*, was
published by Secker & Warburg in 1994. He
has also written radio plays, short stories
and television screenplays and documen-
taries. He lives in north London with his
family.

MAURICE LEITCH

Poor Lazarus

Minerva

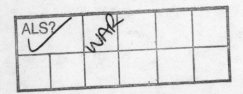

A Minerva Paperback
POOR LAZARUS

First published in 1969
by MacGibbon & Kee
This Minerva edition published 1995
by Mandarin Paperbacks
an imprint of Reed Consumer Books Ltd
Michelin House, 81 Fulham Road, London SW3 6RB
and Auckland, Melbourne, Singapore and Toronto

Copyright © Maurice Leitch 1969, 1985
The author has asserted his moral rights

A CIP catalogue record for this title
is available from the British Library
ISBN 0 7493 9658 X

Typeset by Deltatype Ltd, Ellesmere Port, Cheshire
Printed and bound in Great Britain
by

For Bronagh

"I don't understand you, you don't understand me, and we don't understand ourselves."

"What a ridiculous fool I am! I go about playing the poor Lazarus day in, day out."

Anton Chekhov: Ivanov; Act III

1

FOR THE THIRD TIME in twenty minutes Young John Joe asked the same sly, stupid-seeming question – "Begod, are them boys in earnest at all?" and Packy, his side kick, squinted delightedly towards the laocoon on the television screen. The bald wrestler – the one with the eye-patch, and wearing a black leotard – tightened his leg around his opponent's throat, and the unseen crowd in a hall somewhere in Manchester bayed its sudden approval.

"Bejasus, I wouldn't like to meet up wi' any o' the two of them turks on a dark night. That I wouldn't." Again from Young John Joe. This time not seeming to care if the nudge he gave Packy was noticed or not.

Yarr smiled but didn't answer; he was experiencing a new pain beginning in his head and he wanted to concentrate on its unfamiliarity, explore its boundaries, before it ebbed away and another took its place. It was four o'clock on a Saturday afternoon and the morning feeling of muzziness he awoke to unfailingly since he had stepped up the phenobarbitones was leaving him, and then this new ache had struck, or, rather, nibbled, tentatively at him, as if it wasn't sure if he was palatable enough.

And he felt he was being crowded again, by the two pressing him and then withdrawing, pressing, withdrawing; by the flickering and roar of the television; by the relentless commentator's voice. If he could only slide out from beneath all their weight, away to where he could concentrate, concentrate . . .

"An' wouldn't ya think now they'd cripple the other? The great force o' them landin' on one another like that."

But they were watching *him*, two louts, leaning over *his* counter, in *his* shop, and watching *his* tee vee that he'd lugged up from the kitchen to help kill time on this slowest of all afternoons. And they were thinking to themselves weren't they the great bloody men to be taking the hand out of Yarr.

When they tired of him they would bicycle leisurely to Mallon's Cross where they would stretch on a bank with their Woodbines. They left great bruised channels behind them among the coltsfoot and daisies where they had lain all day, restlessly, like courting couples. And there they would shout at passing girls or pull other youths from bicycles whom they accused of "looking" at them. And if there were no distractions Young John Joe would torment Packy with a nettle until he wept and then thump him and by then it was time for the milking.

Yarr straightened up from his hard chair behind the counter and, proffering his twenty packet, said, "Have a smoke, boys", when what he would have liked to have done was pelt them out into the village street with the tinned ammunition from his shelves at hand bounding off their thick heads. Two years ago, a year ago even, he wouldn't have seen them in his light . . .

Outside, Ballyboe's single street sat sullenly where it was – other streets in other parts of the world *run* because frequent passing of people, vehicles and animals communicate even a brief life to the stones; but since noon Yarr had only tallied two breadvans, four cars, a tractor, a pony and trap, a dozen or so passers-by and a few skinny dogs which had passed and re-passed with longing hungry glances into the bacon-smelling depths of the shop.

The street door was pulled back – a pair of wellington boots (his new stock of seconds, military green, and not selling, bugger them!) holding it open. He had started the habit of keeping it wide like that all day in all weathers the time the I.R.A. campaign was at its height on the Border a few miles away, and his predominantly Catholic customers took their trade away from his – the only Protestant and therefore British – shop in the village. But the inviting interior didn't invite. They walked past to Hickey's, or Reilly's, or McAuley's. Now of course the explosions and the siren's shriek from the police barracks on the hill and the tender's rattling rush through the village to the point of attack were night sounds of the past – well two years ago anyway – and business was rising, not much, but rising . . .

The day was a soft one, full of airy murmurings that barely stirred the dust on the street and the few dead leaves that had strayed in from open country on people's boots and tyres. Yarr noticed a thin withered line of them against the far wall of the shop edging out from behind the open door. *Christ*, he thought, *does that lazy, red-headed lump of a bitch ever use a brush in this place. That rubbish was there yesterday as well!* Without thinking, he shouted, "Bridie!" and the eyes above the counter flickered from his face to each other's, brightening.

The shout had set off inside his head a sickening echo that seemed to bump clumsily off flesh and bone and he waited for it to die. Despite the pain he held reins on himself till she should appear, turning over in his mind with rapidity how he should speak to her and what he would say in front of these two. He knew they would distort it anyway but the desire not to please them was strong.

The kitchen door opened at the end of the passage leading up to the shop, and instead, he heard the sullen slip-slop, slip-slop of *her* slippers. She made the distance in between seem like a hundred miles as they waited for her to appear.

"Hello, Young John Joe," she said, sighing, "Hello, Packy. Isn't the weather awful close?"

They touched their caps. "Hello, Ruby."

She turned her head round to look down at him, sitting on his kitchen chair. The way she spoke, the way she moved, did everything with such self-pity, made him hate her.

"What'd you want Bridie for?" Slow, slow bloody martyrdom. *Look at me, you did this to me . . .*

He asked, "Where is she?" without expression, his eyes fixed on the ugly patterns on her smock. Her hands in the pockets stretched the cotton fabric out slantingly from beneath her breasts and over the bulge underneath.

3

"I told her to take the afternoon off – to go to the carnival in Slaney."

"Oh I see," he said mildly, while underneath raging white-hot. *Told*, by god. *She* told her.

Packy said, "I seen her talkin' to Tony Molloy on the bridge a wee bit after dinner-time. He's home from England you know."

"Ach, an' sure it wasn't all that important, anyway. No matter now," he said.

It fended them off for only a second, then their attention swung back again, like a ball on a chain to crush him. He felt bad for a moment, longing for the shelter of the privy out in the yard with the white-washed, newspapered door shut tight on him and his fingers in his ears closing out everything but the comforting red roar of blood. Or in bed, curled knees to chin, with clasped shins. He had always loved to dream about living in a barrel, or a burrow – a furry little creature – or steel-ringed and rimmed forty thousand leagues under, the way it was in the school reader. *She* laughed at the way he slept. *She* lay like a man full-stretched to her meagre size in their bed.

Young John Joe said, "Give us a quarter o' your best caramels there, Yarr," and he rose thankfully, toppling one of the big screw-topped jars towards himself off the shelf. The sweets slid, dropping into the silver scoop in a handful, then in ones and twos as he shook, until the red-tipped needle swung steady over the 4. He searched for a paper bag off the pile beside the scales but Young John Joe stopped him with a lazy flow of the hand.

"Save your bags. They'll do just as well in the oul' pocket."

The sweets lay on the counter untouched, until Young John Joe motioned Packy forward to creep like the weaker, more cowardly brother-jackal to the bounty. They wore khaki British Army jackets, lighter working shirts of the same colour, bib and brace dungarees, folded down wellingtons and black schoolgirls' berets on their heads. They stank of sour milk and pig manure and their red swollen hands – the ugliest part of them – had nails tipped dark blue. Yarr looked at those hands, pickled with daily delving into steaming mashes, and then thought of his own condition. A morning prize-fighting pose before the mirror and looking passable until the buried muscles relaxed and the true flabbiness revealed itself. He thought of his body hiding beneath his clothes, an ugly fraud, and shuddered . . .

4

She said, "I didn't know Tony was back, Packy. I thought he was over there in that Luton place for good."

She was leaning forward on the counter on her elbows, eager for gossip, and Yarr could see the dirty-pale backs of her legs and the veins just behind her knees. Her right blue bedroom slipper was worn down on to its heel. His view of her matched the rest of what he could see beneath the counter, the empty sham side the customers never saw. For weeks he had been seeing ugliness where before it had been turned away from him. He looked at the width between her legs – they were splaying more and more each day to support the growing weight they were being forced to carry. He wanted suddenly to push a hand up her clothes, not from desire, but to tumble her composure. Then he felt disgust at the thought. He went back to listening to what they were saying. Young John Joe was belittling the returned man and she was encouraging him by pretending to rebuke him.

"You shouldn't say things like that, och sure it's not right now," she kept saying after every jibe about the length of Molloy's hair, the cut of his trousers or the high heels on his boots, or his new accent which had been acquired after only two months' sojourn away from Ballyboe. He knew she was loving every mean-minded, envious witticism.

Packy said, "Bridie now has the great notion of young Molloy, so she has."

Ruby sniffed but said nothing. The peace was uneasy between her and Bridie. They circled each other warily in their day to day work in the shop and the house. Each was dependent on the other, reluctantly, for Bridie was the only local girl who could be persuaded to work in. And Yarr knew something that his wife didn't know – that Bridie had a cheap school notebook in her handbag that kept score of each pound that brought her nearer to the fare that would get her across eventually to her sister in Hammersmith, the Josie one with the club-foot. He knew it because he had gone through the bag one of the times his wife had stayed overnight with her people in Armagh. That memory of over a year ago had blurred like so many others lately – he couldn't remember things well any more – but the stained emerald lining and the pent-up smell of powder and perfume when he'd carefully opened the clasp (for she was asleep beside him, one bare freckled arm lying out over the eiderdown of her bed in the spare room) and the pathetic contents were ever-bright in his mind to plague him.

"They say she wrote a big long letther to him ivery week he was away. What do ye think o' that now? On pinky ruled paper she bought in Hickey's, and – with S.W.A.L.K. in the corner of the envelope!"

"What sorta ballocks is that atall?" growled Young John Joe.

Packy didn't notice the displeasure in his master's voice and face. "You mean you never heard of it?"

He was hopping with elation, having pulled off his beret instinctively. His hair was twisted cruelly, a sweaty tangle of spikes and flattened glistening planes. A wild musty smell of the countless cows, it seemed, against whose sides he'd leaned his head, flooded the air. Yarr felt sick. The stink of the two of them seemed to have been exuding steadily and relentlessly into the atmosphere since they had entered.

"Are you sure it wasn't S.A.G. now?" put in Ruby seriously. "Saint Anthony Guide, you know."

"Not atall!" snorted Packy and his eyes squinted more painfully than ever. "It stands for – *Sealed With a Loving Kiss!*"

Young John Joe hit the counter with a flat palm and the collecting box for the African orphans leaped with a jingle.

"God, you're the right oul' wumman!"

His face had an ugly flush to it. Young John Joe was jealous. That was it. For a moment Yarr forgot the pain in his head and felt himself drawn out of his routine, remorseless introspection.

Packy's beret was a twisted black rag in his sweating hands by now. He couldn't make out how he could have offended Young John Joe. He tugged desperately at the strangling collar of his shirt, and a button flew. "John Joe?" he pleaded, moving instinctively into the other's angry aura. Doomed.

"Oul' *wumman*," growled Young John Joe, shoving a shoulder up at him. "Oul' wumman." There would be unparalleled savagery at the Cross later that afternoon.

Ruby coughed, and Yarr knew she was searching for something to say – in appeasement? But, no, for she snapped, "Packy Traynor! Carrying tales indeed!" with a sly try at outrage. Tears were starting in the eyes that beseeched each face, for Packy spent his days in a perpetual state of bewilderment, reeling and then recovering from each senseless quirk of his fellow creatures. He was like a pitiable raw recruit, trying vainly to fall into step with his marching, machine-like brothers as they swept through life in glorious order. Yarr stared thoughtfully at his ugliness – the turn in one of the eyes, the acne, the rank hair, the dangling red joints of hands, the humps and hollows of his work-racked body – and hated him with the others. Packy was for hating. Yarr knew that if Packy ever got *him*, Yarr, in a pit – the way he was now, he wouldn't show pity. No, the sticks and stones would rain down as savagely from him as from the others – pounding and thudding, crashing and thudding . . .

Yarr rose to his feet; he felt shaky. There was a blackness before his eyes and an intolerable thirst in his mouth, and the pain behind his right temple threatened to burst its way out after every rhythmic, padded drum-beat.

"Where are *you* for?" asked Ruby.

Young John Joe laughed. "A policeman wouldn't ask you that, Ruby," he said, smirking.

"Where the hell do you think?" Yarr growled, avoiding the bright curiosity of his wife's tightening gaze. He moved clumsily past her and his coat dislodged a shallow tilted box of pencils. They scattered over the floor, rolling, their red lacquer setting up sparks of light.

"Where the hell do you think?" he repeated louder, angry at the disorder he had caused.

He left them with their laughter boiling up at his heels, even Packy's dry-throated but strengthening croaks joining in gratefully.

Up the short, linoleum-covered passageway and then left, one step up past the door of the tiny kitchen and into the scullery with its crammed shelves reaching up to the low, pink distempered ceiling. He lifted the latch of the back door and moved out into the air. A startled thrush flew off from the iron lip of the water-barrel and he watched it rise like a lazy ball over the wall between his yard and Hackett's. The bird's feathers had an unseasonal fluffed-out look. He had often seen them the size of young chickens moving in dazed jerks about the place when the cold came gripping down from the heavens. He stood for a moment thinking about the bird and its existence and then moved through the tangle of mineral water crates, soggy cardboard cartons, Calor gas cylinders and paint tins without lids, all half-filled with rain water and cobwebs. Ugliness and waste all around. It was all there to remind him of projects planned but never undertaken, opportunities lost and, above all, this deadening lack of energy.

7

He had stopped mentioning it to Doctor Mac because what had all his pills and tonics accomplished? He had lost faith in the old man when he began to notice how he would reach wearily for his prescription pad even before he had finished his account of how he felt. And how could you put into words, anyway, the subtleties of sensation? What was the use?

There was little ground at the rear of the houses on this side of Ballyboe's single street, for the entire narrow village was built under the lee of a ridge of high land – the bottom step on the ascent to the South Armagh hills. Each house on this north side had a stumpy yard which seemed to rush blunting itself up against the steep swell.

He kicked at a tin that had fallen on to the narrow trodden path before him and it bounded from his foot in a low arc to strike the big lean-to shed at the end of the yard. The roof jutted out from the overhanging mass where whin and pale dying grasses tangled inextricably.

He opened the door and moved into the gloom. In far corners forgotten objects rotted slowly. More reminders. He noticed casually that the white tubers on the Arran Banners had sprouted another foot. When they reached the rafters would they bend softly and grow like a roof, towards the light at the door? A flicker of interest in the phenomenon briefly illuminated in him and then died as he moved listlessly across to the privy which stood – one shed inside the larger shed – in a corner. The door swung inwards at his touch and the familiar strong odour rose from the round blackness in the middle of the wood. He sat down quickly, sealing off the hole and the brimming bucket below with his clothed thighs and buttock, and lit a cigarette. In a few seconds the pungency had retreated and he leaned back with his head resting on a wad of cut newspaper squares that hung threaded from a nail above. Light had begun to seep back through cracks between the boards and under the door until he could even see the fine slowing mist of wood dust that his entrance had shaken from the crumbling, riddled structure. He held out a hand in a ray of light and watched the tiny grains dropping into his palm so soft, so fine, that there was practically nothing to blow away when he brought his hand up to his mouth.

For a moment he felt peace, then the thoughts began coming again, like a stream of peevish insects striking on a windshield. It was always the same. He would ache for a place of quietness away where he was sure he would be able to collect himself, slow everything down, and then what would happen when he reached it? The same turmoil of thinking, beginning again; yet not thinking, just a rapid turning over and over of his mind until he thought he would go mad. He smiled bitterly to himself. That again. The word. Mad. One used lightly around him. *That bloody madman! He's mad. Yarr's mad.* Aye, there it was. Des Hackett worked as a male nurse in one of those places outside Wolverhampton one time. In the country, with a big wall around it, like a demesne wall to keep them in . . .

A man in dressing-gown and pyjamas running for it with two others in white coats after him. The first man screaming as he runs, a high steady stream of sound lifting frightened birds out of the trees. Then doubling back to the doctors' quarters and they swing round after him panting over the turf. The man in the dressing-gown getting a ladder, putting it against a balcony, climbing up, into one of the doctors' rooms and barricading himself in. Des Hackett going up after him and looking in through the window. The man inside has got hold of a whiskey bottle out of the doctor's cocktail cabinet and, while Des is watching, breaks it and begins jabbing himself. Face, throat, arms, chest, stomach. Systematically. Blood, blood, blood everywhere. Three hundred and seventeen stitches later.

He starts to shake. He looks down at the jerking cigarette in his hand and stills its movement by bringing it up and putting it into his mouth. Inhales. Closes his eyes. Leans back against the soft pad of paper and breathes out blue-grey smoke which changes slowly in colour to soft brown, melting like wreaths of chiffon in the light, drawn upwards to be trapped by the cobwebs. A shout from the house, startling cruelly.

"You're wanted in the shop!"

He rises clumsily, guiltily, for some reason, and fat red motes swing before his eyes. He shouts back, *"Okay"*, and his voice assails him in the cramped sentry-box.

Out into the shed. Out into the light. Rain, or rather some kind of evening mist, brushing his face as he plunges towards the back door which is open. In the shop the three look at him curiously. He senses his face is flushed, damp with perspiration, his eyes and mouth ugly.

9

There is a stranger standing in the shop eyeing him like the others.

A voice, an American voice, says, "My name is Quigley. I would like very much to talk to you, if you could spare me a little of your time. I've come a long way to meet you . . ."

WELL HERE I AM IN PADDY'S LAND – the drunk's song on the Boeing coming over, until the stewardess shut him up with her Swedish-steel stare. Poor old mick in his cheap wrinkled seersucker suit. Yet I pretended to be asleep as he came reeling up the aisle, looking hopefully into every closed face. He could have been my old man ten years ago, the same iron-grey hair, the same paws, the same hurt dog eyes. But even their own children avoid men like that. All those red-faced men you meet in bars back home, one minute weeping unrestrainedly on your shoulder, the next wanting to smash your head in, when their little black devil arbitrarily jabs. Yes, the Irish are feared abroad and rightly so. The smell of madness hangs about them. A bell should be rung before them.

My first moment on Irish soil. If the old man had been alive what an emotional bang that phrase would have given him. My father. Terence Aloysius Quigley, expatriate gael and stock character out of a dozen Barry Fitzgerald-Pat O'Brien movies. Not the roarin', drinkin' type – more the mouldering romantic weeping nightly over Count John on our old H.M.V. phonograph.

Belfast. The old man hated Belfast – black, bitter, British Belfast. The papers he had sent to him, thick heavy rolls squeezing through our letter-box on East Delaware, were always Dublin papers. He read each month-old edition with devotion – obituary columns, even the fat-stock prices, I suspected. I preferred the photographs of priests, bare-headed invariably, and young girls at race-meetings who, as invariably, wore head-scarves. Did all Irish women wear them, I wondered? Or was it because they were always going to or coming from mass? There is an Ireland peopled by bare-headed priests and young girls wearing scarves bought in Brown Thomas and Switzer's. My father's Ireland.

Just how many Irelands are there? I've been trying to count them since I've landed. And I must find one for me, because time is running out. *Three months! Three months to do what you have to do? I don't want* THE BIRTH OF A NATION, *laddie. You have six weeks to wrap it up. Good luck.* That silver-haired old timber-wolf snarling behind his glass desk on the top floor of Trans-Film in

11

Toronto. MacLachlan. Mac the Knife. Give him the excuse he's waiting for, and Quigley's head will plop into his out-tray. NO ONE IS INDISPENSABLE – in fine eye-straining stitching in a maple frame on the wall of his office, facing him. The sampler (he says it's his mother's work. Ho ho, not the work – but him having a mother) is the only antique piece in that glittering modern suite. For sentimental reasons, he says, he keeps it there. Just who does he think he's kidding?

But I thought I had exorcised that old demon coming over on the jet. So, conserve the energies, keep the nerves purring. But *six weeks*. And not an idea in my head. Good God above! Calm down, Quigley. Think. What did that journalist say in the Belfast pub? Something about his typical village, he'd once discovered. And close to the Border. He seemed to think that factor gave it added appeal, for someone wishing to tap Ireland's pulse. Bally – ? Ballyboe. And the man? Yarr. *Yarr is someone you must meet. Even if he isn't the man you're looking for, Ballyboe is certainly the place you're after. And Yarr is an experience. At least he was. I haven't seen him for years. A character, a real character.* Ireland seems to be bulging with "characters". If they were in any other country they would either be in gaol or in the state nut-house.

I've been looking at the map, hoping for something to rise from the brown and green contours, the red and black lifelines. There is high land to the north of this village, there is a nameless river draining into a nameless lake, there is an ancient monument, and the little green afforestation symbols tell me that the land around Ballyboe must be poor. That is all. It isn't mentioned in the *Shell Guide To Ireland*. Not even the ancient monument.

The old despair again. What have I let myself in for? Why not take Mac's word for it? *Of course, laddie, if you don't feel you're quite up to this assignment, well, we might let young Silvers take it over. He may not have your – eh, racial qualifications, but he has flair, he has flair.* You bastard, MacLachlan, you've a lot to answer for. You've fucked me up proper.

A memory. The old German cameraman who tried to tell me what it was like. An alky with tears in his eyes and me, the young invincible at the time, buying him drinks, listening and thinking that failures were a separate race, and that I, *me*, Edward P. Quigley (that's when I thought it would look good on the back of a director's chair) had been born white, gentile and with unlimited talent. He'd worked with Fritz Lang. Had been the most famous cameraman in all Europe. And now he couldn't get work because his hands shook. The sort of man MacLachlan would enjoy humiliating.

Little consolation, but I can pin-point the exact time (month, week, day, hour), when I lost my nerve. Yes, as animal an attribute as that. The steeple-jack, lion-tamer, fire-man, skin-diver — makes a slip, puts one foot wrong, once. And that's enough. Just once.

Timmins, Ontario, was my slip. Shanty town, with the biggest copper strike in history. Three millionaires inside a week. Population doubled inside a fortnight. Prospectors, adventurers, con-men, prostitutes, newsmen sleeping in cars, hallways, on tables, in the town's gaol. MacLachlan screaming for the first man to get there before C.B.C. did. *The syndicates will give their eye-teeth for one half-hour of black and white. Get north, Quigley.*

In the helicopter my plan for a "significant" work of film art. I would intersperse my live shots with stills of the '49 Gold Rush. Stills I had lusted after since I'd first seen them collecting dust in Montreal archives. Rows of bearded, foreign faces frozen for the camera. I would thaw their curious stares, merging them with delicacy into modern faces, then back again, an effortless mingling of past and present. I would do all this – and more. My film would be the definitive documentary on The Still Living Frontier. It would be Jack London, Whitman and Bret Harte all rolled into one. It would win prizes, by god!

Arrival. The rain, the mud in the streets, the babble inside the Mackenzie Hotel. Cajoling, threatening, begging for a room, a bed then, a telephone line, food, whiskey, a jeep, a guide, oil-skins. C.B.C. already there and shooting. Also British Granada TV, 'C.B.S. TV, French-Canadian TV . . .

Second day. My new cameraman, Oscar Dorsey, with the biggest hangover on record. Rain on the lenses. Bad light. Tape recorder faulty.

Third day. Dorsey a bastard. A twisted, embittered lush. A wrecker. But my responsibility. All mine.

Fourth day. Very frightened. MacLachlan yelling on the phone for a progress report.

Fifth day. C.B.C. pulling out. Smugly. Fist fight with Dorsey. His eye closed. His *eye*!

Sixth day. Shooting myself now. Anything and everything. Who cares?

Seventh day. Recalled. *Bring home the bacon, Quigley*! Ham, ham . . .

The rushes in the viewing theatre. Silence in the darkness from MacLachlan. Leaving, his face white. Not a word. Nothing. Literally. Then or later. Everyone connected to him through inter-office in-trays. His written word wafting down from his penthouse suite four times a day, to settle in those olive-green trays. The armour-plated glass of his desk symbolic. Makes us feel this floor (our ceiling) is also made of glass. Looking down on us in our boxes below. A single ant inside each cubicle. With no existence outside of him and his memos. Only in my case the flow from above began to dwindle. Tray empty. Finding myself sitting tense, watching that shiny emptiness with hate. Fantasies breeding in my brain. Leroy, the office boy, looking at me in a strange way. Night after night under the desk-lamp. Ideas, treatments on paper choking the waste-paper basket. Then out to a late-night bar in Yorkville. A single glass and bottle that telepathic bar-tenders place, without speaking, before hopeless cases as soon as they enter their dark dens.

Then the day, Leroy, by mistake, left a sealed memo which was for Theo Dunning on the floor below. Requesting him to attend a major programme conference in a few days, to discuss Trans-Film's big new series *THE OLD COUNTRY* and to receive an assignment. From the routing at the head of the yellow flimsy I saw that I would have a copy sent to me. I re-sealed the envelope, returned it to Leroy on his next visit, and waited right up until the day of the conference. No memo. Elation for the first time in months. I had still a chance. My reasoning – because my name had not been omitted from the list of producers to receive a summons, then he, MacLachlan, wanted no one to know what he had been doing to me, and if I didn't appear that afternoon, and all those other afternoons too, most likely, it would look as if it was my fault entirely, that I was deliberately disobeying his orders for some senseless reason of my own. The reason did not matter. He would hint at something, and all those around the table would manufacture their own solution, and Quigley would be put easily out of all their minds for good. Neat.

But – I went to that conference. My fellow producers. Fat young Horstmann, Theo Dunning with his English regimental tie, tense La Rivière, Silvers – ivy-league suit, ivy-league mind, Ricciola, blond bland Jensen, Tiny Kovacs – MacLachlan's hand-picked U.N. of talent. No sign on his face when he entered, saw me, but probably making a mental note to fire a certain stenographer. Then the ritual. Unzipping the crocodile-skin brief-case, the abstracted sip from the glass of iced Vichy water, the pale blue eyes fixed on a distant corner of the ceiling. All of us waiting. Hanging over our own private precipices. Divide and conquer – his rule. His worker ants never seeing each other. Single frantic insects inside transparent boxes.

Gentlemen, this project could well be the biggest thing that Trans-Film has ever tackled, and for that reason we must not fail. My panic. Thinking, if it's so big, how can *I* thwart his desire to have me out of it? And big, the only word for it. A dream of an idea, in series form, which already had been sold to half the TV stations in the world. THE OLD COUNTRY. Each "shot" to deal specifically with one European country and its modern image. His editorial brief – a glossy treatment verging on the romantic that would sell abroad, yet satisfy the millions of nostalgic immigrants at home. Clever, like him, fool-proof, not art, but very lucrative. Horstmann to film in Westphalia, Dunning – the English Midlands, La Rivière – Brittany, Ricciola – Lombardy, Jensen – Sweden, and Kovacs – the Hungarian Plains. Leaving Silvers and me. Pause. His move. Then, zipping up his case, clipping his gold Sheaffer back into his breast pocket. The business at an end. *Thank you, gentlemen. And good luck.* The others opening their sealed instructions around me with carefully concealed excitement. Silvers smiling to himself.

My voice croaking out suddenly, despairingly, in the rustling silence. *Is no one inter-ested in the dear ould emerald isle atall, atall?* Silence. Painful. Then, MacLachlan, softly – *Come up to the top floor, laddie – now – for a wee talk.*

Exit of headmaster. Silvers still smiling. Ricciola's troubled brown eyes. One fat hairy hand outstretched across the table to me, apologetically. But bastards all of them. None of them worth a damn.

Close the door behind you. The headmaster's study. *Come in, Quigley.* All the furniture cold surfaces and geometric planes. Thirties Bauhaus. Coming into fashion again. Like him, waiting patiently over the years for the big come-back.

His voice very low to start with, but sharpening to an edge. Laying it on the line for me, harsh and heavy. A numbing catalogue of my shortcomings over the past three months. Ineptitude, arrogance, disloyalty, jealousy of colleagues (Silvers?). I had really achieved something, no doubt about that, to succeed in getting into MacLachlan's hair. Which was no consolation, at that time. For – I was all washed up. My future – ironic word – a downward looping chain of humiliation. Lower and lower down the echelon from producer at the top to god knows what at the bottom.

When I stood up he went pale, thinking I was coming for him. My first advantage, for then he had to listen to what I had to say. If I was going down I was determined to make some sort of splash before sinking. MacLachlan sitting there, graven, after his initial shock. My voice rising and falling above the insect-hum of the air-conditioning. *My* voice? The strangeness of listening to it, convincing not only him, but me, that I was good – not just good – but goddamned brilliant, the best producer that Trans-Film was ever likely to have the good fortune to employ, a man who would bring them fame and respect in later years, for having encouraged him in his early career ... And beginning to believe it myself.

16

Taking me back two years, a year, when I went around feeling ready to explode with the force of something inside.

Let him do what he had to do, this sinewy old Scots creep, with his stories of how he worked behind the camera with Flaherty and Grierson and how his name would have been up there alongside theirs today too if it hadn't been for the breaks not breaking his way. Christalmighty, I was too good for this hick outfit! Screw MacLachlan and his boy scout troop! Screw all of them!

The cold, untouched expression on his old man's face. I had aged him somehow. Something at least before I emptied my desk drawer for the last time. But my own revelation still buzzed in my veins. All else, a dream.

Then another awakening. His strengthening voice, heavens, offering my job back; not that it had ever been taken away, not formally anyhow, but amounting to that. And wanting me to confirm for him how good a job I was going to do on this Irish project. Those *were* atavistic rumblings when I thought of the homeland and the film I was going to wrest from it. My invincibility.

But not all a runaway victory. The Silvers angle tried. Weakly, but still tried. *Don't make the tears run down my leg,* or words to that effect. *A Toronto jew to do a treatment on rural Ireland!* Conveniently forgetting my absence from the oul' sod since the age of five. Still – defeat accepted. Details worked out, mutually. A cigar offered.

One small mistake on my part, however, before leaving. The asking for three months. His reference to it not being a Griffith's epic. Getting his old bite back again. My departure at that point, not because of draining confidence, no, just a decision, mine, to leave and down to my own little office. Because I felt like it.

My door closed behind me. Feeling replete. As after a satisfying meal. The room itself having reverted to its former friendly ordinariness. Feet on the desk. A glance at my nails. Savouring it to the full. Wonderful . . .

*

Later I thumbed open a gazetteer, until I came to the right map. It looked back at me, the neatest shape of an island in the world, a friendly green doggie, begging on short back legs. I studied it – and it was then that I felt the plug being pulled out somewhere stealthily and the leaking away of everything I had felt a minute before. All the confidence ebbing away and leaving me weak and weakening. That serrated coast swam before my eyes, changing into the wavering boundary to a frightening dangerous foreign country. Oh sweet god, I began to pray, what have I done? What am I going to do? There in that place, I'll be lost, lost. I haven't been there for *twenty-seven years!*

2

GALLERY'S COMMERCIAL HOTEL was as deserted at seven o'clock on a Saturday evening as on any other week-day. It wasn't the place to do your drinking in on any of the six days out of the seven. But on the seventh a curious change took place in the grey peeling building in quiet Erne Square at the bottom end of Slaney's Main Street. If you passed by you couldn't help but feel the emanations of restrained excitement and illegality wafting out into the peaceful Sunday air, for inside, in small, dark airless rooms, men were drinking secretly. Guests had been known to find their bedrooms occupied by ranks of solemn-faced countrymen lowering bottles of stout with such dedication that Gallery's three poor daughters couldn't keep pace with the whispered orders hissing like jets from every room. They moaned to each other about it constantly of course but they realised that it was the only way to keep the place going because Daddy was drinking the bit out these days and if they barred the door of a Sunday he would drink them and himself and their small brother Dominic out on to the street in a matter of months. So Sunday was hysterical and the rest of the week was one long yawning match.

It was because of this that Yarr had brought Quigley into Gallery's after they had met. He wanted to get the Yank on his own so that he could find out exactly what he was after without any interruption. There was no place he could be sure of in Ballyboe so he had got him to drive the distance of five miles to Slaney, the nearest town.

Yarr now sat on the greasy red leather bus seat which was one of several around the walls of the empty lounge and waited for your man to return. He had gone out through a door marked *Fir* (Gallery was a fanatical native speaker. His great friend, Sergeant Breslin of the garda, wore the gold *fainne* too and that was why the hotel was safe from legal intervention on Sundays).

Facing him, over the fireplace in the opposite wall, was an old-fashioned fly-blown mirror with *Mitchell's Old Irish* in faded red and gold curlicued script. He could just make out the top of his head in the strip between the bottom of the glass and the lettering. While he was waiting, he stretched himself up until, at intervals, his forehead, nose, upper lip, mouth, chin and finally the knot in his tie, were reflected. To get all this in he had to lift himself clear off the spongy leather on splayed fingers. He looked at his reflection with sharp interest.

Of late he found himself unable to pass a mirror or a shop window, for that matter, without surreptitiously studying his reflection. Sometimes at home he even carried a jagged triangle of looking-glass from the scullery with him in his pocket when he visited the privy. Propped up on the horizontal middle bar of the door, it framed a fragment of his face that he could study in peace. The habit had become an obsession; he wanted to break it out of vague ideas that it was effeminate or, worse, that someone might discover him at it, yet he found it irresistible.

He examined the face, seeing only details – the thinning patch of hair square above the temples like a baby's; the freckled pouches under the eyes, fleshy jaw, a scar and pit or two, the shiny stretched skin of the nose (the pores couldn't be seen at that distance – in his shaving-glass his nose always had the ugly texture of a strawberry) a soft swelling doubling his chin. Details. Never could he fit them together to form a face, the way other people's were. Other people's faces seemed to *belong* to them, to be complete. He had even tried glancing quickly at photographs he had of himself, trying to catch that "something" unawares but it never worked, for immediately the elusive image broke up, separating like a blob of oil on water. Still, he found himself keeping on searching for that *other person*, as he thought of him, just out of sight . . .

Des Hackett had told him of a woman where he worked, a beautiful-looking piece like Elizabeth Taylor, and one of the male nurses, a chap from Tralee, slipped into her room night after night. He told Des she loved it, so didn't feel guilty, despite what the doctors had told them when they first arrived. Anyway, he said, they weren't past having the odd bit on the sly themselves. But this looney, the following morning, used to tell everybody, *Charlotte was a bad girl last night again*, giggling and nobody ever took a blind bit of notice of course because it was always – Charlotte did this and Charlotte did that. Charlotte must have been her *other person*. An abnormal case of course. Extreme. So perhaps *his* now was . . .

Suddenly trembling, he sucked a deep draught from the glass of whiskey before him. Why was it, he asked himself, could he never go the whole way with *that* line of thought. Why? Why under god's name, could he not still the shaking and fluttering?

He took another drink – it was neat, and he screwed up his mouth against the concentrated bitterness – and when he had downed it and put back the empty glass on the table, Quigley came out through the lavatory door. As he came across the worn carpet he turned his head to look back at the inscription over the door. Laughing, he said, "It's just as well I happened to know what that particular word meant, eh?"

Yarr smiled, nodded. Lowering his voice, he said, "The English language isn't good enough for your man here. He has to go back to his ancestors. A right oul' eejit. Wait till you meet him but . . ."

"Do a lot of people speak Gaelic in these parts?" Yarr looked at him, sensing the professional's search for information. He now wished he hadn't spoken about Gallery the way he had. After all he knew nothing about this guy. He might be anybody. You had to be bloody careful what you said and who you spoke to. They could be touchy around these parts. And they never forgot things either. Bloody teagues, all smiles when they met you, but their heads together the minute you left. Maybe this guy was one himself. Quigley – a Catholic name all right. Had the looks too. Funny how you could tell a peter nine times out of ten. But that was jumping the gun a bit.

21

"Well?" Quigley seeking his answer. He was wearing a pale-grey tweed sports jacket with patch pockets, blue shirt, narrow navy tie, charcoal trousers and black shoes. The shoes were the only thing that would have told you he was an American.

With his eyes still lowered, Yarr said slowly, carefully, "I don't think there's anyone left – not now. Of course the Government's all for keeping it alive, or so I've heard tell."

Quigley looked puzzled. "But I thought it was only in the South of the country that that was the case."

"We *are* in the South."

"But we didn't cross the frontier."

"We did."

They looked at each other. Yarr was curious to see how he would react. At the time in Quigley's hired blue Anglia, directing him along the maze of by-roads between Ballyboe and Slaney, he hadn't given the Customs a thought. It was subconscious, because he would no more have dreamed of driving around by the long route – a good extra eight miles on the clock – along the approved road to the barrier than would have anyone else in the village. The Customs was only for strangers, greenhorns. A nuisance certainly – but only a nuisance to those who let it be. It was only when they were approaching Slaney up the buckling bog road that brought a sudden view of the Church of Ireland rising high out of the middle of the old grey town and the steep strips of gardens dropping down from the back walls of the houses that he realised what he'd done. He snapped a quick glance of alarm at your man in the driver's seat at his side, oblivious, concentrating on the unfamiliar road ahead, and silent. Sure, when it came to that, hadn't they hardly exchanged more than a dozen sentences since your boyo had first introduced himself back in Ballyboe, and Yarr had taken him down to the back store-room where they'd be out of range of the eyes and ears of the three they'd left behind in the shop. *They've ears as big as elephants in this cabin*, struck the Yank as funny, and Yarr had liked the way he laughed and pushed his way good-humouredly after him through the flawed fatigue jackets swinging like corpses from the low roof.

But Quigley hadn't explained himself very well when they'd eventually been brought face to face among the fusty-smelling stock. What the hell did a "documentary" mean anyway? Of course he didn't want to let on he didn't know what it was, so he'd marched him out to his car, pronto, past Ruby and Packy and

John Joe, all with their tongues hanging out and raging mad at him for not standing his ground in the shop with the stranger; and away went the two of them into the 'State and Slaney.

Yes, to be true, when the thought had first struck him that he'd involved this stranger in something that he wouldn't understand, that might easily anger him because of an instinctive fear of cutting across the laws of a strange country, that most people from outside had, he had felt disturbed. Then he thought, I'm doing *him* the favour, if he doesn't like it, okay, nice to have met you, fare you well, inniskilling, nothing lost. But then – if I have something he wants, this is the time to see how badly he wants it.

And so, when Quigley eventually smiled after the pause, a knowing smile, Yarr felt pleased. He usually made up his mind quickly whether he liked someone or not. And didn't change that first feeling easily.

He edged forward on the seat and, touching him on the knee with a light forefinger, confided, "Watch what you say in front of this crowd about here. I know them. You don't."

"You mean about – the frontier?"

"The Border, you mean. No, no, I didn't mean that in particular. Rule number one – eyes and ears open. Don't tell them anything about your business. Not that I want to know it either but –"

He paused and waited for his hint to be taken. Smoothly, the Yank relieved him of his burden – the slickest of baton changes, by protesting, "But I want you to help me. At least I hope you can help me."

"Fine, so let's get down to brass tacks."

He knew he was jumping the gun, he could have spun out the skirting, butterfly-like oul' chat for a week or more for hadn't he been trained in the art from the first day in the cot, but he no longer delighted in such play now. Of late he craved directness, plain speaking out; the intricate manoeuvring of the life around him was too slow, too slow. "I don't see how I fit in with your plans. Sure I don't *know* your plans. We never got that far, did we now?" He waited, invitingly.

Quigley gazed back at him. His eyes were blue-grey. He coughed, then smiled (he didn't show his teeth when he smiled) and said, rising to his feet, "What about a drink? Eh? Before –" Pause and another smile – "we get down to those brass tacks."

He stood, looking down on Yarr, waiting. Yarr tightened himself just once more, then – ach to hell with it, let himself go,

23

subsiding like a spent balloon. He nodded his head and Quigley strode across to the bar, reprieved. Yes, reprieved – most definitely. Now what in hell's name was up with him, thought Yarr, as he studied him.

Quigley, finally, tapped the top of the bar with a coin edge and the noise sprang loud in the empty room.

"Hit it another blatter," called Yarr lazily from his seat. "Sure they're as deaf as all get out in this oul' place."

Their eyes met and then Quigley, with an exaggerated gesture, brought his half-crown – crack, crack, crack, down on the polished wood so hard that a shiver of glass touching glass rolled along the shelves at the back of the bar. Yarr gave a snort of laughter and, after a brief pause, Quigley joined in. They were both hard at it, over loud, because of the excuse it gave to sweep away the feeling of tension that had built up out of nowhere, it seemed, when Gallery himself came through the door. Their laughter choked off.

He had his usual unkempt look about him, as if he had just been disturbed from some lair or other, dragged up out of the depths of some old horse-hair sofa somewhere in the back regions of the hotel. Indeed he carried the bunched remains of a newspaper in his hand – maybe he had been sleeping with it over his face. He shambled across in an erratic line, muttering to himself, unshaven as always, the hair on his head a bristling ginger cap and the small blood-shot eyes of him dulled with drink and his obsessions, which left him no peace day or night. It was a rarity for him to serve anybody whenever any of the three big daughters were about and Yarr thought to himself that the noise must have been awesome to rouse him out of his hole.

He watched him rooting about behind the bar. He had ignored them completely, especially Quigley who still stood waiting, a foot away from his moving bent, cropped skull.

"How's the health these days, Eoin, eh?" he himself called out patronisingly, the way he would to a child or an old dodderer. But Gallery was neither and he impaled Yarr with a swift glance from under his hairy eye-brows. Yarr suddenly felt he had made a bad miscalculation.

Gallery suddenly cried out in a loud agonised voice, "Will them dirty, back-stabbing English gets niver leave us in peace? Oh, if we only had the one good man back and living on this earth that would have been able to turn the pin in all their noses."

He raised bleary eyes to a reproduction of John F. Kennedy that hung above the fireplace. He saluted it, holding the gesture while Yarr and Quigley exchanged glances. Then dropped the hand lifelessly to his side. He placed a pair of much abused spectacles, their frames fattened with Sellotape, on his nose, and, groaning, searched the newspaper until he came once more on the source of his despair. "Young fella," he said to Quigley in pathetic tones. "Young fella, is it anythin' but right that them garbage merchants across the water are allowed to defame and desecrate this country as they please?" Quigley looked down quickly at the paper and read quietly to himself. His face didn't alter.

Yarr called out from where he was sprawled. "What is it?"

In a quiet voice Quigley read slowly out to the room, "*Had Malcolm X Irish Ancestry?*" There was silence as the words dropped home.

Yarr said, "Well, had he?" and Quigley looked at Gallery behind the counter.

The old man stirrred from his abstraction. He pulled at his grease-stained tie as if it had tightened suddenly on his neck and the collar-button plopped on to the counter. He looked at it for a moment. It lay in a patch of wet on the mahogany, dazzling the eye, miraculous in such drabness. Then he swept it away before him resentfully. His words flew after it, out at them. "How could a buck nigger as black as that grate there have Irish blood in him? Tell me that now?"

Quigley said innocently, "Well, it's quite possible, you know . . ."

Yarr smothered a roar of rising laughter and busied himself by frantically brushing off imagined grains of dust from the knees of his trousers. God, this was gas. A regular bloody tonic.

Gallery leaned forward, his red-rimmed eyes tightening to dots. "*You* wouldn't be English yourself, would you?"

"No," said Quigley, "I'm Canadian – although I was born in –"

"Oh, from Canada is it?"

He turned away and they both felt the contempt in his voice for any country that had its chance of independence but still kow-towed to an English queen.

Quigley said, "I was born in Derry," and Yarr thought *oho* and added the information to his slowly growing store. But old Gallery had ignored him and was snuffling at the newspaper once more as if to smell out more cleverly concealed jibes at the homeland. Finally, "*Ach*", in disgust from him and he flung it from his hand,

25

the pages slowly unfolding in the air to land strewn like several newspapers over the carpet, on a table, and overlapping the tiled hearth.

"That's one dirty rag," he spat. "One filthy sheet. If I had me way I'd have ivery single one burned on the Dublin quays as soon as ever they came off the Heysham boat. Imported bloody foreign dung!"

He went to an upturned bottle of John Power's fastened to the shelf, and measured himself a glassful. Quigley looked at Yarr with his mouth dropping, and then, as the old man shudderingly drank, he winked. It was slow, deliberate and mischievous and Yarr felt a return to the past when care and worry and this thing inside, whatever it was, hadn't been imagined, and he'd spent his days and nights with people he liked and who had liked him in turn. A string of names and faces quite suddenly slid through his memory.

One name, one face jerked the string taut. The recurring image swam up into his consciousness and *the slowing circling of the blue light on the parked police car, the smell of freshly crushed metal, oil on the grass, the crushed Triplex on the road like gleaming demerara, the leaking upholstery, the two brown shoes, still laced, in the hedge, and the blood everywhere – under the mats, in the carpets, pockets, ash-trays – pools of it, congealed streaks, blobs, wet-tipped baby stalactites, black stippling on the headcloth – oh where did it all come from? not all surely from him – he was a small man – but yet, it did, they told him at Daisy Hill hospital . . . spurting and then silently bubbling out through nose, ears and mouth as he lay draped among the scrap metal waiting for them to come to plug him . . . his phone ringing downstairs at three in the morning; they'd found the number in his diary (Telephone No. Of Friend) . . . then driving fast enough to join him, urging, swearing, towards a lighted island at a cross-roads in a strange quiet country place – there were corncrakes calling as the figures moved in and out of the lights, lifting, pulling, bending among the wreckage . . . when he arrived the ambulance had been there and away again and voices called out after him as he ran back to his van . . . his chest felt cold, his pyjama jacket had unbuttoned and he had done nothing about it . . . he flogged the van on along roads he didn't know, driving past finger posts, then screeching back in reverse until his mind seized the staring white letters, numbers, then on again, skidding, grazing – god, god don't let him die –*

until the square buff back of the ambulance with its two sinister
blobs of windows held him and his speed in check . . . he drove
stuck a dozen feet from its tail-light, christ, christ, christ – only fifty
miles an hour – he wanted to ram it, burying the nose of the Morris
deep into the great broad arse and force it along, blowing it faster
and faster along the white roads like a following wind until it
screamed and screamed . . . even at the hospital they kept him
waiting – o fuck them – he wrote the word fifty-six times (he kept
score) on the waiting-room wall on a shady bit of the plaster until
his biro ran out, to punish them for their indifference . . . his best
friend – wee darling Joe – the only man he ever loved – just another
bit of butcher's meat to them . . . one of the doctors, his coat
spattered, was laughing at something a nurse was saying to him in
the corridor outside the morgue – for, yes, he was dead when they
let him see him . . . he had to weep before they would let him, weep
tears that they watched in silence before they shifted about
muttering among themselves . . . Joe – drained old bit of tubing, he
wasn't worth giving a transfusion to – lay on the flat padded board
as if part of it and there was no trace of red anywhere about him . . .
but a pink sponge and hose hung in a sink in the corner . . . and the
tiles had smears . . . when they washed his face it must have been
like washing a rubber mask – it giving under the rubs and dabs –
wobbling, dimpling . . .

He almost shrieked, for a real false-face seemed to be hanging
just a few feet away in front of his focusing eyes.

Then Quigley said, "Hey, are you feeling all right?"

He said, "The oul' stomach's playing me up again," patting
himself and faking a belch and a grimace.

Christ, he thought, *that was a near thing*. Now he was angry at
himself or, rather, that part of him that was weak and couldn't be
trusted. He felt the fatigue weighing down on him that resulted
from unfaltering vigilance.

"What about that drink we didn't get – to settle it?" Quigley
was looking at him with sympathetic eyes.

Yarr smiled strongly back in spite of his inner churning, and,
rising to his feet, said, "I tell you what. Let's go somewhere else –
where there's a bit more life. It *is* local colour you're after, isn't
it?"

The Canadian (now don't forget that, he told himself) sucked in
a deep, rallying breath and gestured for him to lead the way. At
the door Yarr turned – Quigley too – and they both looked back at

Gallery who had found another newspaper beneath the counter. He was riffling through it short-sightedly. "Up the Rebels!" called Yarr and the old man snarled "Aghh!" at them and shook the paper. He said something in Irish that sounding like the chokings of someone drowning in mud, and, beneath his breath, Yarr muttered in reply, "And up you too, y'oul' anti-christ."

As he walked along the dark passage smelling of onions and dirty feet – Gallery's Commercial Hotel special blend – towards the outer air he could hear Quigley chuckling, and brightened up. The small pressing wind that always seemed to arise when the sun sank met him up the passage and felt cold on his temples. It dried the sweat and dispelled his pallor, or so he believed anyway. He glanced at his profile in a hall-stand mirror to check as he stooped to go outside. He felt back to normal except maybe for a softly dying flutter deep in his stomach.

To the right of the door outside was a wooden bench of the park variety with wrought-iron ends and faded lettering across the top-most plank. Once it had been bright with green paint and the gold inscription advertising the hotel plain to see. But now, like everything else under the present management, it only sighed neglect. Yarr sat down and stretched his legs, his heels raking the dust of the Square. Beside him Quigley searched in his pockets, found cigarettes and held them out to him. Yarr shook his head; the other lit up and then breathed out smoke into the stillness. They were silent. The Square was empty, a criss-crossed expanse of fine dry gravel so thin in covering that cars kept continually rubbing the asphalt bare, then others covered the tracks in turn and so on, a constantly shifting grey skin.

Facing the hotel was a long high bare wall with *Tierney's Monumental Works* painted on it in foot-high Celtic lettering like that employed on the forest of inscribed crosses behind waiting in readiness. Further along was *Breakfast, Dinners and Teas* to advertise McKenna's Café at the corner where Casement Street, the town's main thoroughfare, ran erratically uphill to the other and larger Square. Nothing moved anywhere – the children who had been playing noisily out in the middle of the waste when they'd entered the hotel had been called off to bed.

Presently a chapel bell began to peal rhythmically in single counting strokes from the distant top of the town. Yarr had no idea what it signified. To him it was only another manifestation of the intricate foreign ritual that occupied these people's lives all the year round. They were always being summoned and reminded by bells – all hours of the day and night.

He said suddenly to the air straight ahead of him, "They're all mad you know, ravin'."

Quigley looked startled. "Oh?" Puzzled too.

Yarr continued slowly, "I knew a man once who blamed it on the water."

He halted again for the other's reaction. It came obediently, predictably – a silent questioning opening of the mouth.

"Everywhere . . . water. More of it here than in any other county in Ireland. Lakes. This fella claimed it had something to do with them being mad. Affected their nuts, you see. I think he had a point."

The other showed understanding at last. "Oh, I get it. That old guy back inside. Yeah, he seemed a proper screwball all right. And you say there's a lot like him about?"

"Any quantity. The outside world would not believe the things they get up to. Straight up. As you say – screwballs." Then he laughed and slapped his knee. "By god you've hit it," he said. "Screwballs. That's the best I've heard yet. Screwballs."

The other quickly joined in the laughter and Yarr thought – that pleased him, me saying that. But he still didn't want to go out to him, not just yet. Some old warning nudge from the past, that time with Joe and what happened and how he had been crumpled – too easily – stopped him.

He said, "But if you're here for any length of time, sure won't you be able to see it for yourself?"

Again his tentative pussy-foot, and again the backward withdrawal.

"I guess you've got a point there," from Quigley.

Yarr had a moment of impatience. Then he relaxed. He felt good. Why poil it?

There was a great stillness in the air, a brooding peace. It was as if an enormous bowl had been silently, gently lowered from the heavens to cover the town, enclosing it and its somnolence. The air felt rich and thick with sleep. The bells, birds and the muffled wheels of slowly passing traffic somewhere out of sight only seemed to draw the quiet closer together. Sitting side by side on

29

the bench, with their eyes closed, they felt their lids bathed by something unseen. It was one of those rare miraculous evenings when he felt that the true sleeping heart of Ireland was not too far away. That if he travelled towards it there was a good chance of finding it – a wooded enclosed haven in the green, green centre.

Yarr always thought of it like that; something like Gleason's old fort over the fields behind Ballyboe. After school was out he used to go there by himself and lie hidden on the top of the mound in the long grass and listen for fairies deep below. But although he concentrated, observing faithfully the rituals laid down by all the old people he had ever heard on the subject, never once did that thin unearthly sound rise through the warrens of rabbits, foxes, and badgers to the surface air and his sensitive ears. It was just another of his dreams that withered on the stem of experience as he grew older.

"Did you know, for instance, that they still believe in fairies? Fairies! I mean what can you do with people like that?"

Quigley swung a sideways glance at him. He was polite. He said, "You know I once read something about that, but I thought it was only way out in the far west of the country that those beliefs still hung on."

Yarr shook his head. "No. I can take you to people right this minute who leave out a saucer of milk every night after they finish in the byre for the wee people and . . ."

He stopped, sick of the whole charade – fairies, Finn McCool, Gallery. Christalmighty, this guy must think him a real candy man, because he knew that this couldn't be what he was after – the leprechauns, thatched cottages, donkeys humping panniers of turf, barefoot wee gets, colleens in green and gold and all that shit – no, that was for the tourists, the stupid ones who knew no better, who didn't know their arse from their cine-cameras. *But what the fucking hell did he want?*

"Look, Mr Quigley" (the air seemed to ice at the sudden formality). "Look. Is it folk-lore you're after?"

The other shook his head. "It's not. So" – Pause.

"Well if it's not that, what do you want me to show you? You name it. I'm at your service."

The other revolved his cigarette rapidly between his finger and thumb.

"Basically I want to make a film about Ireland. The trouble is – well, what sort of film I'm not quite sure at this point . . ."

"I see."

"That's the way I work. I can't –"

His voice had risen to explain. "I need time before I can see a starting point. Do you understand that?"

Yarr said, "Sure, I follow you."

He smiled to show he was sympathetic, but the other had his eyes on the ground. He was pawing at the gravel with his toe. Makes life difficult for himself, thought Yarr, then – *Christalmighty, would you look who's talking* . . .

"How long are you going to spend here?"

"Just over a month."

"And then where are you heading for?"

"Back home after that, I guess."

"Oh."

There was a pause. Their minds worked on their separate problems, shredding, sorting the facts.

"Tell me," began Yarr. "Have you your camera with you?"

Quigley began to explain the technique of his art – the preliminary observation stage, the shooting script, the filming period with him directing the borrowed camera crew and sound recordist, the processing of everything in the can, the first rushes and then the inevitable last minute panic over loose ends – film re-takes and sound-over recordings and all the other items which should be remembered and aren't – only in this case a return journey of three thousand miles wouldn't be on.

Yarr allowed the flurry of jargon to die. The last words fluttered down like wreckage from some aerial combat. And he felt as if he had been involved. Quigley looked exhausted. There was sweat on his brow. Yarr thought to himself, *I certainly can pick them okay*, but it was with fondness. He had felt the same way once about a magpie with a mangled leg. He had nursed it back to near-normal and then watched it fly over Hackett's old tin shed, forgetting him.

He said, "You haven't much time."

"I know, I know." Quigley was puffing white explosions from a fresh cigarette.

"Well," said Yarr rising. "If that's the case, we'd better get started then. Tonight."

The other looked up at him. Still puzzled.

"Now. Right now. So. You want to see things? People? What goes on here? Tonight? Right?"

"Right."

31

"Well then – you couldn't have picked a better time nor place. No sir. It'sss –" he stretched out the word as he looked down at his wrist-watch – "nearly a quarter to eight. So, say in another two hours, this place will really start to hum."

His arms took in what they could see and what was hidden of the town.

"Tonight, Mr Quigley, is the first night of Slaney Carnival. Yes siree. Your luck is in."

Quigley looked up and Yarr felt like patting him on the head. He was proud of himself and his capabilities. Single-handed he had fought his way to an understanding of the man and what he was really after. Again a feeling of fond superiority washed through him. He would help this man, yes, he would, give him what he wanted. *He* would be left of course, but it was all going to be different – no, not different, like the old days, yes, that was it. Like the old days when he was king of the castle, and Ruby and people and this snarling thing inside him were never any threat ... never.

"Boss," he said, grinning, as he lightly clapped his palms together. "Boss, it's all ahead of us. Let's you and me take our way up the town. And I'll show you Slaney – and what makes it tick. Okay?"

A QUESTION. How long before I make up my travelling time loss? A simple arithmetic problem i.e. three thousand miles equals five hours – because that's how far Toronto is behind me etc., etc., or a purely physiological one? For, no doubt about it, last night Quigley was one very tired old man. Nodding off in his arm-chair after dinner in the residents' lounge of the small country hotel. While the only other guest talked across to him tirelessly about his house, his car, his credit cards *et al* back home, for, irony of ironies – how do you do, Mister O'Neill, returned emigrant "boy" from Philadelphia. Grey-headed O'Neill who *shook (shuck?) Kennedy's hand once at Massey Park, did you know that? By the bloody hand!* Follow that, Quigley. All for the benefit of our dark little barmaid.

But enough of the old malice in Quigley to put O'Neill down as a retired mick cop – despite all his talk of real estate deals – home to dazzle the natives. His night-stick swishing days now only a suppressed memory. You don't impress the locals any longer with the rewards of three uniforms a year and hero-worship from little old ladies waiting to cross at the lights. Or do you? Some of those old Pat O'Brien B-pictures might still be circulating . . . Of course Americans abroad always resent one another – it's like Columbus finding another paleface in the bushes. Still, I find in myself, as I say, a certain atavistic spite towards this man – something not quite natural. Leading me to question, examine certain personal characteristics. Am I of a "celtic" temperament? Dreamy, intuitive, given to gab? I'm not concrete and practical, that's for sure, my moods certainly see-saw, words are more important to me on paper than in mine – other people's mouths. Perhaps a score of eight out of ten? Perhaps.

Thinking about it this way leads to the curious paradox of people like O'Neill who should have their Irish-ness diluted by the American way of life but haven't. The thick, stubborn concentrate guarded zealously by fathers like mine (Christ, that time he got the family to learn *The Soldiers' Song* in Irish . . . I sang it at a neighbourhood concert and was ribbed on our block for months afterwards. Which brings up the other point too of never being allowed to forget one's national strain by one's fellow Americans.

The biggest fight I ever had when a kid was with Ted Koppel, the rabbi's son).

O'Neill, of course, later on in the evening turned all my theories upside down. I was drinking more than I bargained for and, pressing me to drink even more at one stage, he said, *Aw, come on, drink up. Thank god, there's someone like you to talk to. This bloody country's drivin' me nuts. The sooner I'm back in Philly the better I'll like it. I'll give this place back to the bogmen any day.* A revelation. Where now the proud gael wetting the hand of John F. K. with his tears? The staunch brother of Philadelphia's biggest and greenest G. A. A. Club? The subscriber to *Ireland's Own*? The singer of songs on Saint Patrick's Day? The rantin', roarin' expatriate Monaghan man? The scales had fallen from his eyes on this trip back to the homeland. What would such a return journey have done to my old man? Killed him? But who wants such thoughts when there's Maeve, our ministering brunette barmaid, so patient with her two tipsy customers. When we chaffed her she blushed becomingly and her black eyes sent out burning glances. Like a Victorian heroine with wildly beating breast, her starched apron-front and eyelashes fluttering like frantic moths. Maeve mavourneen, my little dark Irish rose. Arousing the moustachioed villain in me.

Who knocks at my bedchamber door at this hour?

It is I – Master Quigley.

Och sur, och sur, for pity's sake, have a thought for a poor helpless young colleen's honour.

Open, I say!

Och sur, och sur.

Open!

Withdrawal of oiled bolt. Another one here for insertion. Ha ha. In. Darkness. Palpitating rustle from the bed. Ah. *Ah*. Ahhh . . .

Destined to go through life as the working-girl's Don Juan. Or the chambermaid's Casanova. Michèle's phrase. The vinegar of her accent making it smart the more. *Poor Edward, I see your fate so clearly. You'll be so pathétique. A fat, bald chambermaid's Casanova.* Or, as that blonde Calgary waitress put it so genteelly – *a lousy, damn bum-toucher* – after I left her in the morning in true travelling-salesman fashion. I look in the mirror. How's the hairline, the gut? The glass doesn't show philandering tendencies.

Michèle, ma belle. I knew her before the song. Can't think of one about Eddie – for her. Maybe I'll write one. Mail it to her with – *remember the ducks in Huron Park?* She used to chase the leering, raggy old seagulls away when they muscled in on her beloved family. Standing there in her pony-skin coat shivering – me too. The dark glasses – the biggest to be found and her face, the tiniest – the patent buckled shoes, the perfume. *Mitsuoko.* When I put my nose into the hollow between neck and shoulder . . .

The small loft apartment above her mother's shop. Six flights up and *ssh, Edward,* because no one was to know she lived there because of the fire insurance. Later, one bare arm out to snap off the light and a few hours with that beautiful body. She modelled her mother's creations in the boutique below, striding about, her face a cold cutting instrument in a wind of Italian silk and chiffon. The buyers watched her from their gilt chairs. Did some of those old dikes fantasy what was underneath all that *haute couture* as she whirled past? Only Quigley knew of that fine prickly fuzz, the legacy of a recent appendectomy, certain moles and beauty marks, nipples that waxed and waned under his blowing breath, her liquid envelope.

And Quigley, the boy from the wrong side of town, also loved the parties, receptions, the balls she took him to. Toronto society still remembered her father had once been Irish Ambassador. And her mother still dressed all the women with icy tyranny. Those red-faced businessmen and their wives – a short, brutal generation removed from peasant Scotch-Irish ancestors – fought for the privilege of having Madame Lynch and the beautiful Michèle on their invitation lists. Quigley stood aside while the polite conversation roared around his two female companions and enjoyed the women's magazine element in his love affair. Of course Michèle's old lady hated him. That finely-boned French-Canadian nose soon detected the mick in him right off. And Quigley hated *her* then. A laugh now, of course, and cold objectivity concerning his true motives. Poor Michèle. His relationship with the mother much more violently passionate. And always was with the ones who didn't capitulate right away. As soon as he had them hooked – like Michèle – a loss of interest . . . Yes, it was all clear. He saw his workings like the insides of one of those skeleton clocks. It would be nice, wouldn't it, to perhaps meet the next in that long list – he knew it was going to be long, all right – here, in Ireland. Perhaps a *colleen bawn* to augment the world-wide sorority?

QUIGLEY WAS MOONING ABOUT the yard at the back of McCann's, sniffing the night air, a contented grin on his face, when he went to look for him.

"Hey, boy, we were nearly sendin' out a search party!" shouted Yarr with huge glee on sighting him. "*Hey!*"

Quigley turned, screwing up his eyes. From the pub back-door Yarr laughed loudly, then moved across the debris-littered expanse to take his friend by the arm.

"Come on in," he said, lowering his voice as he approached. "You're missin' the best crack back there. There's somebody I want you to meet. A V.I.P. no less."

The thought of it made him giggle, eyes squeezed, mouth wide, hugging himself. Then, with him at a trot, along the narrow cat-piss smelling passage with its brown varnished dado sticky to the touch, through the crowded back-kitchen, the range covered with glasses of stout and into the roaring bar. Only it was quiet now – waiting. For them. The faces all had that same expression which children have when they've conspired together and are not sure if they can keep the secret to themselves very much longer. Quigley was blinking and smiling uncertainly. He seemed to be half-expecting them to roar out, "Surprise! Surprise!" in deafening unison when he sensed that he was the only one present not in on it.

Then Yarr swiftly, theatrically, stepped aside just inside the doorway to reveal a figure standing facing them in a cleared space in the middle of the sawdust. Old Carbin in his long stained raincoat, the dirty, lined face, the clapped-in toothless mouth. As soon as he saw Quigley framed in the door he moved his arms jerkily and went into a very slow soft-shoe routine back and forth in the sawdust. He looked like a bit of broken-down ancient clockwork that had been wound up and set in motion by the stranger's appearance. While he performed in silence all eyes were raised to fasten on Quigley standing on the top step. Yarr had stepped down into the crowd to enjoy the spectacle more. Finally, the old man came to a trembling stop, his knees sharply bent, the cracked shoes ploughing two long gleaming tracks on the floor, his arms describing some half-remembered fragment of music-hall gesture from his past. He seemed to hang there ridiculously for a long time while his deep dark eyes stared

37

hungrily at his one-man audience. There was silence. Quigley cleared his throat out of nervousness and the room erupted as on a signal, in a frenzy of ironic applause. "Good man yourself, Johnny." "By god, Johnny, you can still show them a t'ing or two!" "Take a bow, Johnny!" "You'll be on the fill-ums yet, Johnny me lad!" A great laugh at that and the eyes darted up at Quigley and then slyly back to Yarr.

How would he take that, wondered Yarr? For it was he who had tired unaccountably of all the mystery bubbling in their wake in every pub they had passed through that night and he who had arranged this little show, with the co-operation of the crowd, when he had got Quigley out to the lavatory. Anyway, wouldn't the whole town know his business, even to where he had shit last within another twenty-four hours? No harm done.

Quickly he said, "Johnny, who was it taught you that?" with the right amount of simulated awe. Again the hush, the expectancy. Men held pipes, glasses from their lips, waiting, holding in. The old man twisted with his hands deep in his pockets and barked, "Fred Astaire, who fuckin' else?"

Yarr led another great roar that burst out, washing the glasses and wood of the room, then draining. He clutched himself with crossed forearms while tears squeezed through the folds of skin around his eyes. The old boy stood unmoved, enjoying himself. The eyes were large and lustrous, black with little leaping yellow dots of light in them. When the vast cry had slid away, sighing, he darted across to the fringes of the crowd. "Any oul' combs or razor blades now?" plucking a tattered wallet up and out of his pocket. Coppers were reached to him good-humouredly and he collected them in his lean palms to be stowed away down in the lining of his overcoat. He gave no articles in return and none were expected.

Then Yarr sidled up to him and touched his shoulder. He swung round, mock affront on his face. "Niver do that, Mister Yarr, the last man done that was a big Arab in Sidi El Jib. An' I had to shoot him. God help us so I had, him and three other of his mates, big brutes o' fuzzy-wuzzies as black as your boot. That was the time I was in the Foreign Legion you know. Ach god give us strength but youse young fellas have no inklin' of the terrible ordeal we had to go through. I seen me marchin' through the desert till the soles was wore off me boots. A pair of new boots issued to us ivery fortnight. Ach god help us, times were bad, times were crucifyin' for a good young green Irish lad brought up in the best county in

38

Ireland. Och, merciful mother o' god, look down in your infinite mercy on poor oul' Johnny Carbin an' give him rest after a lifetime of wanderin' the stones o' this world ... Syria, Mesopotamia, Abyssinia, Algeria, Alexandria, Tunisia . . ."

The stream seemed endless, pouring out past those twin discoloured blunt fangs, hissing and spitting on the delighted faces of the mob. They swayed, happy grins on each raw red mug. Ranks of befuddled cobras. Some of them stole glances at Quigley, still standing on his pedestal, winked, then nodded conspiratorially over at the shuffling wreck in their midst. Yarr saw one of them, Owenie Quinn, a small man with screaming blue eyes in a round sweating face touch Quigley on the arm. He heard him whisper up at him, full of seriousness, "Shell shock in the Big War." His hair clung to his moon of a forehead in a schoolboy's damp wisp. Yarr felt contempt for him. And his ingratiating ways. He even had on his Sunday best clothes specially in honour of the big man from the movies. The fool!

He stole a glance at Quigley and his eyes ran into the other's gaze. He had been observing him. The look of bewilderment on his face sent him off once more into a huddle of merriment, his arms biting into his biceps, a wrinkle-faced bear. Then, master of the entertainment, out again in the centre of the floor with his hands on old Carbin's shoulders, with a big solemn face on him.

"Now, Johnny," he began gently, "this is Mr Quigley and he's come a very long way to see you . . ." Yarr looked up and winked. A smile came slowly to the other's face and Yarr knew he had understood the joke. "Now you *could* be in this film, you could be, it's entirely up to yourself. But now don't let us all down, Johnny, give him the best performance you can. You know what an audition is, don't you? You must dance a wee bit, you must act a wee bit. Johnny, you must sing."

The crowd vibrated on cue. Eyes darted at Quigley, faces cracked, grinned, and Yarr saw the last doubts clearing from his face. He knew the score and could now enjoy the performance that had been mounted specially for him. So on with it.

In the middle of the floor he and the old boy stood looking into each other's eyes. "Is it for a fill-um part?" whispered old Carbin.

"A fill-um," said Yarr, "a movie. Could be a starring role. Maybe. Maybe not. It's all up to you."

"What'll I sing?"

Yarr loosened his hold slightly on his shoulders. He screwed up his eyes. "Well now – ach, Johnny, don't you know better than I do what to sing?"

But the old bugger had lost his nerve. He couldn't rise to the bait as he'd hoped he would. Instead he began to shuffle after him, hen-like, anxiously trying to pen him while he, Yarr, strode rapidly around and around the grinning circle, just out of reach, pretending he wasn't there. The stern mien and Chaplinesque pace he affected for his audience set them guffawing once more. He could see Johnny shooting glances in Quigley's direction. But at last he could bear it no longer and, calming his rubbery old face and swerving eye-balls, he halted in the middle of the cleared space, took off his hat, held it reverently in front of him and lowered his lids. The noise from the crowd died from the centre outwards. Cries of, "Order, Order! The best of order there!" chastened those noisy spectators on the outer rim who couldn't quite keep up with events as they occurred in the ring. Whispered word was relayed back to them that old Johnny Carbin was about to sing. When all was silent, McCann and his fat wife, lowering rinsed glasses carefully on to a spread cloth, while miming to the crowd their enjoyment of the proceedings, Yarr announced neatly, "Gentlemen, I give you Mr Johnny Carbin for his pleasure . . . Mr Carbin." A very brief, very restrained bark of applause, then a deeper, more respectful silence than at any time.

The old fellow now looked as if he were praying and the long grey hair and bent poll strengthened the impression. His greasy coat-tails weighted with coppers hung perpendicular, almost to the split uppers of his shoes. He revolved his hat once and a deep swelling croak started somewhere in his chest, rose and issued from his barely parted lips. The song was one Yarr had heard him sing before in market square and pub.

> In a dreary Brixton prison
> Where an Irish rebel lay,
> By his side the priest was standing
> 'Ere his soul should pass away,
> As he faintly murmured, "Father,"
> As he clasped him by the hand,
> "Tell me this before you leave me,
> Shall my soul pass through the land?"

The verses rolled on monotonously. A few of the crowd swayed drunkenly with eyes closed, the rest leaned or stood impassive with great patience on their faces. Then the last note made its high journey up and out into the smoky air, tumbled and was gone. The applause boiled up and old Carbin lowered his head before it.

Yarr was staring. Surely to god he had imagined what he'd glimpsed a moment earlier when the old raincoat had opened briefly! He looked around him, searching other faces for confirmation. Nowhere could he distinguish a sharing of his own delight. But by Christ he *had* seen it! He *had*. And it was too good an opportunity to miss.

So out again into the arena once more. Johnny ignored him, a proud look on his face, still acknowledging the applause which was weakly renewing itself.

Then, "Johnny," he whispered loudly, "d'you not know there's a lady present?" The crowd tautened.

"What damn nonsense are ye after talkin' now, Yarr?" blustered old Carbin, a trace of fear in his eye.

Yarr glanced slyly over to the publican's wife and clutched himself, giggling. The crowd began to laugh with him, but puzzled. "Sure I couldn't tell you with Mrs Mac present." Under all the eyes the solitary woman began to look flustered. Her husband nudged her and she walked rapidly and angrily away from behind the bar towards the back door. McCann dropped on to his elbows on the bar when she had gone and smiled broadly on his packed house. The jelly bean eyes of him thumbed into a fat child's face perpetually twisted into a kind of suffering smile. Yarr could imagine him dying with that same rictus, the sweating undertaker labouring in vain to relax something that had taken years to set.

The same man now said, "Right then, Yarr, what's it all about? For you know well the oul' lady'll be lookin' for this good man here with a stick if you don't let him get away home to her."

The crowd hooted on cue and the old man grinned back at them in a sickly fashion. "Ach, shite," he said weakly, and again they laughed.

The little episode had pushed Yarr's timing awry. He stood, feeling lonely, out from the edge of the crowd, one hand in his pocket, the other plucking at his lapel, waiting. It became suddenly plain to him how apart he was from this mob. He didn't belong. He was, in fact, on a par with his victim. He also realised, and not for the first time in his life either, how cruelly fast they might align themselves against him if a whim nipped them.

He said quietly, without inflexion, "Johnny."

The old man snarled, baring his gums. "What is it?"

Silence. Then softly, "Johnny, you're hobby's hanging out, Johnny."

Great bellows of laughter beat against the ceiling and four walls of the pub. The old man had frozen into a ridiculous posture, one finger pointed, his slanted body supported on one leg bent, the other stiff.

"Aha!" he cried, "you don't catch me like that, ye fly huer. I'm too oul' a sodjer for that. Hard bloody luck, Mister Yarr of Ballyboe." He waggled the bent forefinger under Yarr's nose.

Yarr stood looking at him, with great pity on his face. "Johnny, oul' son, I'm sorry I spoke. I felt you might have wanted to know. But if you wish to go about the streets that way don't let me stop you. Only they do say, mind you, Judge Corrigan is shockin' hard on cases of indecent exposure."

"*Indecent exposure!*" shrieked old Carbin, hopping. He hurled off his hat and it cart-wheeled into the legs of the crowd. "You dirty Protestant bastard! You black Orange huer's get! You know what you can do, you can go back home across the Border an' lick Basil Brooke's loyal British arse, so you can!"

The crowd roared and this time Yarr felt his share of it. He glanced at Quigley to see if he had understood the significance of the barb. The Canadian was smiling, but that told him nothing. Quite suddenly then he lost interest in the whole proceedings. So he had made a mistake after all. Now the thing to do was to get out as gracefully as he could. He reached out for his glass on the counter, but the old man danced up to him, detaining him, malicious glee still unquenched in his face and his pipe-clay legged gait. "Oho, oho!" he crowed. "Who's laughin' on the other side of his face now, eh?"

"Go away on home, Johnny, an' don't bother me," said Yarr as if he were tired, looking away. "It's long past your bed-time. Oul' Maggie'll be hiding your trousers on you again, if you don't watch yourself."

Another great bellow at this reference to a well-known town joke against the Carbins. The old man spat ineffectually at Yarr who brushed the fine sheen of spittle from his coat-front. Around the room the crowd began to drink up, shuffling and talking among themselves now that the sport was at an end.

But a great hoarse cry of impotence fixed them for the last time and they turned back to the demented figure who was now leaning trembling on the edge of the bar, his two hands whitened with rage, staring out before him. He had every eye in the place on him. His misery was too extreme to be ignored. He held all the converging looks in place with his blazing eyes. Moving forward a step away from the bar, he began unbuttoning his coat from the neck downwards for there it was fastened by a safety-pin. The knuckly fingers moved shakily down to the last button until, with eyes devouring the faces encircling him, he pulled open the coat. He looked as if there should have been a tiny drum roll from somewhere, even a pianissimo fanfare. Instead there was silence – uneasy, lowering.

"Aha! No," he cried hoarsely, with triumph, "I'm too oul' a sodjer to be codded like that, Mister Yarr."

Someone tittered far back in the crowd, the first rip in the atmosphere, then it was slashed to tatters as laughter, harsh, cruel, burst out, up and down the bar. The old man's eyes dropped to his shame displayed for all to see. His shock was so intense he made no move to cover himself but stood, head drooped, eyes boring incredulously. A softly curving fat brown worm peering slyly back at him, uncannily youthful for such an old rackle of bones. Yarr remembered once seeing his own father like that unawares, and the shock that took weeks to heal. The obscenity of such a young man's prick placed where it was. It seemed to have a cunning, self-preserving existence of its own, holing out tenaciously through the years.

Life began to soak back into old Carbin. With his coat wrapped about him, he started backing towards the door. He was shouting. There was foam at the corners of his mouth. "Curse ye!" he cried, tears fogging his eyes. "Fuck all of ye! But especially *you*!" Yarr smiled back at him. "*Your* time is comin'. Some o' these nights you'll get a bullet in you, niver fear, you British cunt . . . *Informer*!"

He stumbled out with the last cry ringing behind him, stinging Yarr with an old half-forgotten memory. He shook himself as if the old man had been clinging to his back. The crowd fell to muttering among themselves. Some of them, he saw, were looking at him with a curious new regard, as if noticing him for the first time.

He walked over to Quigley, his mouth tight. Between his teeth, he hissed, "Let's get out of this fuckin' rebel kip."

Quigley followed as he pushed through the crowd.

THIS JOURNAL NOW. Repository of the day's fragments. Quigley's magpie hoard. Will the day ever come when he dips deep and comes up with the bits and pieces to form a composite – what? Maybe the habit's only a superstitious compulsion. . .

Still he finds it imperative to get down every idea as it arrives. Even if it means excusing himself to go to the can. Like Joyce. *Ach, poor man, the oul' bladder's playin' him merry hell again.* And Jamesey busy, with his wrinkled pants down around his shanks, scribbling assiduously the last half-hour's conversational nuggets from memory.

Not that I've found myself wandering into many bonanza situations since I've got here. Makes ironic mincemeat of the quote from that guide-book I read on the flight over. *And, of course, Irish pubs are a must for the tourist. There amidst the smoke, sawdust and rich old mahogany can be heard the ringing cadences and fantastic imagery of some of the best pub-talk in the world. And it goes without saying that the chat is helped along with liberal draughts of black Guinness porter from the barrel* . . . Liberal draughts of horse-shit, says Quigley. Nothing overheard so far but grunts about the weather, crops, funerals.

Funerals. It was the obituary column in his newspaper my old man always read first. An Irish thing. That Christian end with the full rites suspected to be not all it was cracked up to be. Pagan fears unallayed by a weekly brain-wash. The secrets of all those hushed-up death-beds – (not like the ones in the movies where Father Bing decorously shuttles off another contented soul to its haven. *God rest poor Mrs Morissey, shure she met her Maker with a darlin' smile on her face, so she did*). What about the ones never seen? The wrestling, swearing, kicking ones.

A film about death then. The Irish Way of Death. Opening. Long shot of moving vehicle on country road. Closer. An ordinary old Chevvy or Studebaker shooting-brake model. Black. Closer. Well, who would have guessed it? It's a hearse, for land sakes. One of those Irish ones with the windows and the fleur de lys metalwork up around the roof-rack. But battered and dusty and bald-tyred.

As if it's just completed a corpse-reviving drive over mountain roads at seventy miles an hour. Dying is the big thing here – not death. *Vide* the Irish wake where the stiff was (still is?) propped against the cabin wall, mocked, abused and elaborate jokes made about its genitals. On the main Dublin to Belfast road I passed a bad car crash. A pulped, pressed-in sedan like the one in all those cautionary photographs. It had collided head-on with a cattle truck. Pulled up on the soft shoulder near the scene a hearse. Like the one described. Sheet-covered corpse lying inside casually like a wrapped side of beef. Dollar-sized blood spots. And the crowd rubber-necking at the twisted metal and jagged windscreen. Let the dead look after their own, say they.

But perhaps you're hunting the symbol again, Quigley. Another case in point. While on the subject. Last night – those young kids filing into the dance-hall opposite the hotel. Having the backs of their hands stamped. So . . . Quigley thinks – quick cut to local livestock mart and the stamping of hides of cattle, sheep. Automatic. And slick visual journalism. But Quigley isn't a journalist with a soul of tin. Oh no. An artist. Who must wait until inspiration breathes on *him*. The passion that goes into a morsel of TV pap. All those glassy-eyed, coast-to-coast morons eating, swilling, scratching, farting, screwing (that divorce case where hubby demanded conjugal rights nightly to the strains of Lawrence Welk) while my masterpiece flickers its short life away. *Aw, turn that egg-head crap off, Mildred. These fugging art movies. Who do they take us for anyway, some kind of fairy nuts or somethin'? Open another can a beer and switch over.*

OUTSIDE IN THE STREETS a change had come over the town. Dusty cars, packed with young lads whose heads kept turning after every promenading girl, prowled, bumper to bumper. Their prey strolled arm in arm on either side, ignoring the waves, the smudged faces against the glass, the whistles. They were gay in an awkward giggling way as if they had on their first pair of high heels or were wearing their first brassières. They had on garish pink and blue and emerald and yellow cotton frocks with cheap white cardigans covering bare arms and shoulders which they kept drawing compulsively across their breasts as they giggled to one another up and down their advancing linked ranks. They made Yarr feel old and out of place. Their total absorption in themselves and their own age-group – the cruellest thing in the world.

He said thoughtfully, "It's too early for the big dance yet," and he knew Quigley was feeling the same as he was. "The older people are at the bingo." Then, with new interest, "Were you ever at a bingo session?" Quigley shook his head. "Do you want to go to one?" There was hesitation in his eyes. "You know," said Yarr smiling at him, "I still don't know what I can show you."

Quigley seemed to take it as a rebuke and spoke quickly. "What I would like to do right now is to walk around some more and just see things, things, I guess, you take for granted and which are new to me. Do you understand? Ideas only come to me after a day or two whenever things sort of settle down. Maybe I'm not making myself clear . . ."

Yarr looked at him. He laughed. "I'm getting the hang of it now, don't worry. You'll just have to explain it all to me, that's all. We're slow here. You're a big city man, remember."

"Yeah," Quigley replied, "slow as an express train." It pleased Yarr. He felt light, refreshed again after the bar episode.

"We'll do well together. You've the nice touch. Nothin' to beat the oul' soft soap."

Now he could see it was the other's turn to feel flattered, not that he thought your man believed a word he said, still it was pleasant. It would set them up for the night ahead. Carry them through on a strong tide of self-regard.

They strolled contentedly up the steep street with the young girls brushing past in excited waves. One of them swung a transistor radio by a long, long strap and its rhythm and blues was interrupted by the distorted ship's bell of a pirate radio station and then the disc jockey's over-Americanised spiel as they passed. The music came in waves, beaming in over quiet hills and rivers, lakes, soaring over trees, rocks, white cottages, hay-fields, over the heads of men at crossroads playing pitch and toss, priests on bicycles, bingo players, hurlers, couples languishing in dark hay-sheds among the must, fishermen, bored policemen on country patrols.

Up past the *Luxor* where Scott Brady was playing in *Mohawk* they walked, past all the shops with their windows crammed with lighters and religious statuettes and Kennedy plaques and fishing-reels and spoon-bait made in Japan. It was as if a tip-up truck had backed up to each one and emptied its load into that five by five space and no one had bothered to tidy a thing since. Each little cave, as they passed by, disclosed some old woman on a hard chair knitting or chewing absently and staring out at each new face.

Yarr told a true story about the proprietor of one of the shops that specialised in religious pictures and books. He had a gorgon of a wife who nagged and bullied the man day and night. Once someone went in to him and asked, "Healey, have you *The Life of Our Lord*?" to which he sorrowfully replied, "Michael, sure don't you know well I haven't the life of a bloody dog." They laughed their way up to the big Square, Yarr joining in as boisterously as the other when he saw how the story pleased him.

The Square was larger and more impressive than the low one. There was an intricate Victorian fountain squatting in its centre, with the old Queen's iron face frowning out in four directions – on the houses, shops and pubs on its perimeter. There were ranks of cars parked carelessly everywhere, and old men on benches smoking with brown cupped hands over their sticks, and two groups of young guards on opposite sides of the Square. They kept sliding glances across at four tinker women with their brood who were standing outside a pub. One of the women, a good six inches taller than Yarr himself she was, with a plaid shawl and hard dirty calves ringed with her scuffing wellingtons whined as they strolled up, "Give's a few coppers, sir. Sure it'll bring you luck. Ach, go on now."

Quigley started digging into his pocket, but Yarr held his arm. "Fuck off," he said to the tall woman quite casually, as if it were a greeting. "D'you not see the cops watchin' you?" She moved back a pace as if deflected from their passing bows and returned to her friends with a closed cold face.

"I wouldn't give them bastards the skin of my fart. They'd pick your pocket as soon as look at you." Then he laughed, clapping his friend's shoulder. "You've a lot to learn yet, boy. 'Course they can tell you're a soft oul' touch a mile away."

Then much more quietly in his ear, "Hang on a bit till we see the crack." The old mischief had re-asserted itself. He gestured across the Square to the steps of the ancient grey church where a drama had begun to split the drowsy peace of the evening. They propped their buttocks on the narow blistered sill of a shuttered hardware shop and watched. A few minutes earlier a big sleekly powerful tourist bus had pulled into the Square. On its side was painted THE KENMARE and its tomato-tinted transparent roof stained the faces of its passengers as they lay back in their seats. Their heads rested on prim white slip-covers which strengthened the funeral parlour effect of rows of patient tanned stiffs in a communal glass coffin. When the coach hissed to a halt the passengers started to pile, blinking, out on to the pavement. Some of them were obviously American, but the majority were English – unmistakably so – new-bought Arran sweaters, white pale cotton trousers with their wallets bulging in their hip pockets. The womenfolk wore the same sweaters and shapeless slacks. Harsh North-country accents rang out. "I say, look at this, Glad, it says 'ere 'twas built in sixteen eighty-nine . . . over 'ere, luv . . . The choorch, not that thing – the choorch, you silly fule!"

A group of them with sun-scorched faces were taking photographs with their Brownies when the tinkers invaded them like a redskin raiding party. They fell back in disarray before those swarthy amazons with fierce outstretched palms. Some of them had begun to delve nervously into pockets and hand-bags when the courier rushed up. He was a small dapper figure with a thin moustache and was wearing flannels and a blue monogrammed blazer. Diving at the tinker women with shooing arms he looked like a shepherd vainly trying to protect his flock from a wolf-pack. Yarr started to laugh and slap his knee as the scene began to take on the appearance of farce. The tinkers swarmed around the little courier with impassive faces, tormenting him. Then he accidentally grabbed one of them, an older one than the rest, with a child clinging to her skirts. They saw her arm go back and a fraction of a second after she'd hit him a thwack reached their ears. Stagger-ing, he clutched his face; then, catching him off-balance, the rest of the tinkers, in a swarm, had begun to belabour him, screeching like savages, their mouths wide, their eyes slitted. The guards started running across the Square. A roar of delight rose from the people standing about as the heavy blue-black figures sprinted clumsily with red embarrassed faces.

Yarr whistled and said, "Begod, man, if you had your camera now, eh?"

Quigley nodded sadly.

THE FRAGMENTS CONTINUE to fly in to roost. Quigley content to settle his little flock in their resting places each evening. Latest to arrive with a label in its beak saying *European Qualities. Refer to Incidence of Begging*, which still shocks the non-European or Britisher, for that matter . . . Or American.

On the fast Dublin-Belfast highway . . . young kids at regular intervals offering strawberries for sale. Punnets in their out-stretched hands. The young-old faces showing no emotion as the tyres zip past feet away. Offering themselves perhaps and not their sisters like their fellow mainland *ragazzi*. For, never realised it before – this is indeed the most western European country. Next parish – Boston.

Quigley's black dossier fattens. Ugliness in the eye of the beholder, perhaps? Or Quigley just getting even with his old man? Perhaps . . . How can any man love his "country", as he kept on insisting he did? Ireland – that vast intangibility. Lucky if he can love a townland, a village, a house, a room. But he said he did. Or if he didn't he made the presence of that thing felt. Like a monstrous green plant overshadowing our childhood. Any excitement, any new discovery we brought home to share was immediately relegated to something "back home". *Ach, you've never seen real this or real that. You don't know what the real thing is. How could you? Now when I was your age* . . . and another fable would begin. When we got older . . . savage New Worlders . . . chewing gum, swearing, smoking, feeling girls up alleys . . . we left him to his stories. Our father and his monologues. My mother never had time for such reminiscent extravagances. Her life was geared to dollars and cents and who would wear whose cast-off next.

But I should be charitable. It was his only vice. He could have been a drunk. And here I am back home – and it's not a bit like the way he told it. Ah, da, da, you misled your own son. How could you?

YARR SAID, "Lord Slaney's youngest daughter. Home for the holidays," twenty minutes later as another window-sill detained them and they followed with their eyes the slow, soft, breathing passage of a plum-coloured Mercedes through the streets. At the wheel she sat alone, head-scarf, enormous dark goggles preserving her aristocratic young looks from the crowd.

"Doesn't bother with a bathing-suit in the fine weather. Saw her myself once down at the pool in the Castle grounds. Just lay behind a tree and watched. Buck naked. Great!" He sighed gustily.

It was a lie. Not a word of truth in it. It had just come to him like that suddenly, for no apparent reason. But no – that wasn't entirely right – he wanted to see how your man reacted. That was it. And waited, but he didn't ask for details, like most men would – this one just sat smoking with his mind somewhere else.

Yarr liked observing reactions. Just start on a dirty yarn, or, better still, a bit of *true* dirt and just watch the eyes giving them away. Sharpening into brightness and the voice cracking dryly as they try to be easy when you stop in the middle.

Some of them like Packy Traynor, for instance, got very excited. The hand would dive into the pocket and he would croak, "Then what'd he do? What'd he do next?" Many's the time he had worked Packy up to an unbearable pitch. Chains of yarns hauled out hand over fist for the panting Packy. He could tell a good yarn, he had to admit, could remember dozens, all under topics – honeymoons, size of weapons, prostitutes, big women with small men and vice-versa, of course, greenhorns, medical, farmyard, queer, navy. Oh god, yes, dozens. Once he had spied on Packy after such a bout. He had crept up to the privy and through a knot-hole had watched him shaking the whole structure with his antics, the dirty pig. He had watched the crazy hanging mouth, the closed eyes, the concentration on that part of him which was out of vision. Christ, the way he savaged himself! And the way his eyes turned up fishy-white afterwards, and the flopping down of his shoulders and arms and the quivering of his legs which ran straight through the thin wood into Yarr's own braced palms. He couldn't get over it at the time. There was something frightening in all that intensity loosed inside that small box.

In a way it wasn't like watching another human being at all. He couldn't bridge the gap between them, couldn't fully understand or sympathise with what that other person was experiencing. He was like that with everyone, wasn't he, when he thought about it. There were times, *when he thought about it*, when he knew with a dull hopeless ache that there was something wrong with him that way. All his knowledge of life, all his sharp sly observation of other people that he was so proud of, turned sour in him and he felt very alone. Other people seemed not to feel that way, as far as he could see, never separate, never conscious of being as different as a horse, say, among a herd of cows or a cow among horses; because he didn't feel superior, not all the time, most of the time, yes, because the people he saw every day weren't in his class, he wasn't being big-headed, that was a fact which he'd proved over and over again. No, not superior *all* the time, because occasionally you met someone who was your weight and would make the contest last, keeping you extended full out. Quigley? Yes . . . Yes. But he didn't think much about things like that if he could help it. It brought on the headaches, and, much more important, led you nowhere. You ended up every time like one of those rats inside the revolving cage, thoughts chasing each other's long limp tails endlessly. *You've got to pull yourself out of yourself*, Doctor Mac kept telling him. *You think too bloody much, man. I'm telling you, if you don't stop all this self-indulgence you'll –* No need to finish it. They both knew the final stopping place, that end of the line halt whose name they tactfully omitted from all their conversations. It was unlike the old grey medical man to be a pussy-foot. He had developed that bluff, call a spade a spade surgery manner. But even he sensed how deep was the dark pit that opened up inside his patient every time thoughts brushed within touching distance of *that place*.

Again he turned to the girl whose head and shoulders he could still see silhouetted in the rear window of her father's car as she edged it up the hilly street. The big saloon moved through the careless crowds like a great soft-footed beast brushing them with its glittering body. The girl looked as untouchable as ever within her polished shell, even at that distance. Mysterious. Out of reach. Every woman in every crawling car that had passed him that evening had her share of that quality. The cynical side of him told him that if the cars all suddenly stopped and they got out the allure would fall away from them in an instant, and they would be revealed as red-faced, fat-legged and wearing clothes that had become wrinkled with their hot cramped travelling. But the other side of him ached after them, asking, asking – where do they come from? Where are they going? He felt suddenly defenceless against the potency in the hot night air.

At that moment the recently formed John F. Kennedy Memorial Accordion Band came marching out of a side street and Sonny Dolan, their leader, twirled them flamboyantly into a sharp left turn and up the hill towards them. His silver-capped pole whirled like a wind-borne propeller high above his head and Yarr prayed for it to descend on his thick skull. He had missed the wonderful occasion when Dolan had blacked out the entire town by hurling it up into a power line outside Gallery's. He had been full then but tonight he was as steady as a judge, his chin-strap cutting into a red, solemn jowl, his white drip-dry shirt and gloves immaculate.

Yarr despised him and his ridiculous self-importance. He scorned the whole bunch of them for their stupidity, for their being so blind to the spectacle they were making of themselves and yet so puffed-up at the same time, imagining that everyone in the crowd was envying them. Yahoos to a man. Every outward sign of their bog-trotting mentality registered with him in a cold precise catalogue – the big cheap expanding silver watch-straps, the transparent nylon shirts exposing string-vests, the four in hand ties, the leather belts. This was his way of despising them. He lounged there at his ease, sardonically eyeing them stirring up the dust, dry dung and litter of Casement Street.

Twenty-five brand new button-keyed Höhners played *Boola-vogue* and the music sucked the crowd along in its wake up to the Square where one of the many ceremonies of that evening was to be performed. Yarr chuckled to himself. Pope-heads. But his derision could never quite ease away his hatred. You could laugh at them, fine, but you couldn't ignore them, no, by christ, you couldn't.

He suddenly became aware of an arc of giggling girls just across the street from them. They were jostling each other before Canavan's window, with their backs to them, but they kept looking across at Quigley and himself, and then their eyes would dart off again. One of them was Bridie. She was the leader, he could tell that, by the way her eyes were sparkling and the way her short red hair tossed. She also stood out from the others because of a new rig-out she was wearing that he had never seen

54

on her before. Then he recalled that she'd received a bulky parcel from her sister in London a few days back.

He pretended interest in the disappearing band while watching them closely. Bridie kept drawing them together, holding them in whispers for a moment, then releasing them in a shrieking flurry. They were her acolytes for that one evening because they were in the mood to be led and she felt she could, because of her new-found confidence. Yarr eyed her slyly and took in the short blue denim skirt and the sleeveless sweater with a white anchor on its front and the delicate sandals that made her feet keep lifting light as air. He had never seen her look so good.

He thought for a moment with regret of when he could have touched her a dozen times a day – in the shop when no one was looking or up in the back storeroom among the racks of army surplus, his hands sliding up over the smooth backs of her thighs and under the elastic or down the neck of her dress or into her downy arm-pits. It was like a disease with him. He had to touch, touch all the time and the tiny token whispers of resistance only made the itch all the worse. And the nights he had turned the dented brass knob of her bedroom door so very gently and found that she hadn't put the snib across. How many nights? Five? Six? Maybe more. It didn't matter. Not now. Because he never left his own bed now, not even when Ruby was staying away overnight and there were only the two of them lying above the shop, awake, listening to the weary cracking of the old beams and the crickets below, the two of them lying within two feet of one another. The wall between was one sheet of tongue and grooved board with about six flattening coats of old flowery pink wallpaper on either side. There were nights when he could well imagine their sharp thoughts knifing through to each other as they lay there waiting for something to happen, only he never made it again. Couldn't.

And she had quickly sensed the change in him – those nights, the way he stopped sending her up to the store ahead of him, keeping his hands to himself so scrupulously, even gentlemanly. She smelt weakness and soon began to take chances with him and the more her cheek went unchecked the bolder she grew. And he let her off with it, all of it, even the times she answered back in front of the customers. Not because she might talk; he knew she wouldn't because she would always suffer in the village a hell of a sight more than he would, and that was what really made her hate him, he felt.

55

No, he wasn't afraid of talk; he just was *tired*, simply tired – the only word for it – something over which he had no control, a seeping away caused by *this thing*, whatever the hell it was. Oh, there was a name for it all right, all those glib labels the clever boy in the white coat had carelessly, contemptuously, shoved across the table at him when he went for his consultation. He supposed that he meant them as consolation but he never could wrench his brain into a position to make it believe that there were other people with exactly the same symptoms as himself. The guy in the white coat might be able to see it that way but he couldn't.

On an impulse, he called out across the street, "Bridie!" and she betrayed herself by the quick way her head came round. "I want you a minute!"

She came towards him, her head tossing and her new handbag swinging from its long loop, while her friends hung together behind her giggling with a sudden vehemence. Glancing back at them once with a mock-stern face, she only sent them into deeper fits of merriment.

She was smiling to herself as she finally confronted Yarr. She stood, feet apart, with the little triangular suede bag swinging gently between her legs like a pendulum. "Well?" she said sharply, giving Quigley a darting glance, "What do you want?"

Yarr looked at her snub nose and the freckles which the sun had brought out, then, slowly, arrogantly, he allowed his eyes to slide lazily down over the rest of her. When he glanced up slyly again he saw that she was blushing. He felt a pang then strangely, that had nothing to do with gratification. Instead he was astounded at his sudden urge to put his arms swiftly around her waist, dipping his hands into the twin patch pockets on each of her trim little round buttocks, feeling the heat of her warming his palms until, drawing her close, closer, her arching back from the waist, beating at him, sobbing, pleading, until, until, *until*, inevitably, inexorably he would draw her closer, closer, until she felt the hard bud pressing and then with a moan giving in, pressing to meet it – only there's no hard bud, bud? Eh?

He laughed bitterly and he saw her eyes and Quigley's rush together, then away again. Still laughing, he cried, "Bridie, I want you to meet this gentleman – who's travelled such a long way to meet us!"

He ignored the quick look that he felt directed at him. Realising he sounded drunk, he decided to play on it so he made a grab at

Bridie. "This is Mr Quigley. This is Bridie. You two should meet each other. *Meet* each other."

She pulled away from him and although he felt as tense as a rod he pretended to let his hand flop. He saw her smile shyly at Quigley, then freeze that smile for him. It registered suddenly like a sharp-edged image on a screen. For a moment he thought he was going to feel jealousy, and, sure enough, there was a nibble of nausea somewhere deep in the stomach which he remembered as the way it used to work in him, but then it ceased abruptly and he relaxed. Very old, tired *and* wise, that was the way he felt just then, above it all, all this – that other people felt. This was the way his life slid on from day to day, when he hadn't the headaches or when he didn't let people excite him or when he experienced none of those pin-pricks of old-remembered emotion from his past. Control was the secret. That was it. Control, always control.

"Are you going to the dance?" asked Quigley smiling and Bridie nodded.

"Are *you*?" asked Bridie and Quigley looked at Yarr.

Yarr said, "What would two old codgers like us go there for?" and Bridie, reddening again, said quickly, "*You're* not old." But he knew she meant it for Quigley who was still watching her with that smile on his face. The women go for him, thought Yarr, it's not just because he's a new face or a yank, they'd go for him anyway, anywhere. I wonder does he know it.

He remembered a time when *he* would have had no trouble in getting a woman at dances. They liked his cheek, the dash with which he propositioned them. And very few refused to go out with him – sometimes in the middle of the dance even, to his old van with the spread khaki blanket in the back on which he forced his terms. They wanted it that way and he treated every woman he met the same – except of course for Ruby. *She* fixed him, so she did – sly, quiet little Ruby Tate from Derrygonnelly with her mind set on what she wanted. Him? In a way, yes, or rather, what *she* saw when she looked at him, not him as he was, but *her* version, someone who would provide her with what her secret self had always promised itself. Hard cheese, Ruby, hard fucking cheese . . .

"Okay then, my darling, have a good time an' don't do anythin' I would do," he said, dismissing her. She moved away from them awkwardly, still self-consciously swinging the bag.

"An' keep your legs crossed!" he called out for a parting shot.

He laughed at the venom in her eyes. He could always master her and she knew it. He gloried in his revenge, for he knew exactly how her mind was working at that moment as she crossed the street to her pals. Some of the confidence had drained out of her springing walk already, for she was wondering if he had told, was telling or was going to tell your man that she was easy meat.

Deliberately he leaned forward, pretending to whisper into Quigley's ear, for Bridie's benefit. He told him the one about the chap who went into the pub lavatory and when his job was done discovered there was no paper. *Have any of you lads out there a bit of newspaper handy? Sorry.* Pause. *Would one of youse have an oul' letter in his wallet? Sorry.* Very long pause. Then, pathetically, *Could any of youse give us two ten bob notes for a pound?* Quigley seemed to appreciate it, giving a chuckle with his head back, closing his eyes. Then Yarr saw Bridie fling back her head suddenly and dart up the hilly street followed by her puzzled friends. Aha . . . Aha.

The laughing slowly died away the way it does, reviving fitfully for moments as they glanced at one another, remembering the joke, then going, flaring again, then finally sliding off into silence. People passed; some of them knew Yarr and nodded to him, switching their look swiftly across to the stranger at his side, then back to him. The whole town would know who he was and his business before morning, but Yarr still revelled in holding their curiosity at bay as long as he could. In a way he was deliberately increasing their suspense by his movements that evening up and down and in and around Slaney. Very rarely would he behave in such a way, even on an occasion of festivity as this. He only came into the town when he could help it, for goods usually, which he would smuggle back across the border. Nothing big; he was getting too old for panic – cigarette lighters, a case or two of matches, a dozen pounds of butter, the odd bottle of Power's Ten Year Old; it all depended on the economic see-saw which was very flighty these days. You didn't want to be left with a load on your hands. Cigarettes were safe nearly all the time, of course, and very good payers at the moment, especially with that new fourpence on every English twenty packet since the Budget. They marked them, of course, but he knew one or two chancy shopkeepers up in the far North who went in for risks like that.

At that moment, with a suddenness that shook him, a dove-grey Zephyr with four uniformed men on board cruised by. The

58

men were all young and slumped arrogantly in their deep seats, glancing out of the windows at the people they passed. Guilt raced in Yarr as the one beside the driver stared back at him coolly through the streaked glass. Then the big dusty snub tail of the car topped the hill, sliding into the Square with the twin brake lights signalling some obstacle ahead.

Even though he knew it was stupid to think that way, he half-believed that the Customs' car appearing like that was somehow deliberate. It was just another of his personal superstitions that he employed when anything frighteningly inexplicable happened in his life. They weren't solutions in the real sense, they only occupied his mind until the fear had passed and the event itself had been forgotten.

"I suppose I'd better get a room for myself for the night in that hotel back there. I didn't bother making any reservations for this trip."

Yarr looked at him. "Look here," he said, as an idea started taking shape. "You have to take me back home anyway so why don't you stay with us? It's not the Ritz but we have a spare room if it's any good to you."

They stood up together and a minute later began to move across to a facing pub with everything settled. Quigley had made the minimum of the usual polite noises about not wanting to put anyone out etc., and Yarr had in turn accorded him the traditional reassurance.

CONTINUATION OF THE SEARCH for Quigley's mental Shangri La. In its rural setting. The countryside outside the car windows changing startlingly. But the transition from pasture to woodland to black bog and hill country and back again smooth enough – to a native. To Quigley – a terrain in microcosm. After America the image occurs of one of those miniature landscapes in a bottle. Carboy country. No real stamp – except the famous guide-book greenness. Coming in on the plane – the land tilting up and then away again as the pilot plotted his landing – the patchwork (only word to describe it) quality, the small areas – how can each one be different in size and shade of green? Small fields marching to the blue of the hills, trees like diminishing green explosions, silver water encroaching everywhere.

Later. First signs of human inadequacy to cope in all this natural perfection. Ruined cottages – roofless, yellow fudgy crumbling walls, doors plastered with auction posters, old bedsteads taking the place of gates. A man moodily gazing over the hedge as I came along his road. As if he had been waiting there for ever, just to watch my car go past. A despairing quality about each farmstead. The slovenly exteriors – buildings, yards, outhouses, lanes. Indicating life inside?

Two short reports from a local newspaper I picked up in a bar.

Man Who Killed Dog He Loved Fined £5. Paudge Mallon battered his pet to death with an axe. He said, "I thought it had rabies and I lifted the first thing that came to my hand. I loved the dog and many a time it got half my dinner."

More murder. A young woman travelling across on the boat to Holyhead with her illegitimate three-month-old baby. Threw the child overboard and, when apprehended, said, "He is now an angel in Heaven."

Quigley, can you missionary among these people?

IT WAS FIVE MINUTES TO ELEVEN as they ordered their first round – a Jameson for Quigley and a small brandy and ginger for himself. He had decided to switch his drinks. It was something he would do now and then, not because he wanted to get drunk faster, but because he was feeling festive and wanted to recapture the excitement which used to come from the thought of drink and not its effects.

The bar was new and was still looked after eagerly by the two young boys behind the white formica counter. There were slogans on the walls and clean ash-trays and drip-mats advertising *Harp* and the legs of the stools still hadn't lost their matt black finish. But the best thing was the display behind the barmen's heads. Hidden lighting transformed every bottle into a glowing joy – tawny reds, emerald greens, honeys, ambers, pinks, purples – merging fluidly into one sweep of stained glass which could become more wondrous to the drunken worshipper as the night spun on.

Yarr let the spicy liquid roll down his throat, one thin trickle at a time escaping from a full mouth. It seemed to unloose a warmth in him that the earlier drink had failed to reach. Quigley bought a second round and, from their stools, they toasted one another silently, smiling over the thin rims of their glasses. Then Yarr bought a packet of slim cigars and sensuously unwrapped the cellophane, enjoying the picture of the old Meynheer and the romantic legend on the dark brown and gold box. They lit up and the expensive aroma began to fill the room. The other drinkers sniffed appreciatively and conversation started along the bar about the relative merits of different brands. Men sitting around the walls at tables joined in without any shyness and they were the centre of it all, benign on their round stools. It was as if the room had begun to drift off up into space, into the night, like a lighted craft, full of friendly people talking, laughing, discovering one another . . . and it seemed as if nothing could mar it. Even when the first gentle reminders about the time began to fall on the air the warmth and noise hardly trembled. Yarr looked at Quigley and he grinned back at him, sharing the experience with him. He loved him at that moment because he looked young and happy and clean in a boyish way, with his soft blue shirt heightening his tan.

61

Instinctively he reached out, putting an arm around the other's shoulder. Quigley's smile stretched and, in turn, he touched his elbow into Yarr's ribs. Letting his arm drop until his palm felt the cool edge of leather on the other's seat, Yarr took another swallow of his drink, using his left hand. The tiny pattern of movements seemed so effortless yet so perfect in design that his eyes became moist. He felt purged of all the corroding emotions that beset him, returned to a former age of innocence. All the faces around him seemed to be beaming with goodness. Men were buying drinks for other men and not worrying about getting one in return, or bothering to count their change which lay in heaps before them on the tables. Two old countrymen in tweed caps with gleaming vees of shirt front – the old-fashioned kind, of a sort of soft flannel with delicate hair-line stripes and no collar, just fastened at the neck with a little brass stud – were crooning gently to one another in a corner. They had their wrinkled hands on each other's knees and swayed with closed eyes, remembering in harmony an old come-all-ye from their youth. And not one woman in the place to spoil things. A woman would have hated what she saw around her, would have plotted and squirmed and tricked until she tumbled all.

He said to the man beside him, "It's not such a bad oul' country to live in – betimes."

Quigley raised his glass. "To Ireland. Mother Ireland," and Yarr touched glass, echoing the toast. He felt amazed even more at himself at not resenting the sentiment and the disloyalty it normally implied. Stranger still, the words were taken up along the bar and passed on from man to man without any embarrassment at the possibility of vexing anyone's politics.

Nothing could shake the mood. Nothing that is except time. The anguish on the barmen's faces could no longer be ignored, or their whispered entreaties about the guards, or their apologetic gradual dowsing of lights. In time only the great glass altar glowed, tinging the faces of the assembled drinkers with streaks of colour. As the lights finally dimmed so did the gaiety. Men began to make their way sadly in files to a back door, guided on their way by the whispering boys.

Yarr sighed, "We'll go," and the two of them slid off their stools. It was all over.

But a little of the mood they carried with them up through the cobbled yard under an archway where men leaned, talking softly, their faces briefly illuminated by cigarette points, out into the night streets where, miraculously, all the lights had come on. The sky had retreated into blue-blackness above the sheltering spread of brightness. It seemed very far off, if it was there at all.

Yarr shivered as the cooling air touched him through his thin shirt. He decided to buy himself a five-glass bottle of whiskey to keep the heat in. There was a place at the head of the town where he was known and where no fuss would be made about supplying it after hours. He nudged Quigley who seemed slightly muzzy, smiling to himself happily, as he rocked a little back and forth. "Will we have a look in at the big dance, eh?"

"Good idea. Would love to." He spoke like a ventriloquist, but nodding. Yarr felt pleased at noting how much further on he was than himself, jarred in fact, but it wasn't a malicious thought, more one of sympathetic brotherhood.

Together they started up the hill which seemed to have become suddenly very steep. Both felt like mountaineers, thrusting heavy booted feet forward, then pulling them after.

At Maggie Shiel's where he was to get the whiskey, a pink haze stained his vision and he staggered a little, breathing in and out ponderously. The one step up into the spirit grocer's seemed a further unfair obstacle and the sweaty ball of his thumb slipped painfully off the worn brass door-catch.

Blundering into the unlit shop he became aware of shadowy eyes and pale blob faces watching him warily, for four or five men were lingering at the grocery side of the counter over the last few purchases. The old woman was slicing off some ham on her ancient machine. There was a pile of rashers on the waiting brown wrapping paper, two inches high.

She peered at him out of punished eyes and croaked, "Is it Mister Yarr?"

One of the men laughed as if it were a joke, but it was from nervousness. They were all mountainy men. This was the only shop in Slaney they would have any dealings with. Its old dark mustiness appealed to them, reassured them, as did Maggie herself who hadn't changed for forty years. "Well, lads, an' I suppose youse'll all be off to the big ball, eh?"

He spoke to them as if they were children and they swayed a moment in return, smiling, saying nothing, with downcast eyes. He sat down on an upturned butter box and watched them with a wry grin. But he did not underestimate them. Would never. Their very deviousness thrived on their being treated patronisingly. Out of it grew their strength. He knew they would discuss him with cruel wit, wounding him in his absence, on the long bicycle ride home to their holdings. They were lucky if they had a single sow, or a decent suit of clothes to their back, but still they *knew* they had the edge. At times he had been irritated by this granite-hard feeling of superiority to ordinary twentieth-century men, but then gradually he grew to accept it, even respecting them and their ways.

With a new idea growing he said to the old woman, "I'm lookin' for a drap o' somethin' to keep the heat in on a sharp oul' night like this," but his voice was angled at the group in the shadows.

They stood like conspirators in dark stiff suits, navy-blue chalk-striped for the most part, with their white collarless shirts and irises the only indication of their presence. Great ones for the dark these, never bothering at home to put a flame to a wick while a turf-fire still glowed from the grate. Savers of lamp-oil and candle, except of course for the perpetual red glow-worm before the big crimson Heart.

Old Maggie said craftily, "A wee naggin' of Black Bush might be what you're after . . ."

The men in the corner chuckled for now they knew what he really desired and were enjoying the game.

"I wouldn't think so," said Yarr, prepared to wait. "No."

"No?" asked the old woman, shifting weight on her feet so that a whiff of embrocation, peat smoke and paraffin came from her disturbed clothing, along with other smells that on a hot day could make the stomach slide.

"No," replied Yarr, while his nail traversed a crack in the wood of the butter box. "Mebbe some o' you lads might be able to advise me . . ."

A tall thin one with a joker's face stepped a little out of the shadows.

"Could you oblige me with a light, Mister Yarr?" he said, a Woodbine ready between his long fingers. Yarr struck a match and he leaned towards the flame. His lit Adam's apple was liberally sown with sprouting, lopped ginger hairs and he sucked at his cigarette until the red raced back from its tip. "Thank you," he said, and blew out a vast rush of smoke.

Yarr sat still and stroked the head of a mongrel which had crept out to him from the thicket of legs in the corner. The dog trembled and its nervous heat travelled into his palm. He caressed its smooth head until his hand felt oily. Suddenly it became loathsome to him and he took his hand away.

The smoker said, "It's a nippy sort of a night that, for the time o' year, sure enough," wishing to bring Yarr back to his work again.

"Aye," he replied. Then he winked at the tall scrawny one, adding, "Maggie'd need a good man to warm her up on a night like that." He let his eyes rest on the others. "Eh, lads?"

A soft burst of laughter broke in the corner and the old dame joined in. Then someone said, "Mebbe you'd be the very man for the job yourself, Mr Yarr." Yarr smiled for the sake of appearances, for his mind had quite suddenly seemed to shrink. It was the horror back again, or rather the horrors, because the images rose up like breaking bubbles. *Foulness, stench . . . the old woman spread out beneath him on her awful bed, unmade for fifty years, riddled rotting layers of linen, bolsters like black strings beneath her fanning hair that she'd unpinned coyly for him, her gums smiling, her raddled arms stretched invitingly up to him to draw him down into that wasteland of grey, sprouting tufts and yellow flesh and the smells rising from pits unbattened by desire . . .*

He felt the contents of his stomach stir, was convinced even of a swirl. He visualised that curded broth awash inside him with a vividness that broke sweat out on his face. Gulping, he staggered to his feet, paying no heed to the hurriedly darting eyes. He almost fell down the steps outside, just managing to brace himself on one jammed leg that seemed to ram up into him, a pile-driving motion that added the nausea of pain to the other sickness.

There was a black alley-mouth beside the shop and he half-ran into its darkness, bent double. A pebble-dashed wall halted his palms, stung them as he pushed. With unbelievable delicacy, he straddled his legs apart, settling his shoes into gravel, bringing his head down gently until it pressed between his hands against the wall. And then he waited for the tide to rise to his lips – but it kept hesitating, mere inches it seemed from overflow before slipping back down again to settle for a second then crawling upwards resentfully once more.

He saw himself crouched this way for an eternity, suffering that cruel piston. Tensing his left arm to do the work of two, he took the other away. It felt prickly with the tiny stones from the wall embedded in its palm. He began to push two fingers down his throat, withdrawing them quickly each time he retched. Waiting, then repeating it. The fingers began to feel slimy and cold and he shook from the weakness. He felt as if he were depleting his strength too fast, that what he was doing was dangerous, straining his heart and other organs. Tears squeezed from his eyes, chilling on his cheeks. He felt angry, cursing the sluggish mass in his stomach, then sent his fingers further down than he had previously dared. The reaction threatened to split him in two and his bracing arms slipped weakly, causing his head to rasp down the wall. Then liquid boiled into his mouth and out. Faster and faster he kept bringing his fingers up, into his throat, out, up, in, out, up, in, out . . . He was enjoying it now in a way, calculating quantities, measuring reactions and felt disappointment when eventually nothing but saliva filled his mouth. He spat and it dropped stickily. He brought up his hand to wipe some from his chin and smelt his cold wet fingers. They were distasteful, not to be borne, and, straightening, he felt for his handkerchief and wiped them. Then he scrubbed his lips, but his mouth inside felt raw and bitter tasting, scalded. He must have a drink. Must.

In the shop they stopped talking – about him, he was sure – when he reappeared. His shoes were flecked with vomit and their eyes searched the rest of him greedily for further evidence of his humiliation.

"Look," he said, "no more batin' about the bloody bush. How much?" and he fluttered two notes before the dark closed faces. "You know me," he continued, impatience colouring his voice, roughening it, "we've done business before an' I pay on the nail. Amn't I right?"

They shuffled their feet, uneasy before such directness. The tall one who'd asked him for a light earlier spoke for all of them. "That's no word of a lie now." But he sounded cheated. Yarr had broken the rules, rushing to the point the way a city-man would, because he knew no better, yet now that he had done it he couldn't be refused, for the man knew he could never break the rules himself. They were like fine steel bands securing, yet at a time like this, sorely imprisoning. Their chafing showed plainly in his face for a moment, before he nodded to someone in the shadows, a shambler with a heavy head and hands and two planking great feet on him like something twisted and black out of a bog.

Planting these boots apart, he unslung a khaki gas-mask bag

with a grunt and pulled from it a filled, clear glass lemonade bottle, corked with a screw of brown paper. He reached it to old Maggie who snatched it from him nervously, diving into a recess at the back of the shop. The tall man stooped forward and gently, almost reluctantly, pulled a pound note from between Yarr's outstretched fingers. This he carefully folded into a wad about the size of a postage stamp and then stowed it away in his bottom waistcoat pocket.

Yarr saw that the waistcoat had red piping and recognised it as the sort that postmen wore. Most of their clothing was like that – cast-off articles of uniform from many armies and organisations. He had sold most of it to them himself. Shrewdly, over the years, he had built up the biggest stock of surplus of any shopkeeper in the area.

The old woman was standing behind the counter with something wrapped in brown paper for him. He took it from her, shucking off the covering to reveal a full five-glass spirit bottle of colourless liquid. The label read CORK DRY GIN and he chuckled to himself as he twisted the metal screw cap. He sniffed the oily fumes before raising the bottle to his lips. Above the raised bottle he watched the uneasy faces. Then, swinging it round mockingly, he sighted on Maggie before swallowing. The poteen seemed to char a dropping path inside his throat before igniting in his stomach. He waited shuddering for a moment with closed eyes and when he opened them there was a tumbler of water on the counter. He drained it and the combined tastes of vomit and liquor were washed away.

He looked around him, restored, with the old comfortable warmth spreading through him once more. He felt very pleased with himself. It was a satisfying achievement to have emptied his stomach like that, extending the limits of enjoyment of the night ahead of him. Then – *Christ*, he had clean forgotten all about Quigley!

He bowed to the company, deeply, ironically, and walked quickly out. The slightly convex bottle felt good against his hip, comforting, just like a gun. Outside, in the colder night air, he shivered. Where *was* the man? How long had he left him anyway? It seemed like an hour, but then he thought – time hangs back when you've drink so –

At his elbow, a grinning jack-in-the-box suddenly said, "Hi," and laughed. Quigley. His face looked lopsided, the eyes very far back and twinkling. Yarr felt relief at his condition and replied, also laughing, "Hi," and the other rubbed his hands together quickly up and down before his chin.

"Say," he said, still laughing. "Are *all* the pubs closed around this place?"

Yarr studied him. His tie had become loose and the tiny undercover pearl button gleamed, reflecting light from a street lamp. The hair wasn't as crisp, as trained looking now, and there was a recent stain above the breast pocket of his jacket which swung open. There was also something bumpy in one of his side pockets, pulling the fabric out of shape. He looked very ordinary, drunk, and not at all the controlled sophisticate Yarr had met at the beginning. Yarr felt he would enjoy gently leading him in this state, pressing easily but firmly on the long, loose rein connecting them – so away let us go, my little pony, he thought, and away they went.

In a black entry behind the cinema they passed the bottle back and forth between them three times – three disciplined sips of fire-water – while the distant sound-track rumbled incomprehensibly. The noise made Yarr yearn for glamorous experiences. Somewhere out in the night there awaited him sensations both magical and sensual. He was certain of it. His eyes closed and he leaned back against the brick, listening to the blurred rise and fall, smelling the sour piss, because this was where the patrons relieved themselves at the interval. He remembered when he was young how the girls used to rush out giggling in a clutch to squat with spread skirts while hidden waters burst out mysteriously from beneath them to sluice over the tilted cement to a grating. The strange noise roused him – that and the glitter in their eyes as they faced any boy who had the courage to follow and watch. They were like some breed of fowl, exciting each other – and dangerous in a flock.

"Ahhhh . . ." breathed out Quigley. "Do you think," he whispered in the darkness, "that right now if I took a match, struck it, held it here like this" – he gestured to his mouth – "that I could breathe fire like one of those guys you see in the circus? Eh? Do you reckon? Hm? Well come on, whaddya say, my friend? Have I a future as a fire-swallower or haven't I?"

Yarr smiled as he tightened the cap on his bottle. He replaced it in his pocket with enormous care, patting the bulge several times to reassure himself that it was safe there, buttoned to his hip. It seemed to mould itself to his shape, a friendly little thing, reliable. A song came into his head, one he had learned a long time ago in school, yet it was only then that he fully appreciated its sentiments.

> "Ha, ha, ha," he sang gently, "You and me,
> Little brown jug, don't I love thee?"

Startled, he felt Quigley's exploring hand meeting his own, tightening on it and then his voice breathing on his face softly, sick-sweet with drink. "May I have the pleasure of this dance?"

He stiffened, then eased with him, laughing. "But, of course. But, of course."

They circled around, surprisingly nimble for a moment, over the spongy layers of trodden down rubbish that had been dropped by countless patrons of the *Luxor*. Then Quigley stumbled, falling back, pulling him closer to him in an attempt to stabilise himself. Yarr tightened his arms around the other involuntarily in a bear's hug, his cheek squeezed to the other's and they staggered up against a wall tight in each other's embrace.

He felt Quigley's moist laugh in his ear, his breath coming fast in gusts. "Oh god almighty, this'll kill me," he was wheezing, still clinging to him like a drunk old man, rolling like a rag doll.

He relaxed for a moment, yet gripping more strongly than he was being gripped, certain for the second time of his control over the other. Gradually he became conscious of the other's body. Individual areas asserted themselves – shoulders, arms, chest – and he began to know the man as he'd never previously known him. His smell, for instance. Close up now he could distinguish between the several different lotions that he used, which before had merged into a single personal odour. To his own surprise, he found himself wanting to prolong their embrace beyond the point where he could still shake himself loose and have what they had been doing seem natural. And, amazing himself even more, he stayed where he was. His legs started to tremble as he fought against a lazy warm onrush that was rising in him. Then low down he felt a blunt pressure hardening against his own thigh. He jerked away and the other's arms flopped, released.

"God," he said, "I'm burstin' for a pump."

His voice sounded rusty, unused, and he moved dizzily further along the wall, unbuttoning. Then he heard him at his side lurching a little, unzipping too, then the harsh horse-piss against the wall. Yarr felt embarrassed standing there unable to pee, but took consolation in the other's state. Glancing down sideways he had a glimpse of a pale firm root between the other's finger and thumb stretching out to the gleaming wetted brick. Yarr took nothing out of that for he knew men, he knew himself, from the past anyway, when a dozen or more times a day his own swelling would be set off by even a thought or a stray pressure. No, there was nothing in it.

He began to pee at last and shivered. And he was beginning to sober up again. Another slug? No. It wasn't on because of your man's condition. That one was in a fair way to being footless. Just look at him. His forehead pressed up against the wall as he tried to shake off the last drops. God, but he was making the right ballocks of it. Should he – ? *Christ*, he thought, *am I turning fruity in my old age?*

He briskly did up his own fly, saying, "Let's push on a bit further, boss."

The other mumbled something and doubled up slightly, trying to pop his boyo back in place. More fumbling, then, "Damn this thing . . . I can't seem to . . ." Yarr leaned down like a big brother, but with a dawning suspicion that maybe this guy was a wee bit queer after all, and pulled up the zip for him. But it had stuck, true enough, his left hand brushing for a moment the hard ridge below the cloth, but he pretended he hadn't.

Yarr linked Quigley up the alley, out of the darkness and into a metallic blue-lit side-street which was quiet and forgotten at this hour. Wind sighed through a looping tangle of overhead wires, and the sound made him feel melancholy, bereft somehow. The apex of the evening had been reached and now they, or rather he, was easing down that familiar incline, down, down, towards his normal state of depression. It always waited patiently for his return to its embrace – a cold, drear sucking thing.

He began an attempt to slow the descent. The drink still riding in his blood helped. So, he thought to himself with forced briskness now – I'll not take him to the dance, no I won't, I can't, not now, not in the state he's in, so it's out, for couldn't he very easily make a prize fool of himself and won't he need all the composure he can get in front of the bastards of this town? If he reeled in the way he is now, they would watch him, all mouth and eyes, never missing a thing, and then his goose would be cooked, for they would begin to despise him, and me too, thought Yarr, me too . . .

Quigley was now sadly singing *It's A Great Day For The Irish* as he was jolted along. "It's a great great dayeee-up!" He started it again, this time humming the verse with eyes closed, as his feet flung out in front of him, then falling lifelessly to the pavement, powered by Yarr's strong striding support. Before they reached Casement Street Yarr halted a yard or so beyond the sweep of glare that that bright thoroughfare had scooped out of their own street's shadow.

"Hold up now," he said, squeezing the other's arms in a firm bracing grip. "You're goin' out on to the street now. What you need is a coffee."

Then he gave him a tiny shake – positive enough to show him he meant it, gentle enough not to irritate.

Quigley straightened up. "Okay," he said. "I'm fine, just fine. Lead on."

Yarr looked at him for a moment. The eyes were steady on him. He slapped him on the back with rough love. "Good man, me da . . ."

DEPRESSION DEEPENS. The damned perversity of the whole set-up. I can't look at this place as if it was a *totally* foreign country because there's a thin strain of *déjà vu* in the old bloodstream. Neither can I see it as all home sweet home. Caught in a vice.

And of course I realise (which doesn't help much either) that all this ritual of endless theorising has to be undergone before I begin a thing. Each time it appears, in every film; and the agony never lessens. I've tried to outmanoeuvre it in the past by plunging straight in with the barest of treatments, but then it always sidles up into consciousness half-way through the damned shooting, and that's the worst feeling, brother, the worst.

The creative act. Pregnancy. And each time like the very first painful time. No tricks of the trade to be learned from previous experience. No side-stepping short-cuts. Each child – a different child. What kind of monster is this one going to turn out, Quigley? Top-less? Tail-less? An innocent victim of the sins of his father and his father before him?

Questions, questions, bloody questions and not one bloody answer . . .

THE CROWDS HAD THINNED out of Casement Street and only an occasional late-going car whined up hill in second gear. All the young girls, except for those very young, had gone to the dance, and only a few inveterate corner-boys still hugged the lintels and window-sills. They seemed to be clinging to the last excitement the street had to offer. Their lighted butts glowed in the shadows and every car or footfall drew their heads out of their shelter. Yarr and Quigley walked the gauntlet of all these staring, whispering huddles. Yarr's fists were clenched. His ears were tuned almost unbearably to the merest hint of a snigger, but none came and his hands loosened as they stepped up to cross the threshold of The Reo Café.

They sat down at a table near the door. It was heaped with dirty dishes and empty Coca-Cola bottles, each with its limp lolling straw. Up at the juke-box were four of the corner-boys who must have come in out of the street just before they arrived, for they were now feeding tanners into the corruscating chrome monster. It glowered there, squat and winking, silent except for the clicks it emitted, the only sign of the great complex operation going on in its insides. Through the lighted glass panel at the top they could see the records piling slowly like glossy black quoits.

Then the corner-boys dispersed self-consciously to their table and their Coca-Colas, and everyone in the room waited for the music to begin, with their backs turned to it. The pause stretched. People at the tables began to look then at the monster; one of the boys half-rose to go to it, with a nervous laugh to his pals, then the kicking cavorting strains of The Hucklebuck filled the room — lovely, dark, plump, broth-of-a-lad Brendan Bowyer singing, sounding like a jazzing choir-boy. *And have you heard him singing The Holy City*, said Ruby. *Oh he's lovely. I want to cry every time he sings it.* Yarr hated his pouting good looks, his curls, the smouldering gaze on you from all the show-band posters that were plastered up on every disused barn-door, wall or plank from there to bloody Kerry. Anyway, he had no voice worth a damn. There were no singers now. Screechers the lot of them . . .

A waitress arrived at their table, squat, ugly, with a sticky bee-hive hair-do that looked like a steel-wool wig. She placed her dirty paws on the edge of the table and yawned in their faces. "Well?" she said, bored to death. "What'll it be?"

73

Yarr always chaffed waitresses and shop-assistants but this one was a pig, oh boy. He said, "Two cups of coffee. Make one of them black." Curtly. She shuffled off, the insides of her fat knees rubbing. What a backside. Ugh.

As she passed the corner-boys one of them reached out to pat her. He changed his mind when he saw the look she gave him, and his companions laughed at his discomfiture. Yarr heard him say, "Fuck," loudly which made them all laugh. The other people in the place – a timid old couple in the corner, a man, his wife and their perky little daughter and two old men near the door pretended they hadn't heard, and Yarr suddenly wanted to go over and grab the lout for making cowards of them, himself included, for he sat where he was, allowing the tension to rise inside him.

He glanced over at the two old men who were sitting beneath the mural of a Neapolitan scene painted by the local decorator on the pimply high-gloss cream wall. They looked familiar. Weren't they the two old cods who'd been in the bar earlier singing? But somehow they looked different now. The light perhaps? It was strong in here, beating down mercilessly on their bared grey heads from fluorescent tubes. Their faces were close to their plates as they speared chips swiftly, greedily, as if they feared their food would be taken away from them at any moment. They made him feel sad. He wished people would not let themselves get so frightened, so easily. Their eyes were like animals', streaking from side to side, and they kept showing their teeth.

He wanted suddenly to be violent, cause some tremendous havoc that would jolt them out of their terrors, force them to act without thinking for once in their lives of miserable little things that weren't of the least importance when it came to being a man. A man. Was he a man? What was a man? What constituted being a man anyway? How did a "man" act? Hard or soft, cruel or gentle, by his fists or with his mind? He didn't know, couldn't tell. Sometimes it was one, then it was the other. His head hurt. A throbbing the size of a half-crown above his right eye. Fuck it . . .

The coffee came and the cups were streaked. His had lipstick on the rim but he didn't care. Quigley dipped down too fast into his and scalded himself. His reactions had dulled and he merely muttered something, pushing it away from him to cool. Yarr knew that his tongue would burn later, the tip double in the imagination, irritating, pushing itself up against the teeth continually, feeling itself and its hurt . . .

74

The juke-box rumbled and thudded on – The Hucklebuck, three times in a row, then Elvis, the Bachelors' latest (sickening), the Beatles, Brenda Lee, Val Doonican, Maisie McDaniels, Jim Reeves . . . He liked the Jim Reeves number. It was sentimental – about a cowboy getting lost in a blizzard and dying just five yards away from his cabin and his "Mary Ann". But there *was* a singer for you. He had a voice.

They were on the third cup by this time and the coffee was beginning to taste bitter. When Quigley got up, not quite so unsteadily now, to go to the Gents, Yarr surreptitiously poured himself out about an inch of poteen. The coffee killed it but he still felt it coiling warmly down into him, a slow genial snake heading for the pit of his stomach. It settled there, sending out shivers of heat to his legs and lower body . . .

The waitress was at the door now, reversing the hung card on the glass so that it read OPEN from the inside. She bent down to slide home the bottom bolt, swollen arse presented for their inspection, when faces and palms were pressed suddenly to the glass. She allowed those outside to push her in, and blinking, stumbling a little, four more customers entered. Two of them were supporting a companion. The drunken rag-doll was Packy. Bringing up the rear, hands in pockets, and grinning dangerously at him as usual, came Young John Joe. He had on a cocoa-coloured suit with wide lapels and barn-door shoulders and his shoes were new and orange. He winked at Yarr as he manoeuvred Packy carelessly down into a chair at the next table. Packy's forehead hit the formica with a bump as his supporters let go of him. His nose flattened on the greasy surface, his arms dangled alongside his chair legs and his breath whistled through constricted nostrils. What a hog! He couldn't do anything right, couldn't even get drunk properly, the pig. Yarr had a sudden impulse to punish him for his nature. His hand itched to strike or twist some part of that rubbery mask-like face so close to the dishes. He could understand so well now how Young John Joe felt when he goaded him in what before had seemed an unnecessarily callous manner. Yes, nothing surer, Packy was for hating.

As he watched, an eye opened in that mass of slack flesh. It regarded him with a disturbing mischievous daze. The bastard! The others had seen him too and were laughing. Yarr felt a hotness climb his back. Now he was winking at him slowly, rhythmically – mocking him, by god! He choked on his coffee, spilling it down himself, and the eyelid beat ironic time with his coughing.

Young John Joe called out, "Gas!" and laughter shot up. The waitress was staring at him. She had aligned herself with them against him, although her ugly face hung expressionless. The room started to squeeze in on him, the padded rumble from the juke-box *inside* his head now. He felt that he was about to do something that he couldn't stop.

As he got to his feet, Quigley came out of the door near the counter. They looked at one another across the length of the room and Yarr could see reflected in his face a glimpse of that something that was making him go through with this. He put a half-crown on the table. It felt cold, thin and more real than anything he had ever touched, an icy disc with more meaning than was normal. He crossed to the other table, still not knowing what he was going to do, but certain something was going to happen.

Packy lay looking up at him, a dog's grin now on his face. He gave a mock hiccup and the three sprawled around him burst out laughing. There was a cup on the table three-quarters full of cold scummy coffee that the previous customer had left. Yarr lifted it delicately, almost absent-mindedly, by the handle and held it, weighing it, for a moment. "Packy," he said gently, "you'll not be able to ride the bike home the night, the state you're in. I'm worried about you." The others laughed loudly still not knowing what was going to happen. Then, "Why don't you take some coffee?" – and he emptied the cup over his head – "to sober yourself up."

Nobody moved. Thin trickles ran down Packy's face like brown tears, over his closed lids, down his nose and cheeks and gently into the corner of his mouth. He looked asleep. A pool formed on the table and still nobody spoke or moved.

The other people in the place had turned to watch. The waitress stared with her hands bunched beneath her apron. Quigley was half out of his chair, his eyes fearfully scanning each face for trouble. At any other time Yarr would have exploded into laughter but no, no, not now. The unfairness of it was too much to bear. Why couldn't it have turned out differently? Why couldn't Packy have sprung up cursing, pawing his face to make everyone laugh. Why couldn't the bastards have laughed anyway? They laughed at each other's tricks. They did, damn them . . .

The cup suddenly felt out of place in his hand. He set it down. They were all watching him, penetrating him with their eyes. He was different – that's what their eyes said. His action had stripped him. He could almost hear their minds working, chewing on him noiselessly like grasshoppers. He felt frightened. Not of retaliation, for in a strange way he was begging, had been all that evening, for someone to make a move against him and thus break the thick membrane that imprisoned him, so that then and only then would he be able to leap out released, *releasing* this tension. But it was the look in their eyes, the sudden terrible knowingness – the same look he had seen earlier back in The Cozy Bar after that bit of fun with old Carbin. Fun. But they didn't see it as fun, that was the thing. But it was, *it was*. He wouldn't accept that his fine judgement had gone unsteady. Why couldn't they see it his way? Why wouldn't they – ah, that was more like it – why *wouldn't* they? Yes. They conspired, that's what they did. Suddenly and without any signal he could see, they had formed up against him. Their little dark minds sped messages among themselves he could never intercept. So many times, oh, so many, he had seen those faces closing shut in the same way. Though it was happening much more often now, he told himself, all the time.

It was Quigley who got him out and gratefully he allowed him to push him to the door as if he really wanted to stay. Quigley had played up with a quickness that surprised him, throwing up a smoke-screen of gestures and grunts over the few yards to the door that was wholly credible.

But it was as if those inside had snapped their teeth behind him. And it had been a very close thing. He sensed it. A very close thing. He trembled, more frightened than he had ever been – because, one, he didn't know what the danger was, and, two, when it loomed again he still wouldn't know how to recognise it.

ONCE UPON A TIME . . . once upon a time – but I'm not feeling clever any longer so why give with the allegories? 'S been too easy to be omniscient in this book with the black covers. Still, I can't burn it, or easier, throw it far into one of these deep Irish lakes. Would it hiss and steam?

This village and the man who lives there. The end of my journey? The close of the fairy-tale quest I started out just now to write down? Quigley, like all introverts, you put too much emphasis on what's around the next bend. And like all introverts you're far too bloody articulate about your mental insides for your own good.

A new resolution. To quicken the step, bring an optimistic glow to the cheek. New Resolution. Number Four Hundred and Forty-Three. This year of grace in the month of June, in that country known as Ireland. Resolution. To eschew all neurotic thought of an anticipatory nature. Further – to wallow in all rural experience to come, with mind switched off, critical faculties in deep-freeze. Right? Right.

THE CAR LOOKED LONELY when they got back to it, because without saying anything they had walked together down the hill towards it. It sat alone at the kerb, conspicuous in the length of the deserted street, vulnerable too in a strange way, as a little wind whipped papers up out of the gutter to lay them gently on its dusty bonnet and roof. Yarr waited beside the passenger side, his head lowered, until Quigley had unlocked his door and climbed across the seat to release the catch.

He'd only switched on the engine, when he looked over at him and said, "How do you feel?"

"The best," he replied, "the very best." Then quickly, "Do me a favour, will you? Drive up the street to the Square before we go home." He didn't want to explain it further, he probably couldn't anyhow, because what made him say it was nothing more than a vague itch to cruise the streets one last time. He couldn't leave the scene of his defeat without a backward glance, as if the very bricks and walls and stones underfoot might be holding a hint of what tormented him.

As they slid uphill, his eyes searched hungrily for people who might still be abroad. The drink had all worn off, leaving a gnawing compulsion for some kind of experience. Any kind of experience, even sexual, he thought to himself ironically. Only *one* partner wouldn't do, he wanted everyone who was still in the streets, all of them, an orgy of relationships all at once . . .

Circling the Square, their dipped head-lights searching out doorways, they saw a few people still indecisively hanging around. Yarr stared out at them, willing them to look back in at him with an intensity that made his head throb. None of them took up his challenge. He began to hate them. Then he told himself that they couldn't be expected to sense what he was feeling and match his desires that way. That was logic. It couldn't be altered or argued with.

But in a few minutes as they left the Square and headed out to pierce a hole in the dark countryside around Slaney, he began to hate them again. They drove and Quigley began to talk. Yarr sat listening to what he was saying, carefully, not interrupting, because at last, at long last, he was revealing something of himself, and because it had taken him so long to get to this point he must not miss anything.

79

"I don't know . . . I just don't know –" the start of it, the shake of the head, silence stretching, then hesitating but easing, easing – "Two years ago I made a film on the wheat farmers of Saskatchewan." Yarr nodded in the rushing dash-lit darkness. Somewhere in Canada that place – a name from the old school atlas. "Swedes for the most part. Wonderful people. Big men and bigger women" (laughs). "Blonde hair. Pigtails. You know – I was only there half a day when I knew how I would shoot the film. I *knew*. I felt it. And when the crew and I started I didn't have to think about the next shot. It just kept rolling into the can as if it were making itself. And that film won an award, a Silver Bear at Venice, the best documentary shown on television for 1963 . . ."

Silence once more except for the bounding tyres over the road and the car's rattle in the wind. Yarr knew that the story was still unrolling, but silently now, in the other's head, not reaching him. He sat there patiently waiting to see if the circuit would be re-connected.

He wanted to ask questions, all beginning with why. But he stared ahead into the pacing, travelling glare without speaking. A moment later he had to say, "Take the first fork to the left here," reluctantly, for he felt his voice would dam the other's flow. And as they continued on in silence it looked as if he were right.

He thought a little of what Quigley had said. Most of it had gone over his head, which was fair enough, for he had soon realised that Quigley hadn't meant to share it with him anyway. He was thinking aloud. It was something he did himself when he was worried. He couldn't contain the thoughts milling in his brain so they spilled over, out in words, remnants of his thinking processes that surprised people who heard them. The content of what the other had said meant little to him. What he did grasp and very strongly at that, was the anxiety riding on the man's back. He had no idea what that actual worry was but he felt it, a strong staining sense of despair as much a part of him as his arms or legs or hair. It travelled with his person . . .

They nosed out on to the main Slaney-Monaghan road, Quigley halting the car obediently at the red-bordered triangular YIELD sign. Yarr thought of the Customs' men who might come drifting along silently in their big Ford job any time, the radio antenna bending back languidly in the night breeze. This was their beat, this stretch of highway, smooth black asphalt. They cruised along it listening to the radio and watching for lights quickly doused, then the chase would begin. Over narrow roads, over hump-backed bridges that seemed to snap your car in two at speed, up lanes and through farmyards – anywhere and everywhere once the mad lust got in their blood and you with your foot to the boards, giving her the gun all she was fit, willing her to keep that distance in front. It was like a rope stretched between them and you. *Keep it tight.*

"Let me drive," he said, "I know these roads. Okay?" Quigley pulled over to the grass, switched off and got out. They passed each other in front of the hot-smelling radiator without speaking. It was a black, black night with the hedgerows gently threshing. The noise of the telegraph wires singing in the wind saddened him as it always did and he got in behind the wheel determined to jerk things up a bit. So he was waiting with the proffered bottle when Quigley slid in beside him. "Here, have a nip," he said, and Quigley took it and put it to his lips.

"Whoooo," he said, shivering. "A real river of fire." Yarr thought to himself that that was good as he swallowed. Yes, a river of fire. It seemed to awaken the other spirits he had had earlier and a new warm conspiracy ran through him searching out every artery.

They drove on. The freshly surfaced road felt like silk under them. It seemed to pull them along to a pool of light on the horizon, for ahead was the big new roundabout. Five roads poured into its heart. At night it blazed, and for the first few months people had been drawn to it like moths. They had cycled round and round aimlessly under the tall swan-necked lamps that miraculously went on by themselves at dusk and, as miraculously, died at dawn.

Some of them had travelled far distances for a sight of Piccadilly as it became known locally and after a few circuits had then sadly pedalled home. Yarr himself had driven around it late at night when he'd been on the road home from Slaney alone and the great glaring silence of the place always depressed him for some reason.

He drove cautiously the last few hundred yards to its perimeter. He seemed to shrink as the front wheels rolled into the light. The long shadow of the car in the mirror began to contract and darken the nearer they approached the fenced-off circle of metallic-looking grass in the centre. As he started to bring the car round into the gently banked circle, two figures who must have been lying on the grass, jumped up and waited for the car to reach them. They made anxious thumbing signs. They were two young girls. Yarr squeezed his foot down on the brake pedal. He crept the car towards them so that he had time to think what to do. At first they had frightened him appearing like that, but then as his brain slowed, sharpened on them and their clothes and their vulnerable white blobs of faces under the lights he speculated slyly. He rolled down the window in readiness as he came closer and he could sense Quigley's interest. Deliberately he stopped the car a few yards away from the two and watched them as they ran stumbling, knock-kneed in the way women run, towards them. He could hear them giggling nervously as they came.

The blonde arrived first. "Could ya give us a lift to Slaney, mister?" she panted with her fingers already on the sill of the door. "Ach go on, be a sport. We're stranded out here." Getting bolder as her eyes darted in and around the car. Her companion arrived and flung herself up against her and peered in at them too. Both of them hung on to the door out of breath and Yarr looked down at their bitten half-moons of varnished nails.

He knew the blonde one now. She was a McColgan from Slaney. "Bardot" McColgan they called her about the town because of her fantasy that she resembled the film star. She was supposed to be a guaranteed poke as well. Her mate was new to him, small and thin, with her eyes outlined in black like some clown or other. It was funny how the good looking ones always brought along someone like that for company.

"It's a strange time o' the night for two nice respectable girls to be out of their beds," he said slowly, looking full into the eyes of the big one. She looked back boldly showing him that she understood every possible suggestion underlying his words.

"Hey, I know you," she said, coming closer. Her light coloured anorak opened and she leaned her pointed breasts on the sill. Yarr looked down at them swelling out the white wool of her sweater. He brought up his hand from the floor and touched one of them gently, while still gazing at her quizzically.

She laughed and drew back. "Och go on, give us a lift. Sure you wouldn't see us stuck, would you?"

The thin one laughed nervously, a strained sound that made him take notice of her. She was standing on the grass rubbing her thin trousered legs together. Her anorak looked purple under the light. They both had Aer Lingus travel bags slung over their shoulders. Yarr looked at Quigley. He smiled back, shrugging, and lit a cigarette. But Yarr had already made his mind up. Something was forming in his head. Reaching back he twisted the door handle down and said, "Okay then. Get in." The car shook gently as the two giggling girls jumped into the back seat.

As he drove carefully round under the beating lights Yarr was intensely aware of the scent coming from their bodies. It was a cheap perfume barely masking their unwashed odour but he found it rousing in a cold neutral way. He thought too of the rubbery feel when he pressed in the tip of the big one's tits. She was wearing falsies but he didn't feel cheated. It only added to his intellectual lust.

The blonde leaned forward, her hair tickling the side of his face. "What about a light?" she asked while the other giggled softly in echo from the darkness.

Quigley's Ronson burst alight and the pale head-cloth sprang alive above them and the windows flashed, sealing off the outside world. Yarr sent his left hand stealing back between the two front seats as the girl sucked at the flame. He began to climb up the smooth taut fabric of her stretch pants. She trapped his hand between her thighs, good-humouredly, he sensed that, funnily enough, and then she sat back in her seat and he felt the cold air on his hand as she released him. The two of them laughed together then mockingly and he grinned.

He had the clearest image of himself, baring his teeth like a wolf in the darkness, wily, rapacious, icy cold. He gloried in her young pride in herself, her vain belief in her capacity to outwit a man, any man. It made her all the more interesting, especially when he knew he could make her submit, could do what he wanted with her. He had done it so often in the past, every time. He used to watch them, with a smile on his face, listen to them as they played themselves, flirting, fooling, pretending anger. Then he would tighten himself on them, grinding down on to them, into them, choking off their cries, gripping their beating arms until they subsided, broken, beaten beneath him, and then he would take his time with his own pleasure, spinning out the slow mounting throbbing itch. Afterwards it always amused him the way they clung to him in gratitude with wet faces and cries . . .

In the back seat the two girls were talking now about dances, bands and singers to each other, shutting them out. He listened to them, thinking of the foursomes he used to be part of – the two boys silent in the front seat (that's when he could get the use of a car) the girls in the back talking, talking, talking, in the exact same way about the same things. It was part of their little game of withholding themselves. He couldn't understand it then. Now he knew it for a flimsy cover-up of their true vulnerability. They enacted their tiny toll of revenge while they could, for most men, he had discovered, felt nervy in such a situation, losing confidence in themselves and their power to attract. He smiled to himself at the irony of it, that now that he knew women so well and had such power over them he didn't want to use that power – or couldn't – eh?

The blonde said, "Who do *you* think's the best? Dickie Rock or Brendan Bowyer?" She was talking to Quigley. A passing car lit up her face momentarily and Yarr sensed for the second time that night how attractive women found the man by his side.

He also noticed the spaces in her teeth, at either side of her wide mouth, which gave her a debauched look. Her lipstick too was bright red and stained her teeth. And he smelt her sweet winy breath. All these things aroused him because of the way they seemed to contradict her age which he knew couldn't be more than sixteen. He had always fancied experienced young girls. The reckless things they called out to him in the street and their provocative actions and gestures used to make him tremble. He thought of Bridie . . .

Quigley said, puzzled, "Who are they?"

The blonde asked, "Are you an American?" as if that explained his ignorance, and he said, "No. Canadian."

She then said, "Oh," and there was silence except for the rushing car. Quigley laughed then and asked, "Well who *are* they?"

The little one tittered and her friend also began to laugh. Quigley turned round in the seat and laughed with them. Yarr felt out of it. He concentrated on his driving. The road was full of pot-holes under the trees at that point where the rain dripped on to the tarmacadam.

Slowly, as if explaining to a pupil, the blonde began, "Dickie Rock sings with the Miami and Brendan Bowyer sings with the Royals. You mean you've never heard of them? *Everyone's* heard of them. They're fabulous. Well at least Dickie is . . . Hey, *you!*" She touched Yarr's shoulder and he pretended he hadn't been listening.

"What's that? What do you want?"

"You've heard of them, haven't you?"

"Yes," he said, "I've heard of them. And they're both lousy."

She struck him playfully on the back of his neck. "Aw you . . ."

The other girl giggled again and squealed, "Paddy, you're awful, so you are."

"Paddy?" said Yarr. "What sort of a name's that?"

"Don't you say a word about it. That's a good Irish name."

Yarr smiled in the darkness. She *did* know him, and his religion and politics as well. What a tight wee rat-hole of a town it was. For the first time he thought of his wife and what would happen if she heard over the grape-vine that he'd picked up the Slaney bicycle and her mate at this time of night. But to hell with her. He would cross that bridge when he came to it. He had taught himself to postpone any emotion on that score until the last possible moment – to the time when, in fact, he was tip-toeing upstairs to her on stockinged feet. Then and only then would he allow himself to be drenched in the guilt which asserted itself with such sickening regularity. It was something which was inevitable and he blamed it on her – and hated her all the more.

They were getting close to Slaney by this time. No one else in the car could tell that except him, but something had to be decided. As he listened to the three of them joking and chatting, he felt it unfair that he and he alone should have to manipulate events for the others. In a way they expected it from him.

A mile outside the town he came to a decision. He turned up a side-road that was so bumpy that the two girls began to curse as their heads bounced up against the roof. "Hey, where are you taking us?" asked the big one, but easily, with nothing in her voice except good-humoured curiosity.

Yarr smiled to himself. The reins of the situation now felt snug and secure in his hands. "You mean you don't know where you are?" he called back cheerfully over his shoulder.

The big one rubbed her window. "It'd take a better man than you to lose us two," she said. He knew by her tone she'd no idea of her whereabouts. The other girl began to titter. She sounded strangely excited and again Yarr felt that disturbing sensation of near recognition of something.

He lifted himself half-off the seat as he drove and pulled out his precious bottle. "Here, have a sip o' that," he said, pointing it over his shoulder. "That'll make your toes open and shut."

They giggled loudly and he felt the bottle leave his fingers. "Not too much at a time now," he said warningly, adding, "as the actress said to the archbishop."

The big one choked and he felt spray on the back of his neck. "By god," she said. "What is it? It's not vodka."

"Here, let me try it," said the other one and he heard her swallow strongly. To his surprise she didn't choke. "That's poteen," she said. "I've had it before."

"Aye, like a lot of things," giggled the blonde and he heard the sound of a soft slap in the darkness and more giggles. Again his mouth dried with excitement and he looked at Quigley. He was smiling. The pale green dashlight made his face look sinister. The eyes were black holes, the cheek-bones polished. He was a funny bastard. Keeping it all inside him. Tight. Yarr had a great desire to see him suddenly gaping open, spilling secrets.

"Here, have another jeg yourself," he whispered, nudging him.

To the girls he said, "Could we have our little bottle back, if you please. We'll need something to warm us too, you know, because it looks as if you two aren't going to do us much good."

The blonde put her arms around his neck. "Ach, the poor wee soul. Is he coul'? Maybe he should be home in bed with his wife." The thin one tittered and he thought, *you'll suffer for that, you bitch you.*

The big one then said, "Are *you* married too?"

Quigley said, "No," and she took her arms away from around Yarr's neck. "Change places with me," she said to the other one.

"No, I will not," replied the thin one. They both sounded a little drunk.

"Are you goin' to change places or are you not?"

"No."

They began to pull each other about on the back seat, clumsily, breathing heavily, giggling like children. Yarr felt sorry he had picked them up at all. They had taken over the car, changing the atmosphere in that subtle yet bullying way that women always have. Damn them. He resolved to make them change their tune as soon as he possibly could. He meant to dominate them, or one of them anyway – using the one weapon they could never fight against . . .

Cruelly, he braked the car soon after with more ferocity than was necessary. The two in the back seat, still tussling, were straightened up, then flung forward. The breath was jerked out of them and Yarr smiled to himself. He switched off the engine and lights and looked round with his right elbow easy on the steering-wheel.

"You'll forgive us if we get out and leave you two young ladies for a moment or two. We want to stretch our legs." He nudged Quigley who grunted, and their doors were pushed out together.

They got out, and after closing them, stood side by side for a moment feeling the soft heavy night air brushing their cheeks and temples. It was like plunging the face into the warm folds of a velvet curtain. Vegetation smells started coming out of the darkness too, insinuatingly. Then the wind changed and the one smell alone swamped all the others – the acrid bite of wet ashes and smouldering rubbish. Slaney's tip lay before them, hidden. Yarr could imagine its fat grey march forwards, a lorry-load at a time, into the bog-land, a mashed causeway of burnt-out debris sprinkled with bottles, tins, old bed-springs. When the wind blew papers rushed across its surface like the fluff from the bog-cotton, for it imitated nature in its own sterile way.

Quigley began to pee a short distance away. The sound carried in the stillness and a voice from the car called out, "Do one for us while you're at it!" Giggles then and the sound of the window being hastily wound up.

Yarr gave a laugh for Quigley's benefit, but he was thinking of leaving the two alone in the car, and of the time a prostitute he'd picked up late one night in Belfast had pinched his lighter when he got out for a moment to check on a soft tyre. But there was nothing he could remember having left behind so it was all right. He strolled over to Quigley.

"Those goddamn women," greeted him, and a laugh out of the darkness. "Do you know anything about them?"

"Enough," said Yarr. "Ee-nough."

He was feeling in his inside pocket. Taking out his wallet, he flipped it open like a well-oiled hinge and picked out a neat little filled envelope. It had rode in there for a good six months or more until its contents had imprinted a circle on the worn calf-skin. If anyone laughed when they saw the mark he would look at them very solemnly and tell them that he carried his dead father's medal in there and then their faces would drop and they would be ashamed of their own dirty minds.

The thought of that made him smile as he reached out and gently placed it in Quigley's palm. He could see his face more clearly now. It didn't change. Cool bastard. So he did know it wasn't for stirring his tea with.

"Will they – ?"

Yarr understood immediately and replied, "Well the one that *you're* getting will anyway."

There was a pause as they looked at one another, and then Quigley coughed.

"Oh don't worry, I'll take the other one. I'm not fussy."

Quigley laughed and said, "Okay." Then, "What about – ?"

"You stay in the car. I'll take a walk. You'd only lose yourself in the bog."

They began to walk back thoughtfully. A dog barked some-where out in the darkness, far away, chained in its barrel, in some lonely farmyard – a carping, irritable sound. Yarr was pleased with himself. He felt he had shaped and manipulated the events of the past half-hour or so with artistry – the old Yarr finesse back with him once more. An inspired stroke to think of such an out of the way dead end, the Slaney dump. No one would ever dream of coming here. And they might so easily have been seen if they had parked on even the loneliest of back roads. People in these parts had the habit of noting and identifying the number-plates of any car seen in the district. He did it himself, for god's sake. And then there was the way he had paired off your man with "Bardot" back there. At the outset, he had to admit, he lusted after her himself. Those tits and the fat, firm thighs tightly encased in her shiny black pants and the smell of her. But that had been only fooling himself. He would have been no use to her. And she would have talked, nothing surer. And he couldn't have faced that.

Certainly she preferred your man to him, that was obvious, and he was human enough to resent it a little, but, *but*, he knew he could have had her if he'd put his mind to it. Women like her all wanted to be raped, for god's sake, mentally and physically. And Quigley would never rape. There was nothing of the bull or stallion or rutting boar about him. No sir. And of course *he* had also made it appear, hadn't he now, that he was doing him a big favour by handing over the blonde. In a way he was, he supposed, in a way, yes, yes, for he wanted him to enjoy her.

He began to think of how the other would go about his pleasure when the time came – the whispered words, the caresses he would use. For with him it would be words and caresses. For a moment the old cheating sexual feeling wriggled in him snakelike, for it did cheat, dammit, pretending something it couldn't carry out. Ach, fuck it. He could live without it . . .

They had reached the car and he expected there would be trouble with the thin one, but there wasn't. Meekly she came out of the back seat and walked away with him.

Yarr took a quick glance at his watch when the opening door lit up the inside of the car. It was twenty to one. He would give him until a quarter past. If he hadn't his job done in thirty-five minutes, well, that was just his tough luck. Of course if he was at too delicate a stage to be interrupted when he returned, well, then of course he would just walk away and wait a little longer, but if he was still fiddling about with the preliminaries, well – too bad, too bloody bad, mate.

It was only when he was standing at the edge of the dump, with the girl at his side, that he realised that he hadn't thought at all about what *he* was going to do for the next half-hour or so. The great plan was starting to show signs of weariness. The moon, *a* moon, for he hadn't known it even to exist, had come out from somewhere to light up the unromantic scene. A bumpy, littered, grey wasteland, somehow shrunken since the last time he had seen it.

He looked over at the girl. She had a white headscarf with the names of French resorts haphazardly printed on it. *Nice, Cannes, Monaco* – he read. Like something thrown over a bush, he thought. Then she pushed herself up against him and a silk-covered tussock tickled his face. Christ.

"Let's take the weight off our legs," he grunted, and she said, "Okay," with another of those tight nervous laughs that made him sharpen his glance at her.

A short distance away there grew a misshapen alder that looked as if it had been sucking poison steadily out of the tip over the years. He ran his hand perfunctorily over the cushion of wiry grass that grew at its roots, then dropped down. The girl sat down too then with a sly knees-together coyness that enraged him. She began to pluck and brush off imaginary objects from her long thin legs. He watched her white hands fidgeting until he wanted to reach out and grip them still. They were ugly hands with bitten nails, hands that would always look dirty even after washing. He hated hands like those. His wife Ruby's were the same, the outward symbol of a mean hungry life. Little, pudgy and nose-picking.

The silence between them seemed to be ringing in his ears now. The night sounds around began to prick the velvet softness of the heavy air. Again, that barking dog complaining of something, some itch or chafing that would never be relieved by his sleeping master. The sound depressed him.

He turned suddenly and pressed the girl backwards and down roughly, throwing the weight of his upper body on to hers. He lay with his face over her shoulder close to her hair, grateful for the momentary respite, for every second brought a determined act on his part closer. She lay there still under him. A stem of grass began to tickle his nostril. He could smell the earth and roots close-to, in a painful way, yes, painful, because it brought back to him nights when he had lain out like this when he was younger and the only emotion he had felt was not lust but a kind of nameless fear that seemed to come from the grass and the earth and the immense night covering both bodies.

Crudely he moved his right hand over until it rested heavily on her lower stomach. He wanted to humiliate her by skipping the normal courting procedures. There was a half-formed idea at the back of his mind that if he cheated by slipping to the winning square first throw she would refuse to play at all. Then he wouldn't have to prove anything to anybody. He had tried and that was good enough and she wouldn't talk.

He wondered how Quigley was getting on. Hadn't laid a hand on her yet, he expected. These educated guys were great ones for the oul' chat. The books they'd read had put it into their heads that you had to use charm and soft talk on every sort of woman. That's where they were wrong, of course. For the one Quigley was with, it was be as rough on her as you could. No sweet stuff, no telling her how nice she looked and all about her hair and her eyes and the smooth lovely cheeks of her. It was a hand up her drawers first go off. That was what she was used to. She would despise a man who didn't make a stab at her right away. Yarr thought of her thriving on such brutality and he wished, in a moment of pointless lust, that it was she he had on her back on the grass and not this – this wriggling pipe-cleaner. And, good god, she was wriggling too and moaning and pulling at him, and beginning to shake, the little whore. He found it so laughable that he wanted to roll off and roar. Then he thought, Christ how am I going to put her off? He had hardly touched her, yet here she was vibrating like a bitch in heat. He felt disgust and a kind of disbelief at the performance.

Pressing down on her again he sought to quell the wildly trembling body. She immediately flung her arms about him and began to kiss his cheeks and neck. Her sharp nails began to comb through his hair, biting into the scalp. The warm moist breath gusted in his ears, tickling. He twisted his head to one side to escape her tongue and "Oh, oh," she groaned. "Do it, do it, *do it*."

He had the clearest impression of his own detachment, and this, combined with the illusion she still seemed to be trying to keep afloat that it was he who was forcing *her* to capitulate, made him want to laugh for the second time.

Then she bit the lobe of his ear and he began to feel anger and disgust again. "Easy on," he growled, giving her a thump with the flat of his hand. "I don't like them tricks. Save it."

But it only seemed to make her worse, for she renewed her coiling and uncoiling with greater passion. Christ alive, he thought, this one's a right maniac for it and no mistake. Experimentally he hit her again and again she reacted with moans. Her eyes were closed and he looked down at the solidity of her straining throat. She wore a tiny crucifix on a fine gold chain and the chain had tightened on the neck's pale swelling column. Would she burst it, he thought, almost lazily, as he brought his face down closer to the thin biting wire. "Oh, oh," she breathed and it almost disappeared.

Her flesh had little blood specks on it, like those you sometimes see beneath the skin of an egg when you first crack it open with your spoon. He suspected they were flea bites. Coldly, but with great gentleness, he hooked a finger underneath the chain, managing it when she'd relaxed between spasms, for it was rhythmical with her now. Her buttocks were rising off the bruised grass, pressing upwards ineffectually. He could see how thin she was by the outline through the fine taut fabric of her trousers. Most women had a little mound down there at the vee of the belly, which he had always loved to touch because of its strange mystery. It was to him the threshold to greater mysteries. But he had no desire to place his hands on hers, or whatever she had in its place, because there seemed to be nothing in her case but a flat bony promontory which raced into the meagre swell of her thighs.

He felt disgusted again, but envious in a way too of the blind force of her passion. He had never been able to sympathise with or understand such desire, and he had often thought what marvellous release there must be for people like this afterwards. Then he began to hate her and her brutishness. His crooked finger tensed, feeling the chain bite into his own flesh. Now it was like a contest as to who could bear the pain the longer. "Oooh, oh," she moaned and her thighs pumped. The blood rushed in his head as he got enough slack in the chain to twist. Foam grew at the corners of her mouth and her breath was bursting around his face. *Bitch, bitch, dirty, dirty wee bitch.* The words beat in his brain and his ears were ringing like gongs now. Twist, twist. He didn't feel any pain in his finger at all now. It might have been a lever he was manipulating. Tighter and tighter, he imagined it, and it slicing like the wire on a cheese-cutter into the softness of her flesh, but he welcomed it, feeling passon in his blood for the outcome whatever it was. It seemed to go on and on and he started to shake with the tension. Tighter, tighter. Then suddenly the pressure had gone. All gone. Nothing left.

He must have had his eyes closed for her face, strangely dark, seemed to leap up at him. The eyes bulged like some startled cow's, the mouth hung and spittle gleamed on her chin and ran down on to his fingers. He looked down at his hand. It felt cold and numb. The chain was no longer there. But there was something still around her neck, thin and dark on the skin just like the mark a wire leaves in softest white Cheshire. He touched it with repulsion and she twisted her head away from him, moaning, but differently now.

He held her underneath the jaw the way you hold an animal to look at its teeth. And it might just as well have been the rubbery lips and gums of some sick old cow he was pressing back while his Uncle Thomas stood by ready with a lemonade bottle full of the "drench" to be nozzled down its throat. At first he used to think that the animals at his uncle's farm had feelings and nerves like people, but that soon left him, when the time came when he, too, prodded and jabbed his share. He used to swell with rage, young and all as he was, when the bullocks stumbled and slithered on the wet slats of the cattle-lorry ramp. Their fear and stupidity acted on him, sharpening his aim with his stick to a marvellous precision as he whacked at straining hocks and dung-coated knobs of bone. And after they had been loaded and the ramps screwed up into place his wrist felt weak as water, his stomach swirling, his head beating with strange sounds . . .

"Get up to hell outa that."

She lay, eyes closed, cheek to the grass, one knee raised and drawn protectively over and across her other thigh. She was sobbing. Yarr stood looking down at her. She might have been a discarded piece of rubbish that had strayed somehow from the dump at his back. He touched her with his toe.

"Are you goin' to get up or not?"

"Oh mammy, mammy," she moaned, twisting on the crushed grass.

"Mammy," he mimicked. "Your bloody ma's little use to you now. Will you get up?"

Reaching down, he took hold of her limp hand and heaved. She swayed up on to her feet, knuckling her eyes. The mascara smudged and spread, leaving marks like bruises. They'll say I thumped her when I get her back to the car, he thought, but it only skimmed across his mind like a heavy flat stone on water, leaving the depths undisturbed. Nothing affected him now – her, the others in the car – they meant nothing to him. He'd had enough. A sort of animal withdrawal had set in, leaving him numb and tired, only anxious to get away to be on his own.

He pushed and pulled her back to the car, disgusted in spite of himself at her lack of pride, for she looked limp and bedraggled. Well, damn her, he thought, she's tired me out, so she has, as he walked weakly across to the car and put his hand on the door.

The windows were steamed up and he couldn't see anything or anyone inside. But this was no time for the proprieties. He pulled the door quickly open and there sat Quigley in the front passenger seat, with no sign of the blonde.

"Where's – ?"

They looked at one another and Yarr sensed the other's strong control over himself. It sat on him lightly like a fine cage, firmly moulding his emotions. He blew out a pale funnel of smoke at the glass before his face, then rubbed a hole in it casually with his free hand.

"Oh she's – just gone off for a walk somewhere, I guess."

Yarr got in beside him and, with his palms pushing on the steering-wheel, said tensely, "Let's bugger off and leave the bitches. What d'you say?"

Quigley shook his head slowly. "No, we can't do that. No."

Yarr didn't press it. Then – "Did you – ?" he began, after a pause.

The other shook his head in a wry fashion, eyes set in wrinkles, lips pushed out. "It just wasn't my night, as simple as that . . . Say, is there any more in that bottle of yours? I feel like a shot."

Absent-mindedly, Yarr passed over the bottle, warm from his hip. So. Another myth up the shoot; but he might have known it was a lie about big blondie anyway. It only took one frustrated guy to start the rumour rolling that she was hot. Again he thought of that body and the way her thighs filled out her trouser legs. And a zip too down the front just like a man. He remembered the way her sweater had lifted, baring the midriff band of flesh which bulged over her belt in soft white overflow. And it all going to waste out there in the darkness. And your man beside him, had he tried at all? He felt an urge to get out of the car and find her himself, to roll her on the grass over and over, and peel her of those tight denims . . .

Shaking, he took a savage slug from the bottle, which Quigley had passed back to him. The shivers smoothed themselves out gradually as all sensation concentrated into the hotness lining his stomach. Heartburn clawing at him then, as he should have known it would. It was always the same after such a prolonged bout of drinking spirits. At this stage the alcohol seemed to have lost all its power to stimulate; it merely filled him with gas and made his mouth taste bitter. He wanted to get home and take a couple of Alka-Seltzers in a glass of water. The image of those coiling bubbles rising in chains to the surface to burst, tickling his nose, made him twist the ignition key suddenly, savagely.

"This'll bring her back all right," he growled, as the engine noise rolled out into the night.

He gave the accelerator pedal a couple of darts that brightened the beam of the headlights. Then there she was, shading her eyes, running towards them, her other hand steadying her shoulder-bag, with its white piping and bright legend on the side. Aer-bloody-Lingus. No British bag for her, the rebel bitch. He jerked the floor-change lever angrily into reverse and swung the car back in a sweep, tearing up the grass. Into first, then – your man touched his tense gear-change arm.

"Keep your hair on," Yarr told him, "I'm only tryin' to scare her. She'll not be left, don't worry yourself."

Quigley returned his look and smiled. "You're the boss," he said, and relaxed.

Yarr drove forward a few yards, stopped, waited. There was a beating on the side window. And a touch of frenzy now, which delighted him. Casually, he rubbed the glass with the back of his hand and looked out. A white distorted face stared in at them, mouthing entreaties which were only partly intelligible because of the glass and the engine, which he kept cruelly racing. He dallied with blondie a long time in this fashion, pretending he couldn't understand, then turning to Quigley to have long earnest mimed discussion about it before coming back again to the smudged face – two faces now because the skinny one had joined her friend.

But at last he tired of this prelude and slowly began to wind down. When he had the glass half-way their heads darted in like two serpents – twisting sideways in their haste, eyes popping, lips drawn back from the teeth like wild creatures and their yammer dinning and swirling around the inside of the car. Yarr kept his eyes fixed upon them with a solemn, almost kindly expression on his face, murmuring, "Yes, yes, too bad, och too bad," etc., etc., then slyly he edged his foot off the clutch a little and the car began to move forward. The girls screamed and pulled back their heads, bumping themselves painfully, and Yarr thought suddenly wouldn't it have been great gas if he'd had the wit to swiftly wind up, trapping them, then driving slowly away with them like that – not too fast, of course, just at a nice speed so they wouldn't trip. By god, wouldn't that have cooled them. And, by jesus, the same two blades would never ever open their big beaks again about anybody, especially him.

But he'd had his fun, so he shouted, "Come on an' get in. I'll not ask you twice."

They watched him with frightened eyes for a moment from where they stood a few yards off. Then, after a brief whispered consultation, they came slowly back to the car. Yarr couldn't resist shouting, "Boo!" when the blonde had her hand on the door and she jumped back, cursing him.

"Damn you for a dirty big bastard, Yarr. You're a rotten lousy hound, so you are."

He laughed out at her tauntingly, his chin on the rim of the door. "Ach, for god's sake get in, can't you. Nobody's goin' to touch you. Who do you think you are anyway – Brigitte Bardot?"

He relished the hate in her eyes when he said it. She looked as if she could stick a knife into him, as sure as hell. The thin one, on the other hand, still cowered like a crazed rabbit. He wondered where she would get the courage from to get into the car. Blondie, as if reading his thoughts, reached for her hand and began dragging her into the car. Yarr pushed the door open and sat waiting, with eyes fixed on the mirror above the windscreen.

They got in, the big one first, with the remnants of her earlier swagger still about her, but it was obvious now that it was a pose, thinly covering her ordinariness. She was no different from any of the other girls he had ever known. Her allure had deserted her. He felt sorry in a way, sad, too, that he had stripped her, and so easily. She no longer excited him, her presence, or even the thought of her. He drove off feeling deprived. Occasionally on the way back to Slaney he would glance at her in the mirror, half-hoping for some miraculous recovery, but the two heads together in the back seat, the set lips, the wary and weary eyes fixed on the back of his head gave him no hope.

He dropped them off in the deserted Square at ten minutes to one by the Church of Ireland clock, and even when she shrieked abuse after them as the car accelerated away, his two-finger gesture back through the open window was half-hearted, without bite. *Oh, stuff her*, he thought with a tired mind ... *stuff her ...*

BALLYBOE WAITED FOR them under a quietly moving full moon, warily, like the animate thing Yarr always imagined it to be. It missed nothing, standing guard while its inhabitants slept. Except of course for little Mollie Carty, the teacher daughter of old Carty, the sub-postmaster. There was a light in her bedroom window above the shop. Perhaps she was afraid to go to bed in the dark, but then he doubted that, remembering the hard wee chaw who had come back from training college in Belfast, with her sly lowered eyes and nicotine stained fingers and once, the sweet spicy reek of bacardi and coke he had sniffed on her breath when she'd come in to buy some Wrigley's Spearmint before going in to her old da. He wondered what she was doing with the light on, reading maybe – or something more sinful under the clothes like ...

His imagination played with the thought swiftly, because he now felt wide awake, which was to be expected. He had forgotten about his insomnia until then. The events of the past hours had deluded him. Now, as chastening reminder of his normal state, the first exploratory waves of pain washed in. Head beginning to ache delicately, eyes prickling, as if grit had worked itself under the lids and shivers playing upon him at will. He was taking so many of his tablets now the span of sleep they granted him was tightening more and more.

He could almost work it out, his ration for what was left of the morning. Normally he wakened at five, having gone to bed at twelve, so he would be out – if that was the word for it – until seven, then rise with the after-effects deadening. He felt as if he were encased in a suit of armour until the afternoon, head swimming, hands and legs weighted, skin pricking. Then the thought came to him that the drink would probably knock everything out, cancelling, or worse, changing in some horrifying new way the effects of the phenobarbitone. Christ, he prayed, and how am I going to face *that*! For it was only by anticipating exactly his reactions that he believed he could bear the thought of day to day existence. He had charted so fastidiously all of his symptoms that, in a strange way, he had managed to salvage a certain comfort. But tonight he had smashed down that careful record of continence he had been building steadily. He felt like blaming the man sitting quietly by his side in the now stationary car, but how could he? No, *he* had done it and *he* would suffer for it, by god.

He looked up at Molly Carty's window. The light hadn't gone out, neither had the pink curtains twitched even slightly, so they hadn't disturbed her at whatever she was doing. He had allowed the car to coast silently like a gently speeding wraith downhill from the top of Kennedy's brae, rattling down over the pot-holes, then round the fat sweep of road-bridge over the river and into the village, coming to a halt behind his own parked van, at his own front door. No light, no noise – nothing to bring a sleeper to the window and give him a chance of hoarding away another grain of secret information that might be used at some later date.

As they sat there, quiet in the darkness, smoking, Quigley reached out his closed hand. Yarr looked at it for a moment before opening his own and placing it underneath. Into his palm lightly dropped the wrapped condom he had given him earlier. Nothing was said, just a look passed, nothing needed to be said.

They got out of the car and Yarr carefully locked all the doors, then went around to the boot where the Canadian waited. He put

97

the key in the lock, twisted it, and the lid flew up soundlessly. Inside was a blue suitcase with labels, some new, some peeling, plastered on its side, and a bulging leather hold-all.

They went in, into the hall, walking carefully, not tip-toeing, but still with restraint, as if by unspoken pact, past the open door of the little living-room where the fire still glowed behind its night-guard with great heat. It told him that she had waited up and had gone to bed not long ago. He cursed her and her spite, imagining her sitting there alone through the long hours sharpening her jealousies and hatreds, tormenting herself, crying occasionally, then the hate drying her eyes into hard glinting beads. She awaited him up above now, he knew, stiff beneath the sheets, drawn over to the very edge of the bed in case their bodies touched.

He preceded Quigley up the steep stairs and into the front spare bedroom. The bed was freshly made with a clean white sheet turned down, and that surprised him because he hadn't told Ruby to expect a guest. Could it then have been Bridie, who had anticipated the turn of events? He looked in at the door beside the old marble wash-stand. In there was her room and to get downstairs in the morning she would have to come through this one. The idea of it appealed to him in a cold twisted way, but then he thought that she must be as keenly aware of it as he was. More so, the little bitch, lying in there now, pretending to be asleep with her lamp snuffed, he would bet, and wetting herself with excitement at the thought of spending the night so close to such a lovely big man. *And he none the wiser.* And so she would lie in there all night waiting for him to come in to her, for although she might be dying for it, he knew she wouldn't make the first move.

He had a moment of insight into the mind of a woman, her particular breed at any rate, and the restraints imposed upon her natural instincts by upbringing. Never to act, always having to wait to be acted upon. The same thing that was eating his own wife alive. They all had it growing in them from an early age, except for the rare ones, like his mother. And anyway, when he was born she was in her forties, so perhaps she had reconciled herself, before he was old enough to look for it in her. Her photograph was on the mantelpiece of the room, a wedding group, with his old man fierce and stony-looking even on that day. She looked like a native girl posing beside her master. The sepia tints of the photograph and the old-fashioned dress she wore strengthened the impression . . .

Quigley stood near the bed, easily, one foot on his zippered leather bag. He was a mellow man, even-tempered, relaxed, and Yarr liked the way his eyes had travelled around the room no further, no longer than was necessary when he had first entered it. Many another man of his background would still have been shooting surreptitious and dismayed glances at the bed, the sagging ceiling, the twenty-year-old wallpaper, the thin worn pink linoleum, the chamber pot just visible under the bed – but not this one. It was something Yarr was very sensitive about. The slightest hint of patronising or snobbery towards him or his own registered with the speed of light. So he felt affection for the man, this time strongly and unconditionally. Quigley had passed all the complex tests that one man puts to another before he promotes him from acquaintance to friend.

Yarr looked at him now and smiled. They both smiled, not knowing what to say – they were so conscious of the quiet house and the late hour and their own relationship after the long eventful night together. He, Yarr, would have liked to have left him alone at that point without any word being spoken, but then he felt he must say something, for god's sake.

So what did he say but – "You can sleep as long as you like," (stupid! stupid!) which didn't mean a thing when you came to think of it, and was of no help at all to your man who might so easily want to know something about washing or lavatory arrangements or breakfast even.

At the door Yarr turned. He had decided on something, and it astounded him. Quigley was watching him, waiting for him to speak.

"Here. Have this back," he said softly with his fist outstretched.

Then after a pause, "Come on," he urged, with a gently rebuking grin, and the little dingy packet changed hands once again that night, with Quigley looking much more puzzled than he had done on each of the other occasions. Why? Yarr could see it in his eyes. *Why?* repeated at him.

He felt enjoyment at the temporary moment of mystery he was creating. His vanity, too, took a run-race to itself that he could so easily intrigue this travelled, educated man who was way above his class. He still could take his place with the best of them, so he could. When it came to the old brain-power.

"Bridie," he began to explain in a whisper, pointing at the partition door, "sleeps in there – all alone and very lonely. Just turn the wee brass knob and –" He smiled meaningfully. "Well, I can leave the rest to you, can't I?"

"Such hospitality," replied Quigley, winking, and Yarr was certain that he would take up his suggeston. Unaccountably he felt a pang of jealousy. They said, "Good night," to each other and Yarr closed the thin board door carefully behind him.

On the stairs he was thinking about his action. Telling Quigley about Bridie had come on impulse, yet he knew that there was a reason or reasons for it.

He went down into the living-room and dropped full-length on to the sofa, with his mind busy. The bottle digging into his hip distracted him. He took it out and held it before him for a moment in the firelight. There was an inch and a half left in it – just like port wine it looked, from the reflected glow of the coals. He lowered it a good half-inch, because of the colour, screwed on the cap and carefully set it at his side on the cold rexine of the sofa. He closed his eyes.

Had he done it because he wanted to please Quigley? Because he felt he had let him down in some way over the blonde? That was the most likely answer. And he had taken a fancy to his guest, hadn't he? Would do a lot for him. Even go so far as to serve up Bridie on a plate to him. Of course it wasn't a sacrifice at all really, because he himself was no use to her, was he? Yet . . .

The old emotional possessiveness stinging him. The jealousy which he could always rationalise away but which would still keep arriving all the same to plague him for its short duration. You felt you had it under control, then it slipped in under your defences. But wasn't every bloody thing like that? There must be dozens of poisoned barbs, he thought, that can get past, in and under, doing their damage before you have time to bring reason into play. The image appealed to him, as he lay there on the stiff brown couch, because it fitted certain theories he had recently been rolling around his head. The connection between mind and body, the drip-feed carrying the mental poison to the stomach, lungs, heart, bowels. He was being poisoned, by christ, nothing surer! And he had all the symptoms, the nausea, the shakes, the headaches. And old Doctor Mac prescribed him bloody dolly mixtures, because he could only deal with *normal* cases. And he wasn't normal, wasn't normal, wasn't normal . . .

He lay unmoving, desperate for a moment, with his eyes closed. His dangling hand felt the heat from the fire and began to itch. The rest of him was cold as ice. The back of his neck prickled against the smooth head-rest. The tick of the clock was going through him. And it reminded him of the long sleepless hours ahead. He would sit, lie, stand and walk; would smoke, eat a little, drink too, read a page, look out at the street, up at the sky, but the hands on that damn clock-face would never go the slightest bit faster. Just the three of them—that clock, himself and his thoughts crackling ceaselessly like a whin fire, all the night long.

"Bloody hell, damn and roast it!" He punched the wall in revolt. The *fucking* dead certainty of it. The unanswerability. He went into the scullery, raging, bleeding white-hot rage, kicking the back door, ripping it open, then slamming it behind him with a crash that echoed over the roofs. Why should they all snore in their beds anyway, while he suffered?

But Ballyboe slept on under the fat white moon, which reflected the self-same indifference. Yarr looked up at the slow moving torturer's face, a bland cheese, and his mouth twisted with the thought of the tales he had been fed in school about craters, and peaks just *happening* to form that . . . *that*. The bottle came out of his pocket; he drained it quickly, then drew it back full stretch, feeling it imprinted on his palm as if it was red-hot. Then, with all his strength, he hurled it straight up at that white mockery. The whirling glass flew sparkling, and he watched it rise so high that he felt amazement. Perhaps it would soar for ever . . . perhaps.

But then he saw it falter as if it had run out to the end of an invisible tether. It fell then, exploding on Mulligan's tin roof thinly, without that satisfying bark that light-bulbs make. He used to collect those when he was a boy for a mammoth salvo every few months against some old walls outside the village. Afterwards he felt pleasantly drained. But that was a long time ago, too long. No release for him now. He had a horrifying glimpse of his future. It was like a funnel down which he was sliding relentlessly, with the walls banding him in, squeezing him to an impossible outlet, which wasn't an outlet. And the walls were marble-smooth to his desperate hands. He looked down at them. They were shaking again. He was in a bad way, of that there was no doubt. This couldn't continue. *He* couldn't continue. He put his head in his hands.

A muffled sound like dry retching travelled only a little distance in the night air. Something would have to be done.

3

"Makin' an exhibition of yourself for all the neighbours – at that time of the morning. You think I didn't hear you? Out there at the back."

"Ach, give over, for Christ's sake."

"Aye, that would suit you, wouldn't it? If I never bothered you. Let you go on makin' us the talk of the country with your late nights an' your fancy women."

"You're not startin' that again? Oh for god's sake. Look, my head's openin' and shuttin'."

"Aye, an' no wonder with all that drink in you. Actin' the big fella with your new-found friend."

"For Christ's sake, he's through that partition wall! He'll hear you."

"Aye, an' you wouldn't like that, would you? It wouldn't do for him to know how you treat me, after all the lies you pumped into him last night about me."

"About *you*?"

103

"It's just a pity he knows you have a wife, isn't it? You could have introduced him to a few of your nice girl-friends. But maybe you did. Maybe he's like you. Birds of a feather. Aye."

"Will you never end it?"

"*Never*, Mister Yarr."

"I warn you, you'd better stop before it's too late."

"Too late for what? Eh? *Eh?*"

"Too late before *I fuckin' well murder you!*"

"Go on, then. Do you think I care what you do to me? Go on. Choke me. Here's my throat. Go on. Go on. Go on . . . I'd be better off dead anyway. Nobody wants me . . ."

And then the sobbing; her own self-pity triggering it off this time. At the beginning he used to try to hold himself in check, determined not to say anything that would give her the excuse for tears, but almost always at some stage, he exploded into abuse when she went on and on and on, her voice grinding into his brain unbearably. Then he found he could bear it, as a frozen tooth can bear a jabbing needle. Realising this, she became even more insistent, flapping out at him a dozen times a day, penning him in bedroom, living-room, scullery. He would bow his head or look at a newspaper or book dumbly, while she raged. It took her much longer to achieve the release of tears when he did that. He was beating her, he thought, preserving his nerves and energies while she expended hers. But gradually he grew obsessed with the feeling that, in some secret way, she was still managing to drain him, because he felt emptied of something after each bout. She, on the other hand, after her furious weeping climaxes, gave the opposite impression. Once he heard her singing happily to herself, when a moment before she had been crying with baffled rage, stretched out on the sofa downstairs, her heels kicking dents in the wall. He hated her then and feared her too. She would destroy him if he didn't keep outside the range of that passion.

He thought of what she'd said before she burst into tears. Dead. It happened to other men's wives, through disease or accident; was no rarity. There was always some report in the paper or other. A neighbour, Gerry McQuaid's wife, had died in childbirth in March. She was only twenty-seven, so – but no, no, it wouldn't happen to him. It was like so many other things he had imagined, sudden startling events changing the course of his life overnight, but they never came, his daily existence ground on, spinning out into months and years of sameness. And it was a thought he never wanted to linger over. He had a superstition about it, half-believing that if he did dwell on the possibility of her dying, it might happen. And he didn't want to be rid of her that way. Of course, on the other hand, if it did happen outside his involvement – but that was impossible, wasn't it? He had thought of it. Still there were times when he had let his imagination play about. The house, the shop, his life with no recriminating presence, no dread when he returned late, no tears.

She was still at that, making their big bed shiver. Once the sound of her sobbing would have racked him with guilt, but now it only made him hate her for always finding some way of searching out to his nerves. She lay over on the edge of her side of the bed on her back, with the counterpane over her head, muffling her steady crying. She hated having him touch her, even accidentally. At night when he slid in beside her, she waited patiently until he was asleep, then she got out of bed, tucked the sheet that had covered them under the mattress, climbed in again, this time lying on top of it herself, so that a thin barrier of cotton separated them until they rose in the morning. Sometimes he pretended to fall asleep and he would listen to her grunting with effort in the darkness as she manufactured her little protection for the night. On other occasions, still pretending sleep, he would toss and fling his arms about wildly, rolling over against her, savouring her discomfort. It was one of the few ways he had of punishing her without receiving the usual answering barrage of tears or abuse.

The bells from the chapel began their steady reminder of first Mass. The sun outside was brightening the bedroom's drawn roller blind to an intensity that threatened to bring a brown smoking spot to its centre. The room smelt of its hot linen, stale air breathed over and over again and his own reek from the night before. She had called him a dirty pig, and he had answered her with a laugh. "I'll put you from putting your head under the clothes at any rate." He smelt himself now, a slowly exuding sulphurous stink as the bed-clothes stirred. It was the drink that caused it.

From below he heard Bridie moving about in the scullery, striking chinks from saucepans, delph and cutlery as she prepared her breakfast before setting out for Mass. Secretive wee papish bitch, he thought. Off to her idolatry with all the other Fenians of Ballyboe. Never missing their chapel, not if they were dying, by christ, packing in through the big arched doorway there like cattle at the mart, for their weekly brand of holy water on the forehead. One eleventh of July night, on the eve of his own side's big celebration, he and a few of the lads from the Orange lodge, well jarred, had got into the chapel through a back window and pissed in the font. Quare holy water! No one had ever been any the wiser.

He wondered if she was sore this morning, if your man had – ? His own was standing, the only time, when he woke in the morning. Up before him, as the joke went. It was the pressure of the urine stiffening it, nothing else. He had read that somewhere. He touched its slightly curved length beneath the bed-clothes, feeling the ribbed vein pulsing gently along its underside. A wonderful instrument surely. Not a wonder women were supposed to envy it. What was it the nurse from Castleblayney used to whisper in his ear at the height of her passion? "Oh, let me keep it for myself. It's so lovely and big. I'll take care of it for you if you leave it with me." It was their joke at the time. Of course Rita, from Blayney, wouldn't be so particular about what he had on offer now. It wouldn't give her much pleasure the state it was in these days. Lying there, dreamily fondling himself, he tried to work out when was the last time he'd had a woman. Bridie, that August bank holiday, when Ruby had gone to Bundoran with her people for the week-end. Almost a year ago. It was unnatural, so it was, for a man of thirty-six to be affected this way. He began to think of big blondie from the night before – the swish of heavy thighs rubbing every time she moved in the back seat, that feel he'd had, the bare belly, the lipstick flecks on her teeth, her open-mouthed laugh, exciting in its coarseness – and felt himself, miracle of miracles, for the second time stiffening under his fingers. The touch became exploratory, ascertaining, then settled into a cautious stroking rhythm. His mind chilled with lust, canvassing the possibilities. Her? No. She would enjoy frustrating him. It would be a revenge beyond her dreams. If he had only held his tongue earlier and soothed her then instead, gentling her into an easier, more pliable frame of mind, she might have tolerated something. The normal way would have to be out, obviously, because of her condition but the other . . . The thought of fitting himself in there, a new sensation, angling for a tight grip, while she lay facing away, oh and the position safe-guarding his independence, no distraction from the clever, careful working to his desire's end.

106

He ground his teeth with desperation at the image of what he might have had, *ought* to have had, if she was anything like a wife should be to a man. God, god, god, it mustn't be wasted, this! *She* couldn't know what it meant to him, wouldn't care even if he was able to explain it. Explain – ha! That impossibility, that fucking impossibility, that his attempts at would only end in his being driven mad . . .

He had to still his stroke then as he felt a force bunching perilously. Under his hand the pumping continued for a weakening beat, momentum-driven, then died. He wondered if she could hear his breathing. The pillow was wet under his mouth. His head began to ache, whirl. Then a kitchen chair-leg grated below and Bridie burst in his mind. Down there in her green costume with her tight skirt that showed the bite of her panties through the thin gaberdine. Bridie. On the sofa, a hand over her mouth until the eyes fluttered closed with compliance – or out in the shed at the back, pressed up against the privy door, gently shaking the boards? The image burned for mere seconds. The dangers snuffed another dream.

He squeezed himself cruelly. Punish, punish, *punish*. It was one of those times when he felt like raping, burning, smashing up and down, around and around, inside a flailing circumference until he could fall down exhausted at last, relief sweating through every pore in his body.

With encircling finger and thumb he resumed the journey. It was joyless now. His mind shut off everything but the slow coaxing task he had set himself. A few feet away from his heating face stood the wash-stand, brown veined marble, blue tiles and the big rose-patterned delph basin, the jug sitting in it. Scattered around on the flat surface were his watch and the contents of his pockets – his pen-knife, the keys of the van, change and a crumpled dirty handkerchief. He reached out an arm from his warm cave and felt the chill marble on the back of his hand, as he pulled the handkerchief in under the clothes. One small easing of his mind at least. Not much, but some comfort anyway.

Then, with a sudden wrench, he felt the bed-clothes being pulled away from him and over to her side of the bed. Revenge. Little mean cruelties like this wrapping around herself of the greater share of the clothes, cocooning herself, a large lump brooding on more spites. The suddenness of it had caused him to quiver with guilt. He looked down at his shame, exposed, the spread handkerchief foul-looking on the white sheet, a jumping nerve in his clutching right hand, and *it* like an ugly gasping fish, dying now. It had to happen, no use in trying to bring it back – dying, dying, dying . . . The unfairness of it smote him. Too tired, nothing but a sad sense of loss in him now, he pulled the eiderdown over to cover him, gently, no anger. The cool pink satin slid over his shoulder, touched his cheek.

He lay thinking . . . Quigley. And him. The two of them, last night, together. The rare spirit they had created together. And would go on creating together. Something he had badly needed had come into his life with Quigley. Daft, really, for they had only met for the first time less than twenty-four hours ago. Still, still . . . he could feel it, a change. Something fresh – a fresh start, that was it. New beginnings. He needed that. How and why Quigley he would still have to work out, but it was coming, was on its way, still round a bend, but approaching. And he needed it. God, yes so much – so much. Quigley would help him. Save him? A strong word but – perhaps . . . perhaps.

As if mocking him, he heard Bridie's laugh below. A man's voice joined hers, and he listened, with head held clear of the pillow. It was him. Quigley. More laughter, then a deeper rumble as he said something to which she responded once more with the same bright lift in her voice. He felt a sudden loneliness listening to the two of them talking, joking, with no thought of anyone but themselves. No thought of him, wasn't that it?

What had happened last night behind the wall? To make them feel so at ease with one another? He would never find out. Even if Quigley told him, which somehow he doubted, could he be ever satisfied with mere words? Wouldn't his mind be for ever sorting patterns, fresh meanings out of them? No end to the permutations. Endless possibilities to torment him. True.

The front door slammed and, quite suddenly, the silence in the room below, which he had been too preoccupied to really notice for the past seconds, jerked him alert. Feet scraped on the pavement outside, there were mumbles and the steps began to move away. He swung out on to the floor. The linoleum was cold and he moved swiftly to the window. All his obsessions had been eclipsed now by the cold need for action. Looking out through a cleared triangle at the edge of the pane – he had bent back the roller blind cautiously with finger and thumb – he saw Bridie and Quigley walking away together down the street. Bridie was dressed as he'd imagined she would be, in her good green suit. She wore a flimsy veil sort of covering over her hair. It was the black thing she always wore for Mass. Quigley was wearing the same clothes he had worn the night before.

He watched the two of them sauntering easily along in the sun past O'Hagan's shuttered pub, past Mrs. Morrisey who was standing in her own doorway pulling on her gloves, adjusting her hat, but really putting in time for a good look at them from the rear. The men in their Sunday best at the corner jerked their heads to the side in unison in greeting as they passed, holding silence until they had strolled out of earshot.

Leaning at the window until he could see them no more, he felt a small shocked sickness souring his stomach. Quigley and her going off to chapel. Together. He felt betrayed. Not because of him turning out to be a papish like all the rest of them, he had suspected as much already, but because of . . . The emotion still hadn't a name for it. It was hazy, formless as yet. But the dominant ingredient had something to do with that way they had been talking and laughing together downstairs, then out into the sunny streets side by side, sharing some secret he could never share.

He let the blind spring back from his fingers, rose from his knees, went back to bed again. He felt *her* moving away quickly from his cold feet over to her bed-edge precipice once more. Oh how she enjoyed her discomfort, embracing it with eagerness.

The bells broke out wildly, the last call to laggards, in Father Devine's chapel.

A GOOD OMEN. The first sign that the old cut-his-own-mother's-throat attitude from a professional past still survives. E.g., no qualms about lying to the young Irish rose about the state of my religious soul. *Oh every Sunday, just like you, Bridie dear, of course, but Mass back home is different from the Irish version. You wouldn't mind keeping me right when we get inside the church, would you?* And Edward P. Quigley, God forgive you, despite that good Catholic name, not inside a church door since the age of nineteen, when the scales fell from his eyes, as he liked to put it to his precious young agnostic friends at McGill.

Expediency, and it's expedient now, I've decided, for me to gain entry into the Catholic life of this village. So far I've seen no other. And there won't be for me. Yarr's albino existence among all this fauna isn't what I want to make my film about. But he's my man, all right, my man in Ballyboe, at any rate. Yarr . . . an odd name, definitely not native Irish, probably English or Scots planter in origin. Guttural, primeval in a way. The name of a comic-strip hero. Yarr Among The Firbolg?

Ruby is hardly the luscious adoring strip heroine somehow. A distinct atmosphere in the house. And wasn't that some sort of a fight they were having in their bedroom this morning? I must get young Bridie to put me in the picture.

St Michan's. The local Saint Bridie tells me. A twin-spired, grey-stoned, Irish Catholic church. Hints of at least four architectural styles about it. The priest's house over the wall, built of the same granite. A little inset arched gate connecting his private and public lives. A narrow existence.

Bicycles everywhere, clenched along the wall. A line of dusty Volkswagens, Fords and Austins stretching up the road. Slamming of their doors, punctuating the soft din of the bells. Bird song, sun, dry white road, trees, a faint smell of turf air-borne. Ireland. *It's the fine day, Stephen. That it is, that it is. Will Tipp win the big match? I've a pound says they won't. I must listen on the wireless. So must I, so must I.* You're home, Quigley, you're home, boy . . .

Going inside, Bridie at my elbow, "keeping me right." The drips of water strangely chill. Running down over my nose. Itching. Mustn't wipe with my handkerchief. More important, mustn't appear awkward; move like the others, slackly, automatically, unthinking . . . The kneeler with its prickly horse-hair and smell of dust rising at my descent. Bridie's long lashes quivering delicately on her cheeks as she prays. Which Saint will it be this Sunday morning then? Wise old Church with a Pin-up for everyone. Everyone's private dream or nightmare taken care of. I sacrificed a lot of comfort when I cut the ties at nineteen. But can you ever escape? All my old Catholic memories coming back.

Sister Anna-Marie and her giggling nuns eyeing you with derision in their sanctum at lunch-break. *Speak up, Edward. You're not shy surely in front of all us? A lot of women? Come, come* . . . Coquettes in dusty black and men's shoes. Half-male, half-female – the moustaches, those shoes . . . and Spud Murphy's tale about them having things like a man's under the habits, convincing us that was why they had to become nuns. The Sacred Heart on the wall above our sideboard. The pale effeminate face oblivious of the exposure of His innermost organ. Was my heart as big, as red as that? I used to feel sick after catching a glimpse of that holy haemorrhage. And the prayers directed at it as we knelt in semi-circle before bed. Something pagan there. I had the fear sometimes that if the police suddenly broke in, catching us like that, we would all be locked up for practising forbidden rites. My brother Gerard boarding the plane for the Mission in Africa. A priest in the family. Mother's tears of pride in the departure lounge, and him itching to get out there among all those heathen. God only help them, I thought. That white bony face, the cruel spectacles, the hurtful hand-clasp as he shook hands with us for the last time. Poor Gerry, if his brothers and sisters hated him, how could a pack of howling black savages take to him? Father Malachy who came to tea on Sunday afternoons. His eyes shining as they caught sight of the heaped table. Gluttony, the celibate's vice, as practised by Father Lennon S. J. Ham, roast meat, tongue, salad, four varieties of bread, eight varieties of cake, lemon pie, with cream, all drenched in his stomach by the six big cups of strong tea. *I like to be able to stand the spoon up in it, Mrs. Quigley.* Then Moore Melodies on the pianoforte, played by

111

my sister Dolores. I turned the pages and tried to keep my eyes off that little round reverend belly. The rest of the week it was potatoes and bread for the rest of us. I swore it would be protein for breakfast, lunch and dinner when I became a man. Bread and spuds, like my religion, totally eschewed.

Yet here I am wishing I hadn't been so determined, for how am I going to illuminate this mystery? On the other hand, a certain advantage from objectivity. The innocent eye. If I'd continued to practise my religion, would my senses be so open to all this?

Incense, brass, vermilion, wax, cloth of gold, carmine, jewels, painted statues – baroque prodigality. All poured into one glittering showcase behind the altar rails. The priest and his altar boys, pampered custodians of the mysteries, dipping, mouthing, genuflecting their way through the ritual. Then the contrast. The men and women at this side of the lighted jeweller's window. Poor, ugly, mute, awkward, yearning after the glamour. I wanted to be a priest before I wanted to drive C.P.R.'s biggest locomotive, remember?

Father Devine. Appropriate name. Stern, white-headed figure before the altar. Angry sallies back and forth over the carpet. The altar boys' sea-bird cries rising. Pinging of the little golden bell. Does he adjust his actions to the bell or vice-versa? I was never an altar boy. One of them wears a pair of dirty white sneakers, the ribbed soles visible each time he kneels on the steps. Father Devine's back is marvellously broad, must inspire great trust in his flock. The cloth of gold stretched, squares his width. The back of his neck thick and red, a warning of the solemnity of what he's re-enacting for the ignorant. He will be a tyrant, I surmise, kingpin of anything and everything in the village. Has he been informed of my presence yet? He will have to be cultivated. His sanction granted before I proceed. Wasn't this one of the reasons I came to Mass at his church this fine morning. Another smiling soft-soaper, Fr Devine, for your indulgence. Which won't be forthcoming if Bridie makes her confession, as a good young Catholic girl should to her priest.

Bless me, Father, for I have sinned.
Tell me of your offences, my child.

112

Father, I have allowed a man to share my bed, a stranger to the village, Father. His name is Quigley.

And have you and this man been intimate, my child?

Yes, Father, we have.

Was it against your will, child?

No, Father, I allowed him to do what he did to me.

Did you struggle with the flesh at all, my child?

Only a little, Father. He was gentle, you see, and whispered in my ear. Things.

Things, my child?

He called me his Lolita, his pouter pigeon, his softness, his freckle-faced girl from Kalamazoo, his child bride, nymphet, co-ed, little bum majorette, his colleen bawn – he knows Irish too, Father . . .

No laughing matter, Quigley.

Bridie – eyes closed, mouth moving, as the beads slide with tiny jerks through her hands. Watching her, a return of that old sensation of the night before – *post coitum* etcetera. Only here twenty-four hours – less than that, by god, and I've embarked on my first complication. As if I didn't need all my objectivity. She's half in love with me already. Waking up this morning, I found her watching me. Propped on elbow, studying my face with sad concentration. Unused to gentleness. Remember how wary she was at the beginning. Then lulled, her tiny jerking passion. Not one hundred per cent satisfactory. Could have been if Quigley had submerged himself in the role of slavering despoiler of young pubescent. Couldn't somehow. Sweet kid. Innocent. Despite her confidences about the men – Yarr – roughing her in beds, in ditches, in the back seats of cars since she was fourteen. *Talk to me. None of them ever want to talk to me. Why is that? Can you tell me?* Quigley talked. Igniting himself with his own Irish eloquence. Charming birds off bushes. Little birdies like Bridie. My bed-mate for the rest of my stay here? Shall I stay here – or should I go to an hotel? Glacial well water in a plastic basin to wash myself in the mornings. The pink basin squeezed into the sink, resting on a base of wet tea-leaves. The plastic at the lip has begun to soften. A tide-mark of washing-up grease above the water level. The dry lavatory and the attendant flies. The bed (Bridie's – I mussed up my own unslept-in one earlier with a feeling of guilt) has a long

113

deep hollow in the middle. The sides threaten to close in and over, hamburger style. The mattress tickles . . .

Quigley, I'm afraid you're over-fond of your expense-account comforts. A thought. Would Flaherty, a Grierson now, he deterred by such trivia? Of course not. You should count yourself lucky. Roughing it for the sake of your art. Anyway there isn't a damned hotel for miles. So I'll stay here in the bosom of Yarr's family. Will I? Yes.

And allow him to show me this village. Through his eyes? Wait and see. Amass the material first, then select. Amass, select, amass, select . . . An incantation to stave off fear, Quigley. For don't fool yourself, it's still there. Waiting, biding its time to show its ugly, scaly face. Just why should this bloody film have to be so good anyway? Why? It angers me, by christ, this stubborn mass. Like a lump of stone, and as sullen as hell. I can't get into it. Not an inch. It won't give an inch. Won't show itself to me. But I'll sit it out. Wait, Quigley, it'll give itself away, you'll see . . . Whistling in the dark again, Quigley?

THE X-RAY JACKET *reached his knees, itching him, for he was naked underneath. He could feel his feet and legs prickling damply under the long thick white woollen socks. And two blankets below, two above. He would sweat like a pig, they had told him, running off him in streams, when his time came; so the radiators were up full in the ward and he was like this, stifling in his own steam. His first real fear. Because of the off-hand way they were bundling him about in the bed, dressing and adjusting his body, talking among themselves. For if they were this uncaring – no, not uncaring – ignorant, yes, that was it, ignorant of how he felt now, how could they sense what was happening to him when the thing itself started? He might die and the only warning would come from a rubber balloon and a glass dial. But agony, unbearable agony, wouldn't even register. They wouldn't even know it was happening to him. They had taken his blood-pressure, listened to his heart beating earlier. But, couldn't the nurse have made a mistake? A little fat thing with bad breath, she didn't even think before scribbling something down on her clip-board. Her writing, her carelessness, her inexperience . . . any one of three factors could fuck him up proper.*

Now the atrophine injection, for Doctor Mac had described to him in detail the procedure, patiently answering all his questions until it was burned clear in his mind. A sedative, he had said, first, to relax him. The chill barrel of the syringe touching his arm was worse than the prick. Cold steel. And cold dry hands of the nurse – an older one this time – odourless, sex-less, starched, brisk. He began a joke as she rubbed alcohol into his soft inner joint, then despaired as her bleak gaze never wavered from her task. He knew what he was doing, and despised himself. Everything about him cried aloud for them to understand that he was different. Wasn't it so? From all the others down the length of the ward waiting like him. Only not like him. Of course not. He didn't really need it the way they did. Christ, would you look at them. Wrecks. Pitiful. The one in the next bed now. His eyes out like golf-balls, his chin and cheeks cut useless with razor cuts. Who in their right minds would trust someone like that with an open blade? They should be locked up in his place. And breath bellowing in and out of his mouth. He turned his head away from the sight and sound. The one on the other side was smiling across. Nod back at the old get. His poor

115

ringed tormented eyes smiling sadly. Maybe it'll help me, what do you think, the smile asked. He jerked his cheek off the pillow, holding his eyes on the pale, pearly shimmering ceiling until they smarted. Will it help ME? To keep me from getting like that? Please god, please . . . His eyes watered. Staring at that bloody ceiling . . .

A second injection. Scoline. To counteract the convulsions. Dopey now. Legs melting into the sheets and mattress. His arms starting to grow. Bent at the elbows, falling to the floor, fingers limp hooks. Crucifixion. He could see the long tapering line of his body swaddled by the sheets. Fagan made a bulge half-way. Maybe it would stand to attention in the middle of it all. Giving the nurses a good laugh. Tent-poling up the bed-clothes while he bucked and shook his insides loose.

Screens closing in now. Silently. Taut, pleated panels of flower-printed fabric on rubber castors, manoeuvring closer, with lives of their own, squeezing out the air, the light, to hide his throes from the rest, all watching his little roofless tent, as sick with fear as he is despite their injections, for now the box of tricks itself arrives, trundling softly, velvet-treaded, pushed by the two male nurses, one with a faded green tattoo, Mother And Ireland, on the back of his broad white hairy hand. Their faces swim, pale ovals in his dull drowse, their hands dry as pumice, placing the electrodes on his temples, two chill pennies, two inches lower they would cover his eyes, only he's not dead yet, dead, his executioners, stern, silent, in white coats taking his arms, now they're floating off with them, long blood-distended fire-hoses, out, further, further, it's all swimming, swaying, squirming now, milk-cloudy with streaks of thin pale blue, so thin they hardly stain the delicacy of that haze with its looming shadows of faces, arms, hands, slow swoops in on him, circling without touch, without smell, without colour. A blurring spectrum of crimsons, purples, blacks, yellows, each with a voice and a smell begins to scoop a whirling tunnel into his head . . .

Now what brought all that on? He allowed his head to drop between his legs, his supporting palms spread on the pink fluffy horse-shoe mat fitted to the base of the lavatory pedestal. He rubbed his wet brow with a square of toilet paper, pink like the floor-to-ceiling tiles, the rubber flooring, the bath, basin, bowl. The first time he'd ever been in P. J's bathroom, but mightn't he have known it would be like this. Overdone. Like everything in the house. And dirty. A rime of grease on every surface, dark clots

116

softening the corners where mop or cloth had failed or hadn't bothered to reach, a child's plastic potty brimming with urine and the towels spread on the hot towel rail like thin door mats. On the window-sill were five half-used disinfectant dispensers producing between them a sickly, overladen atmosphere. *Pine Fresh*, he read, *The Sharp Tang Of Northern Forests Brought To Your Home.* A bluebottle – it looked bloated as if thriving on the foul vapours – bumped clumsily off the one small sweating pane high up near the ceiling. He listened to the staccato buzz. It made his head ache, but he couldn't rise, either to kill the thing, or set it free. He lit his cigarette. It was one of Quigley's, some Canadian brand, a bearded sailorman's face on the packet, only not a Players. He tossed the match into the po. It swam in the bright yellow sea. Dirty pigs . . .

But what had brought *that* on? Tiles, heat, disinfectant? The senses combining to remind him? It was like a film. You had to see it all through once it started. Or a nightmare. And this his worst. E.C.T. Magical letters luring him, despite the thought of that fearful discharge passing through flesh and bone, and leaving a residue of – ? Something not even to be contemplated. Too terrible. People hinted, evaded its mention. Even Doctor Mac's brusque man to man surgery chat you felt was his way of side-stepping the dread.

Des Hackett was the only one who didn't go wary on him. Of course he had to be careful to allow the subject to bubble up of its own sweet accord. But the opportunity had arrived and he had listened, trying to evaluate what was truth and what was his man's normal coating of exaggeration. Drink in hand, he'd listened to – *they're only delving in the dark, those boys. Less is known about a man's brain than any other organ in his entire body. I know. Every shock treatment patient is a guinea-pig, believe you me, lad, but how are they going to find out about the bloody thing any other way? Answer me that now. They take precautions, sure, blood pressure, heart, lungs – the lot, but there's always the unknown factor, don't you forget, my friend, that unknown factor which hasn't been discovered yet and won't be for one helluva long time from all I've seen, I can tell you.*

Des thought he knew more about it than the doctors did. And maybe he did too, for none of them had ever mentioned the unknown factor. Inside the blackness of brain a little missing x, a hole the size of a moth's eye, a knot on the cord, a bump, scar, a loose end. You had to visualise it in some form. And hadn't he, endlessly, after his fuzzy month of recovery had passed? He couldn't remember anything except a few flashes of reality from that time. It used to worry him sick when he thought of Ruby, Bridie, neighbours observing him as he blundered about in his mind like a drunken moth. Those recurring questions as after the night before – *What did I say? What did I do? Where did I go? Please, for pity's sake, tell me* . . . And nobody could. An impossibility. One black blank in time he'd never be able to fill.

But fuck that for a line of thought . . . One last drag on the butt and in with it hissing into the bowl. He studied his face for a moment in the oval mirror over the wash-basin, as he zipped his trousers. He was still sweating a little, pale. They would think he had been flogging the bishop. Well let them, what the hell did he care? But, still, just in case, he threw some water from the cold tap into his face and scrubbed with the cleanest towel he could find baking slowly on the hot towel rail. The touch of it was like sacking as he scoured himself. It smelt of curdled soup. It was funny how other people's dirt disgusted you, but never your own.

P. J. was showing Quigley the *Florida's* scrapbook when he arrived. His wife sat on a small pouffe by the fire, displaying her fat white thighs above the stocking line. Without moving, she reached up a cup of tea from the marble coffee-table with a warning touch to her lips. She was dutiful to the point of subservience in the presence of her husband. She knew her place. The tea was cold and the brittle meringue balanced on the edge of the saucer crumbled under his fingers and rained finely on to the carpet. He tried to keep his eyes away from the soft fullness of revealed flesh as her knees opened. He wouldn't charge P. J.'s missus a penny, no, sir, not a wing.

"Of course, Mister Quigley," P. J. was saying, "me and the boys started off in a small way. Drums, tenor sax, accordion, piano. That was in the old days, of course. Strictly village-hall stuff. A fiver a night and glad to get it. But, well, I had faith in the lads. I knew they would make the big time . . ." *Yeah*, thought Yarr, *like hell you did. You got rid of "the lads" the first chance you got, you fat little prick, when showbands started coming in. Who wanted to see four country yokels with short hair, red faces and Sunday suits when you could hire a half a dozen sixteen-year-olds in tight gold lamé trousers with electric guitars for the same money or less?* "If I hadn't believed in the lads when things were tough there would be no *Florida* showband today. But as Carmel the wife says herself, we're more like a family of brothers than a band. Isn't that right, dear? Now that photograph there marks a very proud moment in my life, I can tell you."

"Is it the presentation, dear?"

P. J.'s missus widened her legs even further and Yarr glimpsed a triangle of taut pink silk. Rising quickly, his cup rattling briskly in the saucer, he looked over Quigley's shoulder at the heavy gold-embossed album. In the photograph was the band on stage, all laughing extravagantly around a solemn looking P. J. who was hugging a portable TV set to his chest. It was a flash photograph and half of the faces had the usual drunken, taken unawares expression, frozen by the popping bulb. P. J. was wearing one of his many Dacron draped suits with a silver tie and a lot of cuff showing. The band wore their normal uniform of tight Italian stretch-suits with monogrammed breast pockets, cowboy boots and white polo-necked sweaters. The line-up was three electric guitars, tenor sax, trumpet, drums, organ. Deirdre McGarry, the vocalist, wasn't in the photograph. Perhaps it was too solemn an occasion to have her included. Especially as P. J. was riding the arse off her. Which was common knowledge to everyone except P. J's missus. *My god, that one'll be flashing her lovely round naval yet. I mustn't let her see me with my mouth open.*

"A grand bunch of boys. Grand. I'm very proud of them. All dedicated musicians. They deserve the best, and you know, Mr Quigley, I'll see they get it. I will. I've sweated blood for those boys and the few pounds I've got out of the band game since I've started wouldn't compensate me for all that work. Wouldn't. But sure you don't do it for the money. Love, Mr Quigley, love is what keeps you toilin' away." *Well god forgive you for one little fat lying fart. Your percentage of the* FLORIDA *has set you up as the wealthiest man in these parts. What about your wife's shooting-brake, your own red Volvo, the caravan, the outboard, the racehorse stabled at the Curragh, the shares in that ballroom chain, the four big daughters at the most exclusive convent school in the thirty-two counties. Not to mention the house, of course.*

The house. It squatted half a mile outside Slaney, smugly, inside an oasis of lawn sown thick with painted cement-cast gnomes, rabbits and storks. Its roof was of the thickest, greenest and most glistening tile. It had port-holes as big as bicycle wheels up each side of the front door. Its bay windows foamed with

119

swathes of net, there was a branched antenna on the chimney that would have done credit to a television transmitter, and the double garage was jammed solid with expensive garden gadgetry of every shape and size. Poor-mouth P. J. Yarr's heart bled for him.

"Would there be any likelihood atall now of a little spot on your TV, Mr Quigley. It might lead to an American tour and that would be a great feather in the lads' caps, I can tell you. It would buck them up no end."

Yarr could almost feel the insistence directed at Quigley by the pair of them, for she, too, was hanging forward, soft lips parted, hard eyes sharpened to two appraising dots. For a moment he felt embarrassed. In a way he felt responsible for their behaviour, having brought Quigley here to be introduced. He glanced quickly at him but he was avoiding his eyes.

Quigley began to speak slowly in that tone that Yarr had come to recognise as his "official" voice. "Well I can tell you this much for what it's worth, and that is that this film I'm shooting here in Ireland will certainly be screened coast-to-coast. Now I think you know what that means in terms of exposure . . ."

P. J.'s eyes seemed to ignite. *Coast-to-coast. Exposure.* This was the language he used himself, but hearing it from the source, as it were, spoken by a native of the big-time, impressed him more than anything that could have happened that afternoon.

P. J.'s wife had her plump elbows on her knees. Her red varnished nails dimpled her cheeks. Hot cruel nails against unprotected flesh. So much soft white flesh – throat, arms, thighs . . . Was she offering herself, perhaps unconsciously, to Quigley? With a twinge of bitterness he thought – *certainly not to me.* For he knew with cold certainty exactly how they thought of him, didn't he? That guarded look on both their faces when they had first opened the front door to Quigley and himself. The welcoming joviality in their voices always petered out before it reached the eyes. "Ach, an' how are you, Yarr? Come on in. What brings this unexpected pleasure? How's Ruby? And business? Still coinin', eh? Ha ha." *And the same to you too, you pair of gets, for you're not fooling Yarr for one minute. He knows you and your little brown-tongueing ways. For it's in with the priest now and Doctor Tierney and the three solicitors from the town and the rich Miss O'Haras and old Judge Monaghan and anyone else whose ring it's socially imperative to lick around this town.*

What was it Quigley called them – the new rich, yes, the new rich, after he had translated it for him from some French phrase or other. "Show me some of your new rich," he had asked him. "The new people. It's the new Ireland I want to see, not the old. That's dead and with O'Leary in the grave." A funny way to put it. Still he was getting the hang of it now. Knew what he would appreciate and what he wouldn't. He was confiding in him more as well. Not everything that went on in his mind, of course, he didn't expect that, but a little more each day . . . a little more.

Quigley was talking now in that smooth steady stream that impressed so much. P. J.'s missus was offering him another cup of tea, but he wasn't looking at her, pretending not to see her as he held her husband under the spell of his low voice. P. J.'s head was nodding in time, his short fat neck turkey-red with excitement. Quigley was talking "big-time". *Oh, he's one lovely man*, Yarr thought. *They'd eat the dirt between his toes right now if he asked them. I've been waiting for you to come along for a long time, Mr Quigley.* He felt very cool now in the middle of that over-heated stuffed room with its flowered carpets, knick-knacks and black plastic padded furniture.

Quigley was saying, "I want to see this band of yours at the very first opportunity. Could that be arranged, do you think? On the stand, at a dance?"

"Mr Quigley, the easiest thing in the world, the *easiest* thing in the world. Sure, aren't they playing in this very town tonight . . ."

"ONE OF THE late great Jim Reeves' numbers now . . ." Rest of the announcement washed away in over-amplification. Perched, grinning drummer (all the band seem to be perpetually sharing some joke among themselves) socks out the old-fashioned one-two-three beat, guitars and electric organ emit a throbbing chord sequence, the glass-blowing tenor player and trumpeter train their horns on their shared stand microphone and you think, there just can't be any *more* sound. Coming out of those big Tru-Vox speakers. Bounding off taut marquee canvas. To daze the dancers, who shuffle on a maple floor laid in sections three inches above crushed grass, cow-pats, entombed insect life. (Must get high shot of giant dead yellow print in middle of field when carnival is over.)

Drummer starts to moan, *"Are you lonesome, tonight?"* lips close to the mesh on his mike. He has achieved the impossibility. Has added a *further* layer of sound. Up there a little schoolboy world of japes and jokes of their own on the band-stand. Men will be boys. Some of them older than I am. Carefully brushed forward hair-styles, cuban heels, youthful silver identity bracelets slipping down over wrists. So this is the famous *Florida* . . .

Up near the roof the lights are fluttering. A soft blob of light pulsing inside each bulb to the beat of an unseen generator. Little silver hearts. A gradually lowering cloud layer of blue cigarette smoke. Much coughing. Searching eyes screwed up. A capacity crowd. Jostling, laughing, shouting, ogling between dances. The men packed solid a quarter way up the floor from the door. A self-conscious phalanx. The women in front of the bandstand and spreading thinly around the walls of the tent where stray grasses peep up between the edge of the wooden floor and the canvas. A diversion. Little plump guy importantly scatters waxing powder from a canister on to the dance floor. Loud ironic cheers from all the lads. Little guy reddens, mutters to himself and hurriedly empties the can at random in white blotches. Slips as he strides from the floor. Falls. Louder cheers as he scrambles to his feet, beating his clothes, shooting his cuffs, straightening his neck-tie. Gigantic loss of face. A lull. Someone now being propelled to the front of crowd. Big softie with a red face, dangling

122

hams for hands, old black Sunday-go-to-meeting suit, grinning like a madman. Another butt for the crowd's mischief. Like that old singing guy in the pub. They're egging him on to do something. Can't hear what it is. Suddenly acquiescing, a great leap into the air from him landing on both hob-nailed booted feet, a tremendous shocking roar, then running down the floor, giant tip-toe strides, arms working, mouth open, eyes alight, yelling. Starts his long long slide over the waxy floor. Ponderous skating agility. On one leg. Encouraging cheers from everyone. The band. Me. Yarr with his demoniac grin at my elbow. Puck. He has seen this before. Obviously. The crowd loving it. Convulsed, slapping each other. The girls prodding with finger-tips, giggling, in hysterics. *Oh he's a desperate big eejit, is that Joe Meenan, desperate altogether*, they cry on one another's bare shaking shoulders. Forces of the management closing in on big Joe now. He skates neatly into the crowd; it opens to receive him, then closes against the little fat guy, very purposeful and chastising now, and the couple of white-faced cohorts with Pioneer pins in their lapels. A blare from the band, opening chorus of *Can't Buy Me Love*, the first dancers take the floor, and the diversion is over.

Outside. A thin wind flapping the row of tricolours on the pointed tent-poles, bearing heady scented waves of mown grass. A corncrake rasping, two dogs answering one another mournfully. Standing couples giggling in the shadows, lighted cigarettes flaring briefly inside the parked cars in the dark measureless field.

Cut to Father Devine on a Sunday thundering on about dancing and drink bringing ruin on today's young people. Lascivious thoughts breeding to the beat of African dance rhythms. Girls with no thought of shame, flaunting their bodies. Lipstick, nail varnish, hair-do's, tight dresses, cigarette smoking. The habit of going into lounge bars. Pleasure-mad the lot of them. Destination damnation. The bowed heads receiving his flood of passionate excoriation. White foam at his lips. Knuckles straining on the edge of the pulpit. Goading his dumb Irish oxen until his own blood drips. They outwit him with slow peasant cunning. Enjoying their pleasures. Rolling in the bottom of a ditch of a Monday morning, drunken and fumbling under a full pagan moon. While he strides in his monkish room, his rosary clashing impotently.

*

My nightly gossip to my reflection in the book. Quigley – His Book. Will I ever read what I have written in it, I wonder? Confession. He never kept a diary until he was thirty. Strange twist of retardation. Started off as Quigley's *cahier du cinéma*, to be dipped into for source material, shots, angles, sequences etcetera. Has now taken on a life of its own. Won't be used as a receptacle for the half-formed scrapings of my mind. It dictates. Last night, for instance, a case in point. Despite exhaustion and drink and that soft, trusting young body beside him, what did Quigley do? Sat up with the light on and scribbled his nightly stint. She wondered, *Is the man mad? But maybe this is how educated men behave. Maybe they all write it down first in a big book with blue ruled pages. What they're going to do. Maybe I should have a peep over his shoulder . . .*

A question for you, Quigley. Is this a perversion? The newest?

I saw her dancing. Shaking her little butt with that fashionable bored look on her face. Chewing gum. A yard away from her partner, going through her little motions. The men all look self-conscious. Those pansy wrist actions, whirling imaginary lariats. They must ache for the good old-fashioned bear-hugging waltz. Sweating hands on bare backs. Showing who's the real boss. Grrr . . .

But the band keeps on playing rhythm and blues, grinning at each other, doing their own little shuffle on the boards of the green white and orange draped stage. Three steps forward, two to the side, three back. P. J. sent them to a dance studio in Dublin to learn their "choreography". Yarr says that half the *Florida* are on purple hearts. To give that lift, that zip that earns you your forty quid a week. Tax free. P. J. is his own accountant. Self-educated, but the best. Yarr has an admiration for the lesser Capones of Irish life, it appears. Has promised to tell me about his own smuggling escapades.

We haven't talked much, though. A silent acceptance of each other as he takes me around to meet people, see the things he thinks I might want to see. Either I've explained myself superbly or else he's intelligent. I'm inclined to believe it's the latter.

*

Earlier today he brought me to a tinker encampment, a string of caravans untidily parked along a quiet roadside. But these weren't the traditional horse-drawn, intricately decorated red, blue, yellow and green caravans I had seen on Irish Tourist Board calendars. These were wooden trailers on rubber tyres with four windows and a door and there was a beat-up car or truck to tow each one of them. The hedgerows were strewn with drying washing all right – they looked as if they had been blown there by some hurricane – garish clouts and scraps of things, that hadn't changed, and the little kids still ran about with bare feet and sooty backsides. But there were plastic flowers on the window-sills, and butane gas stoves inside, and one or two portable battery-operated TV sets.

Yarr introduced me to one of the men. He had the best caravan. Made a good living selling antiques – Victorian oil-lamps and horse-brasses for the most part, to passing tourists. Tried to sell me a pair of china dogs, snooty, glass-eyed King Charles spaniels, for three pounds. Said they were fetching up to ten in the Portobello Road in London. That I wouldn't regret my purchase. A good line of sales talk. No pressure, take it or leave it, you know your own business best, no hard feelings etcetera. A big tanned man with greasy black curls and a crucifix around his neck. Wearing a very good watch and ring. Something of a dandy in an unwashed, gaudy sort of way. Voice coarse. A whiskey voice. Offered us some of his Black Bushmills Liqueur from a beautiful old cut-glass decanter encrusted with dirt. The glasses dirty too. Still, a quick swallow and try not to smell the sour reek of children's pee and puke, and the old rheumy-eyed terrier bitch panting in the corner. His wife watched all the while in the shadows with the baby at her bare breast. Had the eyes of a cowed but still skittish doe. A tribal code when it comes to woman's place, these people. I wondered if our gipsy friend will record for us when the time comes. His voice nice and gravelly. A good turn of phrase too. Called his glass of whiskey "a glass of oil-cloth". Use as *voice-over*, while the camera roams the interior . . . the children – little peeking animals, the breast-feeding mother, the stack of unwrapped loaves in a corner, Virgin Mary over the transistor radio, the dog, the sagging bed (for *all* of them?) the pin-ups on the wall – cheeky war-time blondes wearing sailor hats and little else (the man of the house answers to no one when it comes to his pleasures).

Interesting to note own personal reactions to discomfort, not to mention squalor, of these lives I'm sharing. One must deliberately coarsen one's sensibilities. Very difficult. My sympathies alas are with the stock American tourist who must have his Hilton, air-conditioning, showers, room service, ice in his drinks etcetera. I can't do that. Although some producers work from their hotel-suites with fast forays out on to location. Remember Theo Dunning directing a crew in Alaska in pale green suede desert boots, a West of England tweed suit (with waistcoat) and deerstalker hat. Beau Brummell among all those unshaven camera and sound men in stained parkas and army surplus. *I say, you chaps, try to get me a c. u. of that gorgeous old Jack London character over there. So untamed, don't you think?* Poor Theo, keeping the union jack flying wherever he goes. A limey to end all limeys. Very good in his own way. His B.B.C. training of understatement shaping his neat little evocative films. McLachlan only keeps him on because of his ritzy social connections in Toronto. Has brought Trans-Film a lot of business from the right people. And that reminds me. I must send that old buzzard a cable tomorrow. Something about how hopeful things look here. Something like that . . .

Good night, Quigley. Go to sleep.

THE PAIR OF THEM were laughing together when he came into the kitchen.

In his bed above he had listened to the twists and turns they had been giving their little joke for the past half-hour. Silence for a while, then one of them would make some remark he couldn't make out, and the soft giggling would break out again, gradually fade away, another respite, and then the next crack to keep it on the go. Whip the peerie every so often to keep it spinning. Oh it must be good, damn them. For he suspected it was about him. Why else should those two come together? She-devils. Hating him. The only thing they had in common.

He felt under the sofa for his shoes, kicked off last night in his half-drunken stupor after the dance. His head roared with blood for an instant, then felt dizzy, as he came erect. A grunt escaped him. Bridie jumped up from her place beside the fire and went quickly into the scullery. He could see her back shaking with suppressed laughter. Grimly he stared after her, hardening his gaze, for in a moment he would have to face Ruby for the first time that day. If she was still infected by the other's mirth he might be able to keep up this front of heavy indignation already formed, which in turn would help to carry him through the first minutes which were always the worst.

Oh but then, jesus, when he swung his eyes up to her face to meet that familiar glare he might have known that she had too much revenge still unappeased to let him off. Even just this once, he thought, when he needed a smooth entry into the day ahead so badly. The hangover was tightening its claws into him with every tick of the mantelpiece Baby Ben. The hands stood still at twenty minutes past ten, while the red second hand sped around with oiled fury. It was a reminder of how disorganised his life was.

Then Ruby asked, raising her voice, "Was there a big crowd?" The question was for Bridie in the scullery.

He kept his eyes down on the laces of his brogues, his fingers trembling. Air was what he needed most now, deep lungfuls of it to clear this prickling heat out of head and chest, but he stayed where he was. What next from these bitches?

Bridie said, "A terrible big mob. But sure you wouldn't look at any one of them. I don't know why these oul' done men go to a dance atall. They're no good to anyone."

127

She began to giggle. Ruby joined in, but bitterly, producing a strange unpleasant horse-like sound. *That big balloon-bellied mare, not worth a damn to anyone! Christ, if I had the courage to choke her. Both hands round her throat. Then she'd change her jibing tune, so she would. And the other one. He knew what he'd like to do to her all right. And might still, eh? Cocky bitch!*

With a bull-angry roar that surprised even himself, he called out suddenly, to the walls, the ceiling, the pictures around him, to everything in fact except directly to these two mockers, "Am I goin' to wait all day here for a mouthful of tea? While you two yap?"

Bridie said pertly, "Someone's got out of the wrong side of the bed today," and before he could stop himself, he blurted, "As long as you get out on *your* own side and nobody else's, you needn't fuckin' well annoy yourself."

He saw his wife's eyes. Gun-barrel discs trained to miss nothing. And he heard the other one's gasp. Stabbed. But he felt no joy. Victory curdling that moment he realised the consequences of what he'd said.

I am a fool, oh one fool; now life is going to be even more difficult. If that's possible. Quigley will be the one to surely suffer for this. She didn't like him before, but by christ, now when her little mind starts playing about with the image of Bridie and his nibs fooling around nightly in the same bed together, just on the other side of the wall up there, she'll put a rusty knife into him so far that – Most horrible thought then! She could very easily suspect him too. Because if Bridie's at it now with your man, what about the time before he arrived? Eh? And he knew he couldn't bear it if she started again going over calendars and diaries, checking dates, occasions, opportunities, as she'd done that last time. Rows, tears, the nagging, the unceasing surveillance night and day – no, that would finish him. And she wouldn't know a thing about it. What a bloody jungle it all was. You had to keep on back-tracking to keep them off you. When would there ever be the safety of a human-proof bolt-hole?

Feigning fury, he growled, "Forget about the bloody tea. I'll look after myself. As usual," and banged out into the shop.

From the top shelf where the tinned fruit was kept he took down a can of orange juice. He felt easier, less harried here. The top and bottom of the tin were rusted and felt flaky and dry under his fingers. There was no demand for such luxuries in Ballyboe.

Despite the rust, he jabbed a screw-driver deep down through the lid in two places, the sweet liquid spurted and he put his lips to its flow. It stung the back of his raw mouth. He drank on long after the first refreshing pleasure had gone. He finished the can and replaced it in its place on the shelf.

A smile came to his face as he thought of the annoyance it would cause Ruby if someone asked for a tin of the stuff, and she reached up to find it punctured and drained. Not that she served in the shop these days. She spent the time sprawled in her chair in the kitchen, groaning frequently, leafing listlessly through the local newspaper and women's magazines, eating, eating, eating and watching television from the first afternoon programmes until the close-down at midnight. She followed at least eight serials avidly. He would watch incredulously when tears squeezed out from under her puffy eyelids at moments in 'Peyton Place'. Some nights when that square panel of blue-grey was sucking everything and everybody steadily as on a thread towards itself, he couldn't bear it any longer, he had to get up, burst out, anywhere, for christ's sake. The self-pity in the air boxed him in. "Happy endings!" he wanted to scream at her as he charged out. "Don't you know by now, you fat cow, there's no such fuckin' thing."

He thought now of Quigley driving on his way to Armagh to send his cablegram. It couldn't go from Ballyboe Post Office. Just as well anyway, for the more private side of his business should not be made common property. He was still enjoying his role as Quigley's agent, managing him more subtly than the other suspected. Last night at the dance had shown how expert his manipulation had been. A word here, an introduction there, a hurrying off to someone somewhere else when some fool threatened to get too close. And he had to admit also that he'd enjoyed the steady but discreet interest that Quigley had aroused. He was starting to pull himself up out of the cold dark of the past months into the sun again. And not before its time either. Odd how it had taken this stranger to give him his lift up. Of course he had always known it couldn't go on for ever, but those were bad times – he shivered a little – bad times . . .

With fresh, new resolution quickening his actions he opened a drawer under the counter and took out a couple of clean quarto-sized bill-heads and a ball-pen. He circled the dry point across the new paper until the ink began to flow. He would start a list of people and places Quigley should see, that's what he would do. He wrote down – *Cock-fight. Contact Fonsey Meehan* – on the first line to the left of the cash column. It might be a difficult thing to arrange because of the suspicious natures of people like Meehan the publican. And he had to admit he'd allowed himself to slip out of touch this past year or so with the sporting men who gathered in "The Dublin House" each evening.

He knew also that they still regarded him in their deep unreasoning dark way as being in league with the local constabulary. He wasn't, of course. It was just that the lads from the barracks would now and then kill their night patrol by calling in for a packet of cigarettes. They were nervous of going into any of the other shops in the village because they were Prods. like he was. God, how many times had he sworn he would sell up and get himself away out from this rebel hole. But each time he cooled quickly, realising the bitter truth that no other Protestant would be interested in bidding for his business. If it came to hardys he would have to take what he was offered by the others and he knew, oh so well, how they would conspire together to beat him down to rock-bottom. He had seen it happen to others.

He lived his life in an ant-hill, a tolerated guest, ignored, as they moved about skirting him carefully, day to day, but one false move and they could turn on him, picking his bones white any afternoon they chose. God, there were times when he'd felt so tired handling them with the kid-gloves never off. They stood in the shop like sheep, their eyes swivelling around the shelves, around him, and never would they come out with anything. It was a major feat selling some of these characters a pair of bootlaces, so it was.

The ball-point, he noticed, had edged off the ruled line. An inked face looked up at him – triangular, eyeless, open-mouthed. He dotted in the two eyes, added ears and hair on the end. It looked like Packy Traynor. He hadn't seen him since Slaney. Young John Joe hadn't shown himself about the place either. But fuck the pair of them. The loss of their trade would hardly put him in the poor-house. The face on the paper disappeared under a close mesh of needlessly savage scribbles. Then he threw down the pen and propped his face in his hands. He had no interest in doing a thing now – just wanted time to pass him by without anything or anyone bothering him. A terrible way to be – in the grip of this tiredness which could never be eased, but what could he do?

An old woman, a stranger, came into the shop. She said to him, "Would you have a pair of wee boy's sandals – size four?"

He said, "No sandals. My new stock'll not be here till next week. Sorry now."

She stood for a moment. He knew she expected him to show her something else, even rifle through a few boxes first before admitting what he already knew to be true. He watched her with heavy expressionless eyes as she backed apologetically out of the shop, setting the coats on hangers just inside the door swinging. Her legs were shapeless puddings in wrinkled lisle stockings, the back of her coat humping up in an arc from her waist to her shoulders, an old done country woman near her time. She reminded him of his own mother, but any emotion he might have felt was sealed off under all the layers of self-preservation. It was tooth and nail this. Every man for himself. No time for softness.

Then a sound behind him. *She* was there watching him, eyes staring out of her head with hate. She pushed past out on to the floor of the shop to the facing shelves and started pulling out shoe-boxes down all around. Lids flying and tissue paper fluttering among the upturned gleaming soles of new leather.

"Christalmighty, what are you doing?" he cried, moving to halt her madness.

"What am I doing? What am I doing?" she panted. Her hands had torn great spaces in the neat stacks. "Why, I'm only doing what you should be doing – instead of drinking and whoring about the countryside with your fancy friends!"

He reached her and grappled with her. "Will you desist, you mad bitch!"

Her bare arms were slippery with sweat. His hands slid off as she struggled to get back again to the shelves. Then she was scrabbling like a dog for a moment, the cardboard lids landing and piling around her feet before he succeeded in pulling her back and up hard against the counter. His blood turned to water in the instant. He hadn't meant to throw her up against the hard wood so savagely.

Her mouth fell open. Tears and saliva ran down her cheeks and chin, *Oh god*, he thought, *what if something happens to her now, at a time like this*. The unfairness, the bloody unfairness of it!

"O-o-oh, o-oh, oh," she sobbed.

He stood looking at her, holding himself like a steel column, until she had broken herself upon him. His stomach had seized

131

into a hard knot. He felt poisoned. Was there never to be an end to all this?

"Oh god above in heaven," she cried, "what's to become of me, living with a brute like you? You don't care. You don't care. And your unborn child. We mean nothing to you. Selfish, selfish, selfish. Rotten filth that you are. You don't care about anything any longer. Nothing but your own selfish ways. The shop can slip and slide. We all can starve. We may as well put the shutters up while you play yourself – you big dirty pig."

She spat at him, then tried to strike him in the face. He put up his hand and hers jarred into his cupped palm. The fingers closed and he held her straining there. His face was close to her streaming face. He could feel her heat, see the sweat-soaked roots of her thin hair, smell the sappy fecundity of her. She spat again, blinding him this time. He jerked her arm over and down on to the counter as if to quickly win first round in their cruel hand-wrestling bout. For the second time he chilled, as she moaned when her heavy bulk twisted and thudded against the wood. She slipped down from him, pulling him after, her legs folded under, fat pads of flesh spreading out as thigh and calf clamped together. He tried to get his fingers out of her sweaty grip but she held on, entangling him. In a strange way he felt for her then, sensing her helplessness and rage at her own feebleness. The will of her so strong to grind and crush him, imprisoned in that heavy, hopeless body.

She cried out despairingly as he slid finally from her grip. "Oh I hate you. I want to die. I want to die."

He felt fear of a kind he'd never felt before. What had he done to her? How could anyone incur such terrible enmity? He backed off towards the open door, leaving her still on her knees with her upturned face weeping from mouth, eyes, nose, like a child when it has totally abandoned itself to grief.

She began to beat the floor with her palms. Dust rose. If someone came in and saw her – Christ! And the sound must be carrying out into the street. It was a mercy that Quigley was away at any rate. But he couldn't allow her to go on with it. He must stop her some way. More wrenching? God knows how much damage had been done already. Those two occasions when his blind animal side had reacted. But what other physical language did she understand? That was it. You slapped an hysteric's face, didn't you? He'd never actually seen it happen in real life, just on the films, but it was a well-known medical fact. Wasn't it? One slap. *One* slap? How hard? Christ, how *hard*?

Bridie came through the open door behind the counter. "Leave her alone," she said in a flat voice, looking straight at him over his wife's head. "That's enough."

That's enough, he repeated inside his head like a scream, *that's enough*. He glared at her, the sum total of his anger concentrated in his eyes. How dare she? Yes. Force herself to come in and say what she had just said. He tried to pierce her with his gaze, summoning up more threatening power, more than he thought was in him.

She stared back at him curiously, matching him, then slowly beginning to defeat him. He could see it, feel it, for it was in the air. His wife sensed the same steady seepage charging the atmosphere too, for the steady rhythm of her sobbing began to break and falter. They were both watching him now as if to catch a glimpse of something in him for the first time, their eyes colder than pebbles, greedy. He felt a desire to laugh then, strangely enough, for he could understand them so clearly. They were spotlighted dazzlingly for him, their motives as though on a screen, and he wanted to laugh at the simplicity, the obviousness of the things they felt. When he was drunk everyone revealed themselves like this to him, as he sat back smiling at performances through glass. It was beautiful knowledge but it could never be turned to use in your own life. Like now.

He moved to the door, never taking his eyes off the two of them, knowing that something had happened. The full implications would only break upon him later. Meanwhile (that word implied calm acceptance, control, but he hadn't either) but meanwhile where the hell was Quigley? Where are you, you big bastard?

Out into the sunny street and the eyes of Ballyboe watching him.

THE COUNTRYSIDE AROUND HERE is sprinkled with lakes so tiny they don't show on my map. Yet all named. The signposts informing me as I drive. A country sagging under its weight of place names. Every hill, stream, stone and dip noted and anchored in the race memory. My people with their passion for detail, looking at life through a jeweller's glass. A nation of myopics.

Lough Sheetrim. Tear shaped. The surface rippling spasmodically. Is it the breeze or . . . ? Man-eaters in the slushy mud. Down among the decay. I've seen gaunt black canoes dredged up from these same waters in museums. Petrified oak the colour of anthracite, with the grain ridged rough. The slow corroding power of Irish lough water. Like the climate. So much water. Bleeding through the soft crust. Lying in pools and streams, reflecting the changing sky. Such sensitive mirrors.

Quigley in reflective mood himself this fine summer's day. At his ease among the reeds. And very good it is too to be away from all the frenzy of the past two days and nights. First resting place. Time for stock-taking. So . . .

A wedge of geese flying low overhead searching for the inaccessible places. Me, gunless, on my stomach among the water-plants. *Pow*. I make a silent kill. They fly on regardless, beating the air with soft white fans. End of interlude.

So . . . The cable went off today. On his dusted glass-topped desk first thing tomorrow. Will set his mind at rest. That nothing has befallen me. His favourite blue-eye. Pining for me, the poor old sweetie. Tch, tch.

My words concise, yet full of solid optimism. *Have found a base. Stop. See address above. Stop. On to a winner. Stop. Shooting script well in hand. Stop. Estimate budget to be very economic. Stop. Contact Telefis Eireann crew to stand by. Stop. Quigley.* All the cables from his "young lions", as he once termed us at Trans-Film's tenth birthday celebrations, will be the same. I'm the greatest, they yell, love me most of all. *Please.*

*

134

Suggested alternative cable. Why not? To induce his coronary. My service to humanity. *Stoned past two nights. Stop. Perplexed. Stop. Uncertain. Stop. Don't expect shooting script. Stop. Don't expect nuthin'. Stop. Nossir. Stop. Quigley.* The torn yellow pieces flutter down into the dark waters. My imaginary cable.

A water-hen, with her three fluff-ball chicks in tow, ventures out to the further brim. Keep close to mamma, that nervous darting head is saying in water-hen language. They crowd her as the waves reach gale-force proportions out in the wild middle. They make it, disappearing swiftly under a curtain of hanging water-weed, speeding into their dark tunnel of love. Quigley the naturalist. An allegory in every blade of grass, every ant's egg. Who needs people?

Waiting in Fr Devine's ante-chamber for my audience earlier. The elderly maid (Mary) with her moustache and varicose veins. A whiff of cooking surrounding her as she enquires my name and business. *Quigley. Private.* Is obviously used to more respect from callers to the parochial house. A new altar-wine salesman? With the corners still not knocked off him? Father D. will soon see to that. She humphs.

Then . . . *Come in, come in.* The voice through the mahogany door. The old trick. Head bent over some papers on his monumental roll-top. A wave of a hand to a chair. *Won't be a minute, son.* Son! The room dark, with heavy furniture. A smell of wax polish, moth-balls and thick-socked cleric. His pen scratching. Aw come on, you old crap merchant, who do you think you're kidding? St Martin de Pores on top of the big book-case watching all with liquid eyes. My favourite saint. Always preferred him when I was a kid because he looked like a nigger minstrel in the wrong fancy dress get-up. Coon in chasuble.

Well now. On his feet at last, thumbs hooked in the armpits of his shiny black watered-silk vest. Likes to stand, move about, stretch. Dominate through his bulk. Noticed it on Sunday. Photographs of hurling teams on the wall. The athletic type of priest, this one. Best stand seats at Croke Park etcetera. Strong desire to say – *I've a very nice new line in empire burgundy I'm sure you'd be interested in, father,* and just leave it at that, but instead – *My name is Quigley, father, and I thought you might be*

135

able to help me in my research for a documentary film I'm producing.

My standard introduction, pared to neat business card size. Short and explicit enough for one foot to be inserted in the door. Pause now. *They* ask a question next. They always do. Always. Like – what sort of film is it? Or why do you think *I* can help you? This reverses the relationship right away. They're now asking *me* for information. Me giving it. In a very small way doing them the favour. Bridging that ugly chasm of suspicion, softening the cold-eyed look which says – okay, so now go on, amaze me with your miracles. So I wait for the question.

Father D. grunts, *Oh*? then watches me floundering to the dry land of composure for fifty seconds or so. No life-belts to spare from that quarter. Struggle. Good for the soul, my son. When I finish I can't remember what I have said. Humiliating fragments roosting in the corners of the shadowy room. Silence. Then a great clearing of the throat and drumming of fingers on the taut silk of the clerical vest. *I hope you are not going to search for the sordid. There have been some desperate pieces of television lately, desperate. Irresponsible muck-raking by characters who should know better. I wouldn't lend myself to any carry-on of that sort. Filth pouring into people's homes. There are certain subjects which shouldn't be aired before impressionable people. I've written a few letters myself to the papers about our own station.*

The Father's obsessions lurk near the surface. Once more another howling pack of them are unleashed. This time in the mahogany gloom of the very chamber where he lists them on paper for his Sunday salvoes. (What colour ink does he use? Scarlet?) Little wonder they now spring out so strongly at me. Feeling like a sitting duck in a shooting gallery.

The shit I have to swallow! Before I can voice my own tiny, perhaps worthless, point of view on a piece of film. This side of my job I can do without, yet some of my fellow producers love this part. I hear them talk. Silvers, for instance, delights in the buttering up, the cajoling, the deceit. Makes the final screw-you, friend, doubly sweet for him when it comes and it's in the can with it and all of them, all the great buddies and the women you laid and told lies to, and all the cast of thousands who respected you and were prepared to follow and be charmed by you and it would go on for ever etcetera, etcetera, and you would make all their dreams of fame and fortune come true etcetera, etcetera – they can all drop suddenly dead.

Now what is Father's D. angle – because they all have one – all these potential producers of their own private dreams. Father Devine's film of Father Devine's Ireland – a kibbutzy Tir Na n'Og where every young man is clad in G.A.A. jersey and shorts, swings a hurley, is a Pioneer, has no sexual impulses whatsoever and will die a martyr's death for his country as readily as he'll tear off a chorus of the Shan Van Vocht. And where the young women are raven-haired, sloe-eyed, chaste, devout and domesticated and would die if they ever caught a glimpse of a brassière or a pair of silk panties. That's how *I* would make a film, he'll say. Of course I don't want to teach you your job, you know about these things much better than I do, but still I – *I, I, I*.

Another tirade, Quigley. That makes how many in how many pages? A new and dangerous habit. People should be kept in their places – the Father Devines of this world, yes, and the Yarrs, for he too is showing a tendency to feel latent artistic oats. Sweet irony, that after giving him free rein to select for you, you have begun to resent this already. You plant a seed and can't bear to see it grow by itself. Quigley, you may well be in need of a trick-cyclist. But then why pay someone to do a job which you can perform so efficiently yourself. A thought. Or rather too bloody many of them lately. This correspondence (with self) is now closed.

Later. Father D. relaxes hostilities. A few warning bursts still rumble out of that barrel chest of his from time to time, but he is almost inclined to be genial. A bottle of Jameson Ten Year Old and two squat Waterford glasses appearing out of the sideboard. Not a drinking man himself by the way he prepares and fills his own poison. I'm flattered, but still suspicious. Why the old treatment? Waiting for it, with the cool loaded glass in the hand. Lovely whiskey, ripe and golden. The soda squirt gently pene-trates its depths, stirring up a faint languid oiliness. But the good Father (and the adjective seems appropriate now) is merely solicitous in a rough but well-meaning way about the state of my

137

soul. He noticed me, it appears, at mass on Sunday. Who is my priest in the States? *Not America? Oh really. Canada? What part of Canada? Toronto? A lot of Irish there, aren't there? Quigley – a good Irish name. What part of the homeland etcetera, etcetera?* and I am hauled back slowly but surely by that age-old umbilical cord.

After a string of lies on my part concerning fictitious priests and Toronto churches (*they* exist at any rate) it's time to offer me another drink from the tall bottle. I didn't flunk my good Irish Catholic refresher course, it seems. And now we can relax into that state of chummy Catholicism you find from Fiji to Finglas. The whiskey warming the big, heavy, earnest face opposite mine. The eyebrows very black – conté pencilled in on salmon pink flesh. The same black flecking the stiff helmet of white hair. For, curious effect, as if the original colour was white and not black. Tapping my knee, a squeeze to punctuate each of his sentences. My first homosexual priest? For really, cross his heart, young Eddie P. Quigley, strangely enough, never had any experiences of that particular perversion while in the charge of successive Christian Brothers and other men of the cloth.

Of course there was always Brother Maguire from County Westmeath who devised the brutally effective punishment of inserting your finger into a live terminal on the electric meter board high on the classroom wall (he stood you on a chair to do it) if you missed your catechism. Our first young foretaste of purgatory twentieth century style under the tutelage of "Sparky" Maguire.

But perhaps all Irishmen have traces of the old Ionian weakness. For one thing, I never witnessed such a mania for physical contact. Hand-shaking is always an embarrassingly long drawn-out affair and, with a few drinks, the hugging, the shoulder and arm squeezing. The strangers who have had their arms around me, in the last two days, whispering, laughing, confiding, their faces close, always hovering, it seems, on the brink of a kiss. Frigid women of Ireland you have a lot to answer for, driving your menfolk to unnatural acts with each other or consenting farm-stock. Wouldn't the good Father just love a touch of that in the "ould fillum". The roaring trade in odd gum boots in the mountainy sheep areas etcetera, etcetera.

*

138

Yarr's name comes up. *A bit of a character* – and nothing much else from the Father. I nod with him. The implication being, enough said, both of us men of the world, *our* world. A poor heretic that one, first, foremost and primarily.

No one, as yet, has spoken about him openly – if that's ever possible. And it's taking a longer time than usual to form a perfected whole from my scattering of jig-saw pieces.

OLD TATE SAT STIFFLY on the edge of their sofa, his cheeks flaming as though rouged, icy blue eyes fierce, but unprepared as yet to meet his son-in-law's as they roved ceaselessly over the pictures, the wallpaper, the mantelpiece ornaments. He still hadn't worked himself up to the proper pitch of frenzy that would satisfy his daughter and her mother – the old fox-furred she-devil herself. He crouched between them, a little man, showing an inch or two of white wool combinations between trouser bottom and his wrinkled socks. He looked as though he were their prisoner. They glared straight ahead at the opposite wall, seemingly disclaiming responsibility. Yarr felt sorry for him. It was another emotion out of place, for he knew what he was going to have to feel in this situation if he were to save himself.

". . . strange sort of a carry-on for a grown man, I must say . . ." *yes, yes, grind it in about responsibility; you should grunt and buckle down like all the other farting pack animals, oh aye* ". . . have you no feelings at all . . . ?" *that one!* ". . . but then you always were the oddity . . ."

So the eyes had finally come home to roost, had they? – the whites bleeding a little, old man's watery red-rimmed eyes. Now for all the dirt.

". . . always thought you were a cut above everyone else . . . airs, graces . . . big talk . . . no time for the rest of us . . ." It was this stranger they were talking about again, the shadowy double that lived inside his body, wore his clothes, but had all the characteristics of someone else. Still, he had doubts; perhaps the one they saw was not the distorted projection of their own spites and envy. ". . . just because you have a bloody wee huckster's shop that's not doing a ha'porth o' trade anyway, you imagine . . ." He glanced at Ruby – *his wife*, for god's sake, and the closed stone face chilled him. A despair at his inability to appeal either to her logic or her sense of fair play ringed his soul – but then he knew (little comfort in that) that both attributes were masculine anyway.

He felt his scalp begin to tighten. Very soon now it would close in like a shrinking onion skin around the throbbing trip-hammer, and the pain would be transmitted to his whole body in a rhythmical pulverising beat.

"Sure the Yarrs were never anything else but dirt . . ." The old bitch herself had joined in now, her turkey jowls quivering softly.

140

He could see where her lisle stockings ended and the elastic of her knickers began, for her legs had opened out as her fury unfolded. She had on a turban-shaped hat in some green stuff, flecked with little bright stones. They flashed angrily too, in the firelight at every shake of her head.

She was a stupid, narrow-minded, coarse bag. He had always thought so and, accordingly, had felt sympathy for poor old Tate. Even now, despite his insults and the mean outburst he had directed at him, he liked him. The old woman's he could take, but this deep-buried and now released spite of his hurt. He had always imagined old Tate had been fond of him. They had never really talked of course, just trailed around each other vapours of chat about crops, weather, politics, but he had believed then that if an occasion like this ever arose he would have been on his side for part of the time. But then that was only soft-hearted nonsense. His claim on the old man was a weak shadow compared with the pull from the other side. Yarr knew that old Tate loved the woman by his side (how ludicrous it seemed – but it was true) loved that unlovely, heart-scalding fury with a passion almost obscene in one of his years. He had often probed at the relationship in his mind, marvelling. Perhaps it stemmed from old Tate's age – he was a good ten years her senior – and his growing dependence upon her. She led him a life of hell at times, pursuing whims relentlessly until he satisfied them, taking to her bed with imagined illnesses, while he crept around the house with a look of misery on his face. She would kill him eventually, nothing surer, and enjoy her widowhood to the full with a vast self-pitying pleasure.

". . . we were always respectable. I never was happy about my Ruby marrying one of your tribe. That sister of yours . . ." Edie, his lovely Edie, who had to marry George Calvert in a hurry . . . up the builder . . . her swollen face and puffy eyes haunting him when he was seventeen . . . he wanted to kill Calvert . . . now he pitied him, and Edie had turned into a proper snobbish bitch with her kids at grammar school and old George forced out to play golf every Saturday morning . . . that poor suffering bastard in his cardigan and black and white spiked shoes . . . he was down in one shoulder already, the weight of the clubs merely accelerating the progress of his slump . . .

". . . just wait until Sidney hears about this. He'll chastise you, so he will, you filthy blackguard . . ." The big brother was it, the

141

muscle-man, as thick as that wall. He had only contempt for that one and had shown it in the past only too clearly. It was one of the first wedges to be driven between Ruby and himself. *You're only jealous of Sid, so you are. He's twice the man you are*, she used to scream after each of his frequent attacks on "the idiot boy" as it used to amuse him to term him. Looking back on it from this distance, as though through the wrong end of a telescope, he supposed it was jealousy of her hero-worshipping someone else that made him behave as he did. It seemed impossible that he had ever felt such an emotion.

He looked at her now, like an angry pregnant bird she was, perched on the end of the sofa, her mouth ruled, her eyes glittering tear-washed agates. Would she fling in her tanner's worth too, he wondered. Coming at him then from all three angles, this stream of abuse, to converge into a single eroding jet. They were pushing him too far, too far, with their taunts about his "difference". He looked at all of them. *Oddity*. Weren't they the oddities, not he? Surely there must be a society where each member felt and thought like he did and this trio would be stoned away from the gates.

He wondered how long they'd been playing their spiteful hoses on him. He hadn't said a word in his defence or in retaliation either. Had they noticed? What was the use anyway? The course and the outcome were always the same – immutable.

The outside door opened and they stopped, their mouths snapping like traps – all except Ma Tate, who, with eyes still glazed, continued to let slip a few more abusive phrases until the old man put his hand on her knee, squeezing fiercely. She swung a glance at him. He stared back. Her gaze took on a new hardness, for she had a large capacity for revenge.

A cough in the hall. It was Quigley. He always entered the same way. Mentally Yarr cursed his wife, his first real anger. She had made his friend feel unwelcome in his house, *his* house. He certainly wasn't going to allow this other crowd now with their ignorant ways to further embarrass him.

"Your showman friend," hissed Ruby – her first words, concentrated gall. The old man rose shakily, stiff-arming himself off the edge of the sofa.

Quigley had stopped in the hall. He was whistling, rustling and moving papers about on the hall-stand. Yarr sat where he was. He felt calm strangely enough, but the power was there to sweep all of these people out and away in a great gout of anger if they pushed him. He watched them. The old bitch wanted to sit on. He knew her mood well. She wanted to damage indiscriminately. The lust was up in her – would take some considerable time before it fled her system. The old man pulling at her now would suffer for days.

Ruby got up suddenly, stepping over their feet, for the kitchen was a small one, and went out through the door. For a moment he thought she was going to tackle Quigley, but no, he followed her progress by sound, her left wheel at the stairs and then the creak-creak as she climbed stiffly up to their bedroom. He thought of her eyes as she'd left the room. Always her eyes. No longer pebbles, more like ball-bearings now – the latest image – cold, cold, covered with fine film that had nothing to do with tears. Tears were impossible now. She must be damaging herself. But how much could you suffer for anyone else? In his case he couldn't afford to permit even a fragment of any such feeling to flit through his mind. And the unwearying vigilance was killing him. He rested his beating head in his hands and felt the old man and his wife brushing past.

In the hall-way old Tate emitted a grunt or two in recognition of the stranger – he'd still a little decency left – but there was no sound from the old woman.

The street door closed behind them and Quigley came into the room, a disconcertingly smiling Quigley with a folded paper which he slapped on his thigh. "Hi," he said, throwing down the papers, because Yarr could now see that there were several typed foolscap sheets clipped together. "I'm bushed. What a day. But it's been worth it."

Slumping on to the worn arm of the settee, he looked down at Yarr, smiling. With his right hand he felt in his jacket pocket, bringing out his lighter, then his packet of Camels. Yarr studied him in turn, and each step in his smoking ritual. He felt cheated by the other's bounce, for it seemed to him that he had betrayed the earlier mood which he had fashioned for him when he had first heard him fidgeting in the hall-way.

Every time a reversal of this nature occurred now he felt another spike drive home.

"Do you know a guy called Malarky? Librarian in Slaney? Gave me all this historical dope."

The typed foolscap sheets. His thumb running over the edges of the wad exposing their lavish white thickness. Yarr smelt the released richness of print. And again felt his mind chill towards the other. Then angry for feeling it. Analyse, analyse, for christ's sake! And purge it away by so doing. Yes. Where did he get this belief anyway, in the power of the mind, when that very part of him with its unwearying thresh was destroying him. Eh? It made him smile.

Quigley shook his sheets of typescript, smiling too. "You know him? Something about him I don't – but should? Is that it?"

Yarr burst out laughing and the other joined in, watching him with a little perplexity at first, then it melting away, smoothing off into easy good-humour. His face crinkled excessively when he laughed. There was a complex network up around the eyes. Yarr noted the pale tracery particularly. Caused by wrinkling up the eyes against strong sun. A strange thought. For the prevailing weather, which was hot and sunny these past days, had not even impinged on him. He might as well be eking out his life under some lid. He thought of times when he was young and every day brought that stab of anxiety with the first moment of waking and the accompanying first glance out of doors. A wet day in high summer could carry darkest misery with it, or a change to thaw when the quarry-hole was frozen tight to the island in its centre. He had almost forgotten what it was like to be alive then.

"Oh, no, no." He spoke hurriedly, coming out of his abstraction. "He's all right. He knows what he's talking about."

Fancy Malarky and the neck of him palming off that bloody screed he'd been trying to get someone to look at for years. Malarky who affected great airs, had high-flown newspapers sent over a week late from London in wrapped rolls as solid as batons, wore bow-ties, yellow socks and lived on Ryvita and poached eggs. His diet was common knowledge in the town, despite his frequent cries in public about the soul-destroying unimaginativeness of Irish cooking. Oh, he was a great one on the soul-destroying thing, was the same gent . . .

Quigley said, "I'm not so sure though whether a thing like this should have a place in the idea I want." His eyes were puzzled, puzzling out the thoughts of the man sitting opposite. Yarr watched him, no outgoing of assistance possible. *Continue, sir.* "I mean, it's now, here and now I want to – to delineate, if you follow me." *Christ – follow, FOLLOW!* "Though there's no reason why there shouldn't be some strong linking with the past. After all, this place is rooted in tradition. You can't get away from it. You can breathe it, smell it almost. Yeah – an odour, an odour, if you like." *Please god, stop his flutterings. I need calmness so much, in everything and everyone around me. More? Christ!* "But I'm running on about my worries as usual." Yarr shot a glance. *What did he mean by that?* "After all, it's not the biggest picture ever made – I mean . . . ?" *Hurried that piece, but that's what he meant. Back to the dullness and the voice passing over. Nothing but wait until he finishes. Resign yourself to it.* His eyes rested on feet and legs to knee height. He hoped he looked as if he were concentrating. All he saw and absorbed though were the black leather slip-on shoes, navy socks and the grey flannel trousers with their miraculous creases. Such a tidy race. Americans, Canadians insisted so much on things as pressed clothes, clean shirts and underwear and shaving regularly. One afternoon when the other had been out he had stolen a glance at the array of toiletries in green and amber bottles that would have marked down any other man as pansy. But Quigley wasn't, he knew that. Just a different attitude, different values, on what was an essential and what wasn't. He had been so preoccupied with his own torments he hadn't given this man the due proportion of his attention. He tried to concentrate on what he was saying.

". . . I've been damned lucky in finding this place. It's got everything. A real microcosm . . ." Like a little boy in his absorption. What did micro-something mean? Had one until the wheel came off.

"Pardon me for going on like this but –" a hesitation, an embarrassed clearing of the throat. His other side, the opposite of the salesman with the glittering message. How he had charmed people. P. J. and his wife, and now Malarky – although he was easy meat, anyone like Quigley would impress that oul' eejit. *Have you read Joyce?* he would say to everyone, even Coughdrop Kearney the town's fool. *Joyce who?* you answered and Malarky would go off shaking his head, tut-tutting.

"I'm grateful for your help, it's as simple as that. And I hope our partnership is going to continue . . ."

The words, the sincerity in the other's face were warning signals for him to do something, say something quick to shiver the mood. A relieving crack would do it. Then they could both find some ease. But he couldn't conjure even one thin little joke out of the air to put an end to it. His inner despair seemed to inflate every second as Quigley floundered on and on and on.

145

God above, surely, surely there must be a breaking-point somewhere. And now he didn't care, *didn't care*, how unspeakable the aftermath turned out to be. Let it. Let it.

IT'S ALL SEXUAL. The hanging fire until the last possible moment. And the actual creation of the work of art (film, in this case) is orgasm – longer drawn out than in Nature admittedly, but still orgasm. It all fits. Even to that well-known period of lethargy and depression afterwards. Agreed? Agreed. So the longer Quigley delays his old seminal spurt the more telling it will be. Such little philosophic games console momentarily.

Meanwhile, still observing, noting fragments. I have a mania about waste. That's why I put all down here. My ideal is to use every single one of them, no matter how dissimilar, how unrelated they seem to be.

MacLachlan, of course, would love such a line of thought. *Get it straight, once and for all, Trans-Film isn't some wee girls' college film society. We make commercial products here. Speed, economy and no arty-farty nonsense, please.* Once a technician always a technician, with that never-dying distrust of ideas and the "artistic" director, always ready to snarl – *no, you can't get that, it's impossible, it won't work* . . . Theo Dunning's word is "bolshie" to describe his crew. To get the best from them you've got to pick your way through a minefield of their prejudices.

Fragment One. The hand-ball court. In a quiet backwater in Slaney. Hundreds of them all over the island – erected by the Irish government once upon a time to exert the bodies of the nation's young in an authentic Gaelic manner. Only schoolboys use them now. The young men prefer football, hurling, or the ritual of horse-race betting – a bottle of stout, then up the alley to the bookie's for the three-thirty at Newmarket, back to the pub for another Guinness, then the four o'clock etcetera. When the day's race meetings are over the male unemployeds make for home with bleary eyes and empty pockets. Someone must surely win some time.

The court is roofless, three-sided. The formidable back-wall – thirty feet in height, the supporting walls sloping away, all constructed of shuttered concrete – pale-grey, pitted, crumbling. Concrete as old as this looks like Norman masonry. Modern-day keeps. The floor is smooth and stained. Coarse weeds flourish in cracks in the walls. Dogs and drunk men must urinate in the dark, dark corners. But the texture of the shuttering is beautiful – as enlarged as gruyère in places, glittering with particles of quartz, acres of pumice to the palm.

A clap brings to mind Greek amphitheatres. A shout would be unthinkable. I'm in love with it. Would gladly do the complete film here – an Irish *Oedipus*. But will certainly have one scene at any rate.

Fragment Two. The village phone box after dark. An oasis of light. The young bloods of the village gather around it every night. Drawn to it like moths. The excitement of voices along the wire. An illusion of being part of things happening – somewhere – not here (they're like kids in country places the world over – *home is dead, daddio*) but somewhere, somewhere at the end of the long, long wire stretching out from that humid, tobacco-smelling receiver is life and sex and money and things you read about or see in the movies.

Fragment Three. Another of these same young kids riding his bicycle. Along a country road. His coat over handle-bars. It starts to rain. The kid begins to put the coat on *as he rides*. Hands up, one at a time, and into the sleeves. Long, flapping coat-tails trailing dangerously over spokes. But not done to impress anyone, no. Not a spectator anywhere except me and I'm hidden. The Irish temperament at work. Paradoxically practical. This is what puzzles the foreigner who sees such actions as hopelessly illogical. To these people they're not. Simply the quickest and easiest solution to a problem, so why not? Nothing is weighed up. No word or words for pros and cons in the language.

But I must not become bogged down with race theories. These have a habit of contradicting each other in this place. My god, another one . . .

Yarr becomes a problem. The no-bigger-than-a-man's-hand cloud has blown up into a passable storm. I will not, *must* not get involved in his family's squabbles. The atmosphere in this house is poisonous. I've closed my eyes and ears to it long enough. I suppose it suited my purpose.

This afternoon finished it. Kaput. My presence here may not have been the final irritant to set off that bout of recrimination I happened to overhear while in the hall-way, but as they say in the movies, I'm certainly not staying round long enough to find out. Jesus H. Christ! Those three were pulling out his entrails by the yard today. A smell of the slaughterhouse still hanging about that room. And then my big phoney choked-up gratitude act. To console. Why? *Why?* A cheap cheating gush. Be honest, Quigley. This man means nothing to you beyond his means to your end. So don't cover up the shit with a few handfuls of sentimental throwaway. If any time is ripe for you to blow it is now. Yarr is doomed. His wife is doomed. Bridie is doomed. Yes, young Bridie. Her, too. She has changed in a subtle way from that blushing child-bride to someone who still blushes, true, but won't be too long in adapting embarrassment to her own demands.

Playing little games now as she begins to feel out wiles. *Oh no I don't think it's right . . . we shouldn't be doing this . . . you should go back to your own room now . . . ah, yes go on, be good . . . please . . . I'll never see you again anyway . . . you'll go off back to Toronto and forget all about me . . . I bet you've been with dozens of girls like me . . . they don't mean a thing to you . . . how do I know you're not even married* . . . Run, Quigley run.

Another time. In the dark. Her mouth close to my ear. A sudden itch for whispered conversation. Hands on her covered stomach and breasts. She insists on putting her long nightie on immediately afterwards, or, for that matter, not allowing me to remove it at all, so that it gradually rides up into a ridiculous fat, wrinkled halter around her neck. A futile chastity belt. Her moments of passion eclipsed by succeeding spasms of maddening modesty. A sense of the second having the power to cancel out the first. Hot, cold, yes, no.

A bore. I seek total complaisance now. Not this coyness. The texture of her night-thing is curiously repellent-pleasant, betwixt and between, brushed nylon, I think. Silk, moulded to the soft little domed concavity of her belly and breasts, my preference.

149

Would she wear it, if I bought her a present? The slower, more sensual delights I crave not to her liking. She writhes away. Protesting in my ear. Anguish in whispers. Young girls, Quigley, can be unsatisfying intoxicants, didn't you know that by this time? Still that firmness, that smoothness, those unexpected hollows of moist heat . . .

She loathes Yarr. Pouring out her derision in my ear. While he lies conjugally in the next room. While I lie caressing the stuff of her nightie, a hopeful – hopeless ritual. The power of massage works no wonders. I listen, not really concentrating. Out of all the abuse I pick facts.

His debts, to half the country. His own carelessness to blame. Insults customers, won't pay travellers, refuses to open after closing time to late-comers when they come knocking at the side-door; goes off himself for whole days on end (with me?) and to hell with business. Periodically speculates on new lines of stock that don't – couldn't sell . . . three gross of men's trick neck-ties, made in Hong Kong, lighting up to register *Hi cookie*, the American Army surplus steel helmets – the idea there was for customers to pierce them, then convert them into hanging plant-holders for porches and halls – still piled in rusty mounds out at the back, until the next war, most likely. Then there was the instant potato, the peanut butter, Yugoslav honey, the curry powder. And oddest of all (to Bridie) – that order of two dozen pairs of women's silk briefs – four colourways – peach, red, navy and black, embroidered butterflies, dragons and palm-trees on the fronts, and fourteen and eleven (*fourteen and eleven!*). Even at cost price, she herself could only afford one pair, the navy. Dragon, palm-tree or red-admiral? I whisper. A momentary giggle. *Butterfly, you bad thing* . . . Can I stroke a tiny wing? *You'll do no such thing, you're getting as bad as he is, always putting his hand up my clothes, and you can't trust him at the washing-line either. I caught him with a pair of my panties once, rubbing his nose with them, the dirty oul' pig.*

Last night, when the house was empty save for the three of us, he caught her at one point, pulling her down, bending her over his knee as he sat on the sofa. A strange atmosphere. His horse-playing barely concealing his real seriousness. *Bridie loves me doing this, don't you, Bridie, darling?* His hands pulling up her skirt as she struggled, exposing her pants (pink). I sat across watching with a smile on my face. A bad feeling. Her angry eyes watching me while she vainly beat the back of his red swelling neck. I felt the performance had been put on for my benefit. His laughter sounded strange. He made growling bear noises, rubbing and pushing his unshaven face into her breasts, then a glance slyly up at me. God forgive me, I think at one point I cheered him on. A defeat of some kind.

Yes, Bridie hates . . .

Pushed his own father out of the business, did you know that? It was his before Yarr took over. Treated the old man like a dog until he had to leave. Made fun of him in the shop before the customers, played jokes; once he set fire to the newspaper he was reading, then threw water over him – it was common knowledge in the village, everyone knew the story – all you have to do is ask. When he was younger he got two girls into trouble, down the country somewhere . . . it was reputed he was still paying out two bottles of milk and two seven and sixpences a day . . . wasn't that what you had to pay? Then there was that affair with the Donnelly boy, the one who was killed in the crash at Bartley's Corner. He was a pansy sort of creature, they said, had his hair dyed and wore scent, and there were rumours about him and Yarr and their carry-on . . . just rumours, nothing more, but, sure that Yarr, all he thinks about is sex, sex, sex, and there's no smoke without a fire, so it makes you think . . . He's been in the mental place too, you know . . . he doesn't know I know that, but I do . . . thinks it's all a big secret, but I've a girl-friend who's a nurse up there and she saw him in the ward getting some kind of treatment . . . I can't describe it, it's something to do with electric shocks, I think . . . oh, I'd love to see his oul' face if he found out that I know . . . if he doesn't leave me alone I'll tell him straight out, so I will . . . how dare he put his hands all over me, just because I work in his oul' shop he thinks he owns me, but he's another think coming . . . Mister Loony Yarr, I'll say to him, it's time you had another wee dart of the current (giggles). Then there was the time . . .

So Yarr has been treated for melancholia. The Irish malady. My old man had to have E.C.T. too. We were still at school. He used to start weeping behind his *Toronto Star*, then hold it up to shield his face from us as he rushed out of the room. None of us understood. Just kept our peace, our little animal eyes across the dinner-table boring at him. God help him. He had no sympathy from any of us. His trip to Mount Charles finally arranged for *our* comfort, not his. He couldn't remember some of our names when he came out. We used to giggle together, confusing him, until he flew into a crying rage. Only that made us desist. He never was the same man afterwards. Something had been removed, blacked out, atrophied.

4

THEY THOUGHT THEY HAD SLIPPED HIM, the bastards, but they were deluded. Too clever for them still, he was. Still. The rendezvous (an old out-farm at the end of a bog-track, they had said, instead of Duffy's big new concreted yard), the wrong time (half-past four – one hour late too). But he had tracked them, so he had, almost by scent, it seemed at times – the long snaking column of cars without lights, blind man's buffing it as circuitously as possible to the selected main.

The cocks went first in Fonsey Meehan's Volkswagen van. Then came Dickey the vet's car loaded to the roof with his guests and their rugs, flasks of soup and bottles of Martell and Powers, for he liked his comforts, that red-faced swine. Then the other cars, nose to bumper, the drivers nervous, for only the leaders knew route and destination. Invariably some got themselves lost through their engines failing them or starting to drink too early and not keeping their eyes fixed on the big blue Volkswagen's rear when it moved off. They never found the column again, those unfortunates – spent the grey, then brightening morning hours racing over hill and dale for a sniff. Yes. They had thought he would finish up like that, but up them, hadn't he beaten them?

Quigley sat beside him, silent, his knees close in a curiously prim fashion, as their car slipped noiselessly down the old lane. Overhanging twigs and brambles gently whipped the roof and glass. When last had this track been used? The tyre-marks of the procession he had been stalking showed up brutally in the wet silky grass. These forgotten out-farms were used once and once only by the cock-fighting men, then left to sleep.

He felt like a taut string – the dexedrines were at their work. How else could he have found the main otherwise? He would suffer for this twanging later, christ he would, but that was another day's worry.

"Are you sure you won't have one?" He shook his little bottle and the capsules danced behind the smoky glass. "You look as if you need a lift . . ." he said.

Quigley's eyes were tired, stained blue underneath. He had spoken very little on the journey, allowing himself to be shuttled along at a nervous rate right from the start.

At four, Yarr had slid out from beside his wife. She was sweating a lot these nights. Now, ironically, he was the one who held to his own side of the bed with such severity. Her night-clothes were soaked and a damp heat spread steadily out from her. On the cold linoleum he found his pyjamas sticking to his back. Thoughts of a chill made him dress swiftly, angrily. He looked down at her. Her mouth was open, a snail-track of saliva escaping. She flung up her bare, flushed arms and they flopped on to the quilt. She moaned in her sleep and he felt a twinge of remorse. People were cruel to one another, biting and snapping when hurt, like animals. It took too much courage to be the one to sheath one's claws first. You went on snarling mindlessly, day following day, and it became an easy habit. He couldn't remember the last time they had felt or shown any tenderness towards one another.

He thought of their child inside that mound beneath the bed-clothes. It must be almost fully formed by now. God, the idea of that enormous pulsing head, like an anatomical model, with every vein and sinew on display as through glass. A film of the foetus he had seen on television had haunted him. A skinned thing, like a dead rabbit after the fur has been stripped over its head like an

154

elastic stocking, only this one was alive, fluttering at that very moment with closed eyelids. The membrane over the eyes was so delicate. He ached to think of it. His fingertips burned with the unbearable concept. He clung to the bed-rail. Torment after torment. Arriving unheralded at any time . . . day or night.

Outside Quigley's door he had halted, his grasp squeezing in around the smooth cold brass knob. A tremor shook him, leaving his knees a little rubbery at the thought of the two of them in the far inner room. How would they be lying? Him on top? Her on top? Side by side pressing? Perhaps she would have her hand –

He squeezed the knob convulsively and entered, feeling the sympathetic hard budding of his own desire, unreliable as ever. His throat had dried. When he saw Quigley lying there alone and watching him, propped up on one pyjama-covered arm, his voice croaked. He said something stupid like – "So you're awake, are you?" and clumsily moved his hands about in the air before him. Had the other noticed his state? He stole a glance at him now. Theirs was an awkward relationship, each one buttressed up inside his own intense awareness of the other. Mercifully he had got over that stage at the beginning when he had been unable to refrain from making blind emotional rushes, trying to jolt the other into a similar involvement. Ruby had jeered, *you look after him better than you do me, your own wife*. He had caught Bridie smirking. What foulness had she swirling around in that little sewer mind?

Together, silently, they walked down along the long line of parked cars, each one pulled tight to the hedge. He thought, if the police find the main, it's the fields for all of us, running like hares, because there's no turning any car on a track like this. The image of all in full flight, across bog and stream, appealed to him. The shambles, the curses, the un-fit men floundering in holes. Dickey in his expensive sheepskin coat and point-to-point trousers. Ha ha. Swish of wet grass, grey light, myriad spiders' webs cruelly exposed on every bush, and the birds, christ, he had never heard such a racket, where did they come from? A frantic congregation screeching, as if it was their last big chance . . . Yarr felt cold, unreal. This was the time when no man should be abroad. Even revellers had fallen into their beds by now. A cruel time, not for humans.

Around the last bend waited the remains of what once had been a farm. Nettles sprouted from rubble, walls wavered waist-high; what shelter there once had been for farm animals existed no longer. He wondered who the genius was who had discovered this spot. It was like a place on the moon. But tenanted – for there were coats on the walls, baskets and bags which had held birds, a stick or two – and one lone human sitting with his knees up, and his hands shaking loosely and uncontrollably. They passed Tolan, avoiding his eyes – but christ, the mouth! A red sagging slash. He managed to be at every wake, funeral and event for miles around, a figure with the face of doom, giving the children bad dreams and grown men uneasiness. He nodded to him, god knows why, and his shaking accelerated until it seemed his head would fall off at their feet.

When they appeared in the gap above the field where the main was being held, the heads swung up and around. A fight had just ended and even the gamblers turned from their pitch and toss. Yarr felt fear as the eyes swept up to them, cold as the grey water in the river beyond, seeing them and then carrying the information back to the brain to be used in a way he knew not. The elation he had experienced earlier leaked out of him. The bastards, he whispered to himself, the bastards. Will I never be able to best them? All those faces, not showing enmity, just nothingness. It couldn't be described, just had to be borne. On fairdays in Slaney, the same look at a stranger as he walked past them, prickling under his clothes. Behind him he heard the bubbling hiss of Tolan, thrash of his feet in the grass, and he moved downhill in a panic.

The circle had been cut in the sod, the waiting birds hung inside their meal-sacks from a taut rope in the Volkswagen (the complete side of the van opened out to the air on two wide doors) the next two fighting cocks were being weighed on the scales – an old man with white hair doled out weights from his veiny hand, as the owner delicately balanced his bird, only a split second of equilibrium needed before whipping the bundle of feathers on its horny yellow stalks away. Another old man with innocent eyes fed the second cock on brandy-soaked pellets of bread from an enamel mug. He ceased feeding it and began methodically to squirt quenching mouthfuls of water at the tiny fierce head. The horrible little bright eyes of it glittering beneath the spray.

Quigley and he, they walked around observing, and already he sensed a lessening of tension. The ring of gamblers had turned their faces inwards again to the tosser flipping up his laden comb.

156

The coins flew with heavy grace into the air to turn, flashing once, before hitting the turf. There was a smell of crushed grass and fresh dung – the cows in the fields had been roused from their night positions and wandered aimlessly about, chewing, dropping khaki streams. A mist hung inches from the surface of the river, safely clear of the fast-flowing pull of grey water. A dog barked in the distance. And the cocks crowed from the darkness of their bags in a disturbed way, as if the dawn had taken them unawares. They were in the most private place in the whole of Ireland. He marvelled at the way all the men and their possessions seemed to fit the scene, as if they had been there for years instead of an hour. In the same way he could never reconcile the before and after of a circus setting until the tent and caravans had gone and nothing remained save the bruised grass.

The next fight was about to begin. One cock was ready and its owner walked about with it held to his cheek, whispering, stroking, cajoling the little evil head. The other was still having his spurs fitted. The steel points, fastened to the legs with black insulating tape, several tight layers, then twine bound around so that nothing could interfere with the efficiency of the kill. The man doing it held the bird lovingly, his brown, big-fingered hands caressing and moving surely, careful to the point of tenderness.

When both birds were ready – a brown and a white pair – the men holding them circled, darting the birds at each other to enrage them. The tiny eyes glittered like sequins, catching the early morning light and the feathers on their necks stood straight out in a ruff. Then two fast touches to the turf and the battle had begun. At the beginning the spectators held silent, intent on spotting first signs of a supremacy, and it was very still, the sun big and bloated now above the river mist, a red ball, cries of birds and the deadly beating of wings. But in a very short while the victor proclaimed himself. The white cock had begun to falter, falling before the brown's insistence, its mouth agape and trickling blood. Each wound and its position was hallooed by the crowd. The feathers were stained as if by oil spots, a wing hanging useless. The men started mocking the dying cock. Once it was mounted and lay supine under the spurring, pecking frenzy. Ribald shouts rang out.

On occasions, its owner went into the ring to retrieve his bird, the rules of the game allowed him this, and he massaged it, and holding it up, put its head in his own mouth. Its blood ran down his chin. The crowd began to shout for him to put it back in the ring or else call a draw. He ignored them, immersed in dialogue with his bird, intent, it seemed, on still making a miracle out of the soiled bundle of feathers. But each time he laid it in the ring it crouched closer to the ground, as if to scoop a nesting place, shaking mutely under the other cock's attacks. Finally, it fell over on to its side with its talons spread, the blood gargling in its throat.

The winner limped around it still pecking. His little head stretched out like a weapon to probe and be withdrawn at a moment's danger. Someone swished a meal-bag at him and he leapt into the air and away, cackling in alarm. Yarr hated it in the same way he had once hated a weasel he had owned. It had bitten him badly once, swinging heavily from his thumb, teeth buried, like a venomous yellow tippet. He had lost it down a rabbit-hole in McGookin's wood.

Quigley was watching the dying bird being carried off, its head bumping through the grass and cow-clap. Then the good old stretch of the neck and into the whins with it well out of sight, so that no one would ever know a main had been fought. What was he thinking? Yarr wanted a sudden display of excitement or disgust, even, as his reward for showing him this. He watched, recognising neither.

Quigley merely said, "How many fights will there be?" And he said in return, "Oh about a dozen – maybe more. It all depends on how many birds there are."

And then he began to laugh, for no reason. It might have been nerves, then thought – *must* have been, by christ. The tight knots in his stomach when he'd found out he'd been tricked, the killing concentration on reversing the defeat, sweating, sick, asking, asking, racketing the car into farmyards and up lanes, straight over a hen once, by jesus, it hadn't a prayer – leaving its splattered feathery mass stamped into the road, fuck that, shush, shush to Quigley, don't bother me now, *don't bother me*. I haven't let you down yet. Have I? *Have I?* Those bastards, laughing at *him*, laughing. Ha ha ha . . .

They were all staring. Drinking him in, eating him up. Oh oh oh. He didn't know why he was doing it. But it was him – him who was laughing, it was, wasn't it? And he didn't know why . . .

One of the bastards came up and said to Quigley, "You'd better keep your friend quiet. He'll be having the guards down on us. This is a private meeting. We don't want any outsiders." *Him.* A yokel in a tan boiler-suit and wellington boots. Big beef-steak face on him. Now look here, *cunt* . . . But he was still laughing. Ribs sore now. Holding them in tight with his elbows.

Quigley said, "Maybe we'd better –" touching him. He shook loose, still laughing, and staggered a little to one side, seeing at his feet, miracle of miracles, a mushroom in the grass, little white button one hiding itself, holding its breath in case it was spotted. Nice to be a little mushie-room. There in the morning, gone in a day, little pale penis head, so quiet, so calm. He must touch it. Flesh taut, its woody smell, the dark secret gills underneath. The bastards all began to laugh then and the stalk snapped in his hand. He hadn't meant to do it – but they all laughed out loud. He heard them, saw them too. Young John Joe was making cracks behind his palm to them and they laughed hard and cruel on his cues. At him. Dickey the vet, Fonsey Meehan, Packy Traynor, McKnight, Micky Joe Quinn, Slavin, Guthrie, Slowey, Maguire, Delaney, Tubridy, Scullion, O'Hare, Devlin, Glass . . . even Tolan . . . oh god . . . *he* was leaping in the air, his limbs stiffened, a crow-call coming from his lips, getting excited . . . even Tolan.

His own laughing stopped short, and he felt the pain in the stomach and ribs. He stood there on the short green grass looking down, kicking at the base of the mushroom. His toe dug out a hole in the woody fibre. Shreds of the compost flew, and he thought – but he didn't think – this was too much, too terrible (stupid fucking word). He had gone over this time. How long did he stand there? – because he couldn't move – *couldn't*, and how do you explain that to someone? – You in a five-acre field and can't get your bloody legs to move. *Jesus Christ, oh sweet jesus christ, get me out of this, I'm dying and I can't, can't, can't . . .*

They all went back to the cock-fighting. It was like his first day at school, in the playground, after he had been inspected and found lacking in interest, and he stood alone against the stone wall, pressed to it with his back tight, and all the school were playing their own big game away there on the far side, with the sun picking light off the gravel, making the distance in between them and him seem impossibly far . . . but now there was no wall, no hand-bell to ring and suck them all off indoors, to leave him alone.

He felt his arm touched. Quigley put on a little pressure, and his legs fumbled forward. They moved towards the gate. What had happened had been an aberration. True. And up to that moment he had been the only one to know about it, or recognise such a thing when it occurred. But this time, this time, it had been plain for all to see. He wore his mark now for all of them, as plain as a caste mark. So where to now? Where?

YELLOW ENVELOPE WITH the new Diefenbaker ten cent stamps and the Trans-Film imprint on the outside just to prepare me for the blow. Mac says: *You're a lousy bum and how you ever got into my business I'll never know. You conned me o.k. but now follow through or else. I could fire you as fast as it takes this to reach you – but I won't. I know you'll do it for me all by yourself. Don't disappoint me, Quigley.*

My free translation. To anyone else it read that because of "certain fluctuations in the film documentary industry, Trans-Film '(him, *him*, not Trans-Film)' had found it necessary to restrict the series *The Old Country* to six parts instead of the agreed seven. This was regrettable but ... I therefore must understand" – bottom of the page, my god, what's coming – "that each producer already on location should at this stage promptly submit a proposed treatment of his film for analysis and comparison, so that it should be decided quickly which six films should be selected before any needless expenditure on a seventh be incurred." Tailpiece. "You will also understand that the above implies strong possibility of a redundancy in the production staff." Oh, Mac, Mac . . .

Dear Machiavelli or Mac for short – a letter now from me to you (which you'll never see, by the way, but still, never mind that . . .) Dear Mac, received yours of the 12th June and was shocked –shit-shocked, to be crude – at first, but am now in a curiously euphoric state, feeling freer than I've ever felt before (yeah, off his rocker, yeah, I know, *I know*) But to return to the business in hand . . . okay, old boss-man, so I'm fired, redundant, or will be as soon as you receive those treatments to "analyse" and "compare". A mere formality of course. What restraint you show. What cleverness to choke off Quigley so painlessly and privately, without giving him a hope in hell to fight back. However, I have news for you. He intends to fight back – he does – and even from *his* impossible position.

Because. Mind cold, ticking over fast, ruthlessly. First, a phone-call to Dublin to check on the camera crew. Mac will not (or will he?) have countermanded his previous standing orders to that

161

source as yet. Pinning my hopes on the fact that he won't –
couldn't – at this stage, conceive of my madness. The little blind
spot in the grey computer brain. If he hasn't cancelled the booking
of the crew (and, anyway, why should he at this stage? He likes his
little game with Quigley too much, and if he acted now it would
give that game away too soon, wouldn't it?) I have a week, a little
more probably, to shoot the film, blaming my action later on the
eccentric postal service, not having received his letter (letters) so I
have my rushes, shot at speed, and what to lose? Out of a job; but
be honest, Quigley, deep down you still cherish a hope that this
film will be so marvellously good that not even a MacLachlan will
be able to refuse it. Logic horse-laughs loudly, because rushes are
a gamble anyway and Mac is a law unto himself. But still . . .

Now. Purposeful word, indicating a great rolling up of sleeves,
getting down to business. Once it's been said – what? It marks the
outer limits of pipe-dream country – and beyond? – nothingness.
And it's no good pacing up and down, Quigley, sharpening that
pencil, taking a leak, mirror-gazing, scratching your goddam
crotch – *you can't come up with a bloody thing*; so face it. All those
cartoons about the Muse, not funny. That sulking bitch. Probably
having her periods, the slut. Just my luck.

Over and under, in and out, through a maze of notes on the backs
of envelopes, flattened out cigarette packs, a playing card, a menu
. . . Some of the words illegible, scribbled in great drunken
moments of inspiration, when everything fitted into place. Co-
ordinating the cosmos in some bar or other. All those scraps in
front of me now on this bedroom table. Stubborn solitaire. With
nothing better (more fruitful) to do I've leafed through this
journal – this log of Quigley's last voyage. I can see now my
delusion that these observations would be of use. I was merely
putting off the evil day. Drugging myself with the nightly ritual of
words. Or perhaps I half-hoped-believed that one day they would
be treasured as the written thought processes of a great director.
Did I? Poor Quigley . . .

More confidences. You see, I'm hooked. Main-lining merrily. So
what'll I write about? Some more random useless observations . . .
Yes, The Orange Hall Soirée. Yarr's people living it up with
heavy-footed abandon. A dusty, decaying building with broken,

rag-stuffed window panes set in a low swampy place beside the road. The cars parked for a mile along the grass verges of this border cart-track. No man's land. Only recently the spikes marking the line between North and South have been removed. Ripped out like teeth from the tarmacadam. Blotchy scars remaining. Great smuggling country, Yarr tells me, despite the spiked roads. Pigs were drugged – cocaine – to get them across quietly. The myths are already fully-formed. Fortunes made in a single good season. Several of the local lucky-strikers pointed out to me at this dance. Red-necked respectable elders of the church with religious stickers plastered on the back windows of their latest model Rovers, Fords, Vauxhalls. *Jesus Saves. Another Morris.* They are building a new hall at the cross-roads.

The platform festooned with union jacks. A great Orange banner, scarlet and gold, with tassels and fringing, flying frozen on the wall above. A painted Brother Ephraim Gowdy sternly surveying the scene. His oiled hair cleft, his moustache walrus, his watch gold hunter, one hand on the hilt of his sabre, the other brandishing a holy bible. Scourge of the unbeliever. Merciless Mahomet.

A speech from the platform. "Brother Worshipful Master, Brothers and Sisters, ladies and gentlemen ..." Appeals for funds, pledges of undying support for the Queen, the Orange Order, the Right Honourable Member of Parliament for West Armagh. "If he isn't too busy he will make an appearance later to draw the ballot" – (disappointment expressed about the Prime Minister's recent Vatican leanings, hatred for the Archbishop of Canterbury, Cardinal Heenan, the Catholic Inquisition in Spain and South America, the present Pope) ... Solemn faces. Remembering 1690.

Then a great roaring, clumping square-dance, The Lancers, to release tension. The men in shirt-sleeves, braces criss-crossing muscular backs, hopping, guffawing, swinging their girls clear off the floor. Shrieks of *"Stop! Stop!"* Legs slicing the air. One girl flies, peeling off from the ring neatly like a projectile, into a pile of chairs. On her bruised knees sobbing, stockings ripped, plump young face upturned, streaked with dust. Surrounded by stout aproned matrons in a moment, and taken off to the kitchen. Her beau, sheepish, wanders around the perimeter of the floor, hands deep in pockets, shoulders hunched, whistling with the band.

I don't warm to these people. The old atavism again? What would have happened if they'd discovered my religion, the one on my birth certificate anyway. A powder-keg feel in the air. An invisible wind blowing them between extremes. That savage seriousness during the speeches, then the great brutality of the dance. Yarr's people. The Protestant ruling minority. An ugly face. In-breeding? No poet will ever sing for them – of them.

Wednesday night. No further forward. Except of course, that my Dublin phone call paid off as I hoped. Mac boobed. As I hoped. But I don't feel any consolation. The crew arrive on Saturday and will stay as long as I want them – *but what are they going to shoot?*

Today after we arrived home from the cock-fight I couldn't rest. Nerves snapping like terriers. Spent the morning and afternoon mooching about the shop, the house, the shop, the house. Yarr closed up and took to his bed. His wife upstairs too. Bridie gone home to her parents on her bicycle. Just me and the shadowy shelves behind the drawn blind and some old records I found in a dusty box. Fats Domino, Johnny Ray, Nat King Cole, Kay Starr, Frankie Laine, Guy Mitchell – the hits of Yarr's young manhood when he was courting or just married. Hard to visualise these old seventy-eights and their choruses colouring the love-life of that disturbed man lying over my head.

> *I found my thrill on Blueberry Hill,*
> *On Blueberry Hill where I met you.*

I can't even see him having a youth. Why? Yet an early photograph of him in my room. Eighteen or nineteen. Open neck shirt, baggy wide trousers held up by his Boy Scout belt, strong tanned arms folded across chest. An open manly face, staring straight at the Brownie. A summer Sunday snap in the garden or at the sea, or on a country road with girls and other young lads larking and laughing and signalling to him to say cheese. What happened? I compare the framed image with the other, the more real. He's imprinted himself on me. A week, night and day together, until we seem merged. A marriage? We've never quarrelled. Let's face it, we don't *talk* at all. Why? But why why?

164

He's got me all screwed up too, like himself. Whatever he's got it's contagious. Some creeping horror eating him from the inside out. When it pokes its ole hungry head through, don't be around, Quigley. Sees himself now as my eyes and ears. And God forgive me I've encouraged him. But enough of that. Conscience is the one luxury you don't carry in your grips, Quigley. Not you. A few twinges, naturally, for the first day or two after you've waved good-bye to that long line of "used" people, but then the next sucker looms up. So be realistic. Anyway, you didn't promise him anything. *He* built it up, not you. Drop him a cheque, a facilities fee after a few days. He'll be all right. Tell him tomorrow. Yeah, tomorrow. Letting it fall easily, off-hand, cool. *Look, Yarr, I'm pulling up stakes. Must move on. So, see you. Keep in touch. O.K.? O.K.*

Easy? Easy . . .

THE FIRST SHOCK passed through-over him, and he surprised
himself by immediately snapping the book shut and going across
to the door to open it, so that he would be able to hear anyone –
Quigley – come up the stairs, not wolfing what was written a
second, third time in terrible stiffening unbelief *but going
carefully to the door and pulling it open*. It was like putting aside a
tit-bit to save for later. The strangeness of his action pricked him
more strongly, in that moment of time, than the other. Which
hadn't risen far enough in his brain yet like a staining red flood.

His hand rested on the cover calmly, finger-tips registering the
pimpled texture, a single embossed word. And again, inconse-
quentially he thought – *diary, diary*, and the spelling confusion of
schooldays. The drawer he had found it in yawned open. Inside,
exposed, the neat pile of Quigley's shirts – blue, grey, cream, with
soft collars that buttoned down, socks, underwear and his
zippered leather bag. Defenceless, vulnerable – like seeing into a
man's soul. And reading the private thoughts he had written too?

So he found the place again, it was the last entry. He read that
one passage at least a dozen times, then put the book back exactly
where he had found it beneath the shirts, closed the drawer
quietly and – and there ended all calmness and orderly action. Yet
it was strange how one half of his thinking still managed to keep
pace with the other, for skimming the darker depths ran the
thought – they say no one ever hears well of himself – in his case,
now, of course, *seeing* what someone had *written*.

He sat on Quigley's bed and looked down at his hands. There
was a slight shake. He heard his wife whispering in the next room.
She had moaned steadily for the last few hours. That, in fact, was
what had driven him out of bed to go prowling, searching. He
brought his hand up to his face. He trembled. He began to cry
softly behind his hand, his fingers becoming wet. Not tears.
Saliva.

It was a little after twelve o'clock, his wife lay in the next room,
and there were no sounds from below. Twelve o'clock, Friday, the
fourteenth of June, nineteen sixty-seven. It should be written
down. An occasion. Would he remember it? Point to a calendar
and say that's when I – ? Oh, but his head felt as if it must burst
with the growing pressure of thoughts stirred up and rising. His
mind like a bath about to overflow in one of those sums he could

166

never do in school. If it takes a cistern two hours etcetera . . . The stupidest thoughts, yet all adding their own pressure, filling crevices. He pounded with the heels of his hands, then looked avidly in the mirror to gauge the redness of the marks he had caused. Then he thought of the bed. Why not crawl down into the darkness, until the dark cave heated up? But no bed in the house was safe. He would merely lie there trembling, suffocating, then darting his head out in terror. What was that? *What was that?* Oh, please, god, please, what do you do? *What do you do?*

He jumped off the bed and the springs creaked back into place. There was a photograph of himself on the mantelpiece between two brass boots. He couldn't remember when it had been taken. It was foreign to him, could have been of anyone, any of his friends when he was younger. He turned it face to the wall, then couldn't bear the sight of the dusty back, and reversed it again. The eyes looked straight into his, the mouth mocked. Strangers to each other. *I don't know you – don't care to either. Fuck you.* Like Quigley. But he wouldn't think – wouldn't allow himself thoughts. Would keep a cord strangle-tight around this pipe they were pouring through. The image bit into him. Then images. Once again. They came flocking . . .

Wet red tubing, skinned turkey neck, a pulse rippling up and down to the ligature, up, down, a steady press, pressure on the knot, sucking back each time, the thoughts bunched in line waiting for the first one to slither through, soft like eggs without shells, mucus covered, green-streaked, wobbling with the lust to succeed . . . one does, a cone in its passion, inserting its newly pointed head, a stretching sperm, wet plop as its bulbous base is pulled through, now another plugs itself into the moist black eye, another, another, another . . . elvers, thread-worms, evolution in a split second, no let-up . . . inside his head now, each blowing up like a bubble, cramming space, squeezing in each other's soft transparent sides, images, faces inside clawing at the membranes to escape, foetuses, his, his, his own thing with his face and tiny pink paws scrabbling, mouth wide in dumb howl . . . all bursting open now, shelling pods thick and fast, screaming, churning stew, faces and hair washing against his bone . . . they would soon find his eyes, ears, nose, mouth, rupturing those delicate shutters, out to boil through steaming, shrieking . . . aaah . . .

It was his own voice, while *his* hands were clapping ears and mouth, eyes and ears. He stood seeing himself in the mirror, and it was as though something terrible had just retreated from the glass.

He listened. His wife had stopped moaning. He could feel her attention.

He lurched out on to the landing, grabbed for the banisters, missed, his foot slipped on the linoleum, skated between two of the rails, he came down on the back knee, his chin cracking on the hand-rail, and his teeth rang.

In that ridiculous position he remained for a moment panting, feeling his bleeding lip with his tongue. The temptation to stay where he was, as resigned as a cornered rabbit, was strong. A series of bolt-holes held out ecstasy. He could race hunched from one to the next, dodging the horrors in between, a flying man on foot. But he could remain in this one no longer. Someone might appear and he couldn't look into another face, other eyes. He would crack like a dry twig. His leg trembled when he withdrew it. He had to take care as he went down the stairs because it felt weightless beside the other, hollow, papery.

At the closed street door he paused, wiping his brow. The hallway simmered, the pane above the door burning so that he couldn't bear to look at it, there was a smell of blistering paint and a circular that had dropped through the letter-box on to the mat had its edges curled up like a scorched leaf. Deadening heat everywhere, that had him tossing on top of the bed-clothes at night, searching for cool spots on the pillow or on the turned down sheet. Stockinged feet left damp imprints on the linoleum, hands on the backs of chairs, handles and knives. Heat. He swayed. Heat. He thought of water, river-water, brown as cold tea, silk-soft on his shoulders, tightening his skin. He used to feel his balls surreptitiously through the wet wool of his trunks, delighting in their satisfying weight and firmness. Now they drooped, limp skins.

A guffaw from the street started him shaking again. It was very near and he shrank to the wall, his cheek pressed to the cool paint, listening, picking out voices. There were several men. Perched on a window-sill – *his* sill, their legs stuck out before them, spitting and swearing. They were laughing at him. He knew it. He recognised the owner of the loudest, worst laugh. Rocky Byrne – red-headed bully boy. *They had put Rocky Byrne on to him.*

His face was pressed to the green painted wall, nose flattened, lips spread, wet. Maybe they were waiting before they came in after him, to kick him about his own kitchen. He could hear his voice screaming, imploring, amidst the crash of broken furniture. No one to help him. No one. Quigley was out. Quigley. He remembered the words in the book. Quigley. No. Not Quigley. He wept silently. They had him trapped. The world seemed to be poised waiting to close in.

He shut his eyes but that was worse. It was like being in a coffin. He couldn't breathe. He pulled back the letter-box flap on its spring, to see out, but his view was blocked by somebody's green van. He tried to draw air in through the slot, then thought of someone seeing his open mouth and pushing something unspeakable into it. In his fear at the idea he let the flap snap back and it cracked loudly so that the hallway rang.

Now he was on his hands and knees, so that anyone looking in from outside would see over his head. But he wasn't down far enough. Face on the rough-fibred mat, palms on the tiles, his chest, belly and thighs pressed to the same flat plane, he breathed in dust. He sneezed and again the sound reverberated, making him want to shriek. A second time he sneezed, and in the middle of it, his head snapping forward, he heard a sound behind him. It came from the stairs. He was like a stranded seal, couldn't get his head around fast enough, it was filled with blood, his eyes bulging.

Looking down at him was his wife. They stared at one another. Then she began to move towards him, one foot pushed out carefully before the other, ponderously, her belly jutting. She said, "I'm . . . I'm . . ." getting closer all the time. She would crush him, letting fall her heavy weight upon him. He could feel the moist mass of her flesh as it sought him. "I'm . . . I'm . . ." She moaned now. He twisted himself up off the floor, oh god, the blood in his ears roaring like a weir – and fell against the door, clawing for the catch.

Out in the street he ran, doubled over, the sun licking at him through the stretched cloth on his shoulders. The whole street was watching him, all eyes and mouth. It was as if they had sensed what was to take place and so had stationed themselves in readiness.

He ran past Mrs Ryan and her two youngest. She pushed their round black heads firmly back between her apron-covered legs, so they wouldn't see a madman in broad daylight. Stunt their fucking growth. Ha, ha, ha, he choked, then bumped into McDaid the postman, he looked at him dumb as a post – ha ha ha – his bag swung round his middle by the whirling force. On. Around the corner, jogging like a long distance runner, past Nolan's garage, a quick glance into the cavern, the goggled men in their pool of blue sparks. *Run, you poor mad cunt you, run, Yarr.* How far would he stick it? The bridge? The parochial house? The oak with the horse-shoe nailed to it? The old railway station? On. On.

His heart and lungs gave out at Breen's pub. Panting, straining, he dropped on to a bench outside. He put his head back, closed his eyes and waited for the machinery to slow down. The sun stung his lids and he felt sick, the first normal ache he had had in the past hour. His adam's apple was like a knot, so he dropped his head further on to his chest. Then he glanced up. Four men were standing at the corner watching him. They began to laugh loudly when they saw that he had seen them. One of them shouted, "Bang, bang!" and made a gun gesture. The others roared and followed suit delightedly, stamping their feet, pointing their forefingers. A group of children joined them and, after staring from him to the men and back again with open mouths, entered the game.

The noise seemed to fill the air, beating at him. He put his hand over his ears, rocking his body. The children were taking short runs towards him now, then racing back for applause. He heard them shouting something and he took his hands away from his ears. It was a refrain, rhythmical, to the beat of their clapping and stamping. "The *I.R.A.* will *get* you, the *I.R.A.* will *get* you." Old Johnny Carbin's cry. The word had got out that he was marked. *Hunt Yarr. No mercy for Yarr.* "Bang! Bang!" Real bullets soon, tearing his flesh into pink tatters, dum-dum, blood, blood . . .

A child threw a stone. It fell a few yards away and he looked at it as if it were an animal or a crab which scuttled towards him across the pavement. Without taking his eyes off it, he stood up, his back pressed to the wall and moved along sideways, his coat brushing off discs of whitewash.

He found the catch of the pub door by groping and almost fell backwards into the cool porter-smelling dimness. Safe for a little while anyway. They wouldn't follow him in here. Young John Joe and the others, he knew, had a long-standing feud with Mrs Breen about a stolen ash-tray. But it was little consolation. It was like changing feet on a red-hot griddle. He took a drink – whiskey – from the woman without really seeing her. His change lay scattered on the wet counter, and she took away enough for each new drink without saying a word, as he gulped the previous glassful. It could have been water, he didn't taste; some of it ran down his chin to stain his shirt. His back was to the bar, his eyes on the door and the wired window above the shutters, and he brought around each glass from behind him, groping for its wet sides, sliding it over the wood, then up to his face.

He was dulled now, a blanket muffling his brain, hobbling his legs. He moved them, swinging little kicks at the air, rolling his head, all the weight in his face falling down to his jaws. His lips hung like pieces of meat. His face felt brutish, a pig snout and jowl, wobbling. He spat at the floor, and the saliva flew in a sticky string from his mouth. He tried to wipe it from his chin, smearing it across his cheek. Wire brush. He rubbed the back of his hand, moving his chin like a rasp.

An uncle used to do that to him as a boy, taking delight in his wriggling. Bear-hugging Uncle Walton. He smelt of engines and oily waste. He was a fireman on the G.N.R. Dead of cancer of the throat last year. He weighed four stone when they buried him. Cancer was the worst, the worst. Could you have cancer of the brain? The brain was like a plastic bag full of grey jelly, he had read, so the cancer would squeeze the stuff out through the tears in the polythene. It would come through like cake-icing from a nozzle, or toothpaste. He felt his own head, searching for bumps, thin places in the bone. A baby's head had a hollow the size of the bottom of a cup when it was born. The drumskin covering it rose and fell, a pulse. You could puncture it easily. Then the bone grew across and knitted. His own head had a ridge. Once he had a crew-cut and his head looked strange, knobbed like a turnip. He couldn't wait until the hair grew. Now he was almost bald on the top. Eventually the skin would get shiny and stretch. Funny how it never tore. Stretch a yard before it'd tear an inch. That was a woman's thing. They said Mrs Breen was the village bicycle before she got married. Give us a look at your oul' twat, Mrs Breen. Or a bit of your chat. People didn't realise what they were saying when they said that. A commercial traveller for french letters had told him that. He said Gaelic was the dirtiest language in the world. Full of double meanings. Like chat for fanny and other things like that. Americans used fanny for arse. Quigley did. Quigley. He tried not to think of him, but he couldn't.

Why did he have to write that? Why did *he* have to read it? He thought of him and the way he smiled, his unexpected shynesses in company and how *he* had tried to divert attention from him by brisk action and comment and he had never noticed, never noticed. He thought of his skin and his clean smell and the way he coughed with nerves and the way he could get sentimental and emotional when he was drunk. He said direct things, what was in his mind came straight out at such times, and you felt embarrassed at first, then you got affected too and you started saying things you had always kept locked away and you got swept away until you noticed he wasn't listening to you but had gone blurry-eyed with drink or depressed and inward looking. He had charmed you into believing you could fly above heads, and now he had taken it all away. His eyes had a film over them, he felt he could cry easily. Experimentally he concentrated on squeezing out a tear. His eyes swam. Warmth, softness, mushy wetness, lovey-dove love.

He would ring him up, so he would. Why the hell not? He'd ring Quigley up – there was a phone in the corner – and he'd tell him all the things he'd been thinking and had never been able to come out with. He would say – well, he didn't know exactly, but it would come when he heard the voice at the other end. Two three nine, his own number; it was a great idea. He'd ring him and ask him to come down to Breen's and they'd get drunk together, and then they'd go out into the street, and if any of the tormentors were still hanging about, sure they'd go through them like a dose, scattering them to the winds. He clenched his fists and spat, missing the knuckles.

Two three nine. He raked for four pennies among the wet change. The mouthpiece reeked of stale tobacco and his stomach quavered. He dialled – first time. He heard his phone ringing at the other end and saw it in his mind's eye sitting on top of the old red Belfast street directory. It was just inside the room, between hall and shop, he used as a store for the perishable goods of his stock. The smell of cheesy butter that time the Skerrybahn went off in last June's heat-wave. His stomach heaved a second time.

"Hello," a voice at the end of the line in his own house. Quigley's. He knew it would be. Why? Was he at the beginning of a circle of events all working for him, with him? His finger explored the slight concavity of button A.

"Hello, who's that?"

Some sort of noise behind the voice. Other voices talking together. A crowd. Babble. *"Hello, hello, who is that?"* People. In the house. The sweat dried on him, chilling armpits, chest, crotch. His breath began to howl in the mouthpiece. "Yarr? Is that *you*?"

He hurled the hand-set from him. It struck the wall and dropped and swung on the end of the spiralling flex. The woman behind the bar shouted, "Here, what's that?" and raised a white face. "Come back, *come back*!"

But he ran down the dark passageway, bumping himself on the walls. The door opened outwards but he had it nearly off its hinges before that fact dawned on him. Outside he saw a dustbin against one of the yard walls and he leaped for its dome. The lid began to slither, but he managed to get on to the sloping roof of the gents. Corrugated tin and none too safe. From inside you could see the sky through the lacy wafer of red dust. His soles slipped on the ridges as he took the slight gradient in three strides.

The drop was his own height, and he crouched among nettles, broken bottles and delph and tins, chin on chest, panting. He could smell the plants he had crushed. There was whitewash on his hands and his fingertips felt abraded.

He was on the run. Around him the no man's land that circled the back gardens and walls of the village. He would have to get across this waste of weeds and rubbish, a ducking, dodging target, for they were *all* out to get him, he knew that now, oh yes, he knew it all right. His hands clenched fistfuls of green dock as he braced himself with his heels and shoulders against the whitewashed wall. John Wayne at Okinawa. Bullets stitching the air. He was back again with the other children of the village. McNulty's grass-grown dunghill to be taken. Across the fox-hole riddled scrubland. And once he left this wall he would be exposed, a cockroach crossing a lighted room, a frog on the highway. He stood up and his legs were quivering. One last comforting feel of the wall – then he was off running, doubled, his hands dangling, head twisting from side to side. The sun glazed each window at his back to a gold lens. *They* were watching his progress from behind the glass. He kept listening for a sash to be raised. Then he would dive, face down among the weeds and wait for a pain between his shoulders. How long would he have to lie there, rolling about in a shallow trench of his own making? How many wounds would it take? He remembered a foreign film. Man running across such an expanse, slowing, feet stumbling, hands spread across his stomach over the leak. Then down finally among the rubbish, knees to chin, twisting the way a dying eel does when you throw him on to the bank, dirt and grass sticking to him.

An old hoop caught his foot and he fell, jarring himself. His palms were imprinted with grit, his cheek burned. Up again and on, zigzagging. His ears now ached for a sound, the slightest sound, behind him, but the torture spun on and on, no relief for him, his feet lifting and falling like weights on wires. The unevenness of the ground made him stagger, heaped his exhaustion until his eyes misted. Blind now. He ran straight into a pool of liquid dung and urine. McNulty's yard. Upended carts, chickens, dark meal-houses. He had made it. How? Then he thought – *they're playing with me, that's it*. Waiting. No rush. Biding their time until the ripe moment. Maybe they had something special planned, maybe that was it, running him into a trap, down the funnel.

His feet and ankles felt chill. He looked down at his soaked shoes and socks. His footprints in the runny wet dung hadn't filled yet. They led to him accusingly. He lifted a graip that was nearby and dragged the tines through his tracks. Then waited until the wriggling marks disappeared under a watery green skin. A breathing space was all he needed. Time to think. Throw them off the scent and get time to think and plan. That was it. Time. He stood inside the door of a potato-house, hidden, looking out from the darkness, jabbing patterns in the soft floor – thinking. *He couldn't think. Couldn't.* All this talking to himself in his mind about what he would do. Fooling himself. He furrowed the skin on his forehead as if that could help, concentrated on a point beyond and between his closed eyes. *Think. Think.* His head started reeling and he almost fell on to some weighing-scales in a corner. He began to push his foot down, vying with the weights, then fell to taking the brown rusted blocks off one by one until his pressure eventually forced the remainder up – anything to put off the terror.

What was he doing? Playing while his time ticked away. But his mind had stalled. Each time he tried to begin the thought process he grew hysterical at its dead refusal. This business with the scales – what was it but only an attempt to catch the brain off-guard, like a quick reversal of direction? And fuck it, it wouldn't work, would it? No. Christ, but he *had* to do something, go somewhere, now, now, now. He beat his hands in time, *now, now, now*.

174

A rush of wings burst out of the darkness at his back and a laying hen exploded, squawking, up and out of a barrel. He screamed and ran for the door. Into the dying sunlight once more, escaping without direction over ruts and bumps and shaking so much that it seemed bits of him would drop off, so that by the time he did manage to halt there would be nothing left but a torso. Yes, his mind would come up with useless ideas of that order all right, but where, in the name of god, was he to go, to do?

The sound he had heard behind Quigley's phone voice began to chip at him as he ran. People. Why? How? A dozen at least, spilling through his shop, his rooms. Strangers touching things and looking into corners, behind doors, under furniture – examining *him*. Why? A strange sensation suddenly. He found himself torn between an ache to find out and the fear of what he might discover. The struggle roared in his brain as he ran and he couldn't run much longer, this pace wasn't limitless. Would he then have to start circling, plodding around and around behind the houses, slower and slower like a clockwork athlete, waiting for a switch to be turned.

His mouth hung open. He would die. Would that be all that bad? It would be peace certainly, but the ordeal to pay for it. Pay in advance. Collect later. He pressed the thought down deep. *Don't think about it. Don't think about it. Run. Run.* He tried closing his eyes and the jerk when he stumbled was worse than the flames in his lungs. If he could only stop, flop down among the ashy grass-grown mounds and curl up with his hands over his ears, his mouth and eyes closed tight. He might have to go on like this for a terrible period of time. The body held out incredibly before calling its own halt in its own sweet time. Starving or bleeding away stretched on and on. The only way to force an end was to – *don't think about it. Don't think. Run. Run.*

Then suddenly he was in the entry beside Grogan's heading for the main street. He had made a decision. *He had decided.* His feet slipped in the wet pig-swill peelings, his breath whistled, his ears roared with blood, but he had *chosen*.

He reached the pavement, slowed to a walk that carried him, hunched and straining, across to his own side. No one tried to stop him. The phenomenon registered like something blurred on a distant screen. There was no one about – not even a playing child or an old man taking ease in the sunlight, no one, *no one*. Now he could hardly hold himself in check. What was he going to find?

175

Everything that had happened, was happening to him, was sharpening to a fine point, converging on what lay in store.

The shop door was closed. It looked strange, a conspicuous rectangle of faded red set in the lay-out of window and surrounding pebble-dash. He had never seen it like this before. The other door – the house door – was wide open, back on its hinges as far as it would go. The contrast made him smile suddenly. He knew it for something that no one else would see or ever understand.

He stood on the step, ready to run, his head pushed in. The door facing was closed. He could hear voices muffled behind its wood and paint. In the kitchen, that's where they all were – waiting for him? He could go back now. But escape to what? How long could he keep on running? How long before the clockwork wound down? And could *they* hurt him all that much more?

He walked up the passageway, past the half-moon oak table under the mirror. He found himself glancing down to see if there was any mail. The top was bare, dusty, except for one finger-rubbed line. He put his hand on the door-knob and gently turned.

FACES. Eyes. The midwife's bag on the table. Faces. Old Tate's. A taper for his pipe burning unused down to his finger and thumb. *Eyes*. Mother-in-law's weeping ones. Mrs Jack Donnelly's too. All eyes on him. Trained. *Eyes*.

Something breaks inside him. Suddenly. Can't be explained to himself. No running commentary in his head any longer. He slides through, almost swimming across the room, to the step up into the kitchen. Nobody, nothing can hurt him now. He accepts it. Not faces. Not eyes. A charmed fish swimming past the neighbour women making tea in the best blue tea-pot with its Chinese bridge and summer-house. Tea, ham sandwiches, rich fruit-cake. Ritual food for births – deaths. He won't think of that, just swim, swim . . .

Out of the back-door, past rotting garbage, flies buzzing, along the path, swimming through the air smoothly. His arms and legs are fins. Tiny changes of direction steer his course. He is proud of his delicacy of manoeuvre. He is the only fish abroad this day. He will skirt the great ugly anchored things – people and objects – too fine for them, a beautiful tropical deep-sea creature, hair-line of bubbles breaking from his mouth, sipping little morsels of water between his gums. Why has it taken him so long to realise his true nature? And he is Pisces. He swims neatly into the gloom of the shed at the end of the garden, a dark underwater cave, the cobwebs seaweed, mermaids' combings. His head turns delicately to that corner, this, allowing the summons coming to him to strengthen. He begins to move to the privy – but no – that is not where he must go, all that is in the past and buried deep.

He opens a door that is seldom used, the latch sticks with rust, but he moves it without any wrenching effort, still true to his easy feeling. Beyond, a store-house with full racks of dusty new tyres, oilskin capes and yellow gas cylinders. Into another room then, lined with the more immediate part of his stock. He glides past the tinned foods, labels blurring in the corner of his right eye, straight on and down into the shop. The air is heated, light glows beyond the drawn blind. He allows himself time to become conditioned to the rise in temperature. He is delicate and cannot go straight out, so he idles along by the counter, his fingers brushing the wood edge. A notion about the blinds being drawn at this time of day snags his smooth flowing thoughts momentarily – but he doesn't think about that, not any longer, he is free.

177

Bolts to be drawn now, a handle turned, and he peers out of doors, with his head weaving from side to side. He sees Quigley at the corner, talking to some men. He doesn't know them, won't know them, won't know Quigley.

His van is parked a dozen yards away on his own side of the street. He looks at it, feeling his car keys in his jacket pocket, selecting by touch that one that opens the driver's door. Its surface isn't as smoothly worn as the ignition key. He holds the key in position inside his pocket, between finger and thumb, then moves out into the street. His senses stagger a little, sun and dust, and someone is boiling tar. Straight, direct to the van. He concentrates upon the long scratch above the rear wheel, exposing the pale olive underbody. A shout breaks behind him – Quigley – then someone else. He doesn't look up, even when he hears feet moving towards him. The key turns, the door opens, the hot seat stings his hands, engine catches and he drives off – free, *free*. The mirror holds a tableau – Quigley in the foreground, waving, his face perturbed, the others merely staring. He can't read any expression on those blurs – but he doesn't want to, so doesn't. Free. The wind starts coming in through the open window stirring his hair, cooling the interior. He drives perfectly, the car an extension of his moving body, because he is still gliding through air, water. There is no dividing line; the elements have blended into a perfect natural atmosphere for him to travel in. He feels it sliding past his hands and face; he opens his mouth to receive it. His clothes are a hindrance. As he drives – in the country now, but that is of no significance – he begins to remove them – tie, pullover, shoes, socks, shirt, vest, in that order – all come off to lie on the seat beside him, even his trousers and underpants. He is not surprised at the ease with which he manages it. The operation is smooth and unhurried. He uses one hand, knee, a foot at a time. Then the pile of clothes on the seat at his side begins to seem a minor irritant, so he pushes each garment out of the window as he drives. He watches their grotesque flapping in his mirror.

A crowd of children walking home from school come in to sight. He laughs at their faces as his shirt flies into their midst, draping itself over one small boy's head and shoulders. His last sight of them shows them leaping and waving it in the air with delight. Yes, they don't need to have it explained, they know.

He could speed for ever like an arrow, air breaking before his tip, but he has something to do. The words seem too trite for the plan that lies steady and still in his mind. He doesn't try to think when it first took shape. He just knows it grew there like some beautiful flower taking its own calm time, answerable to nothing but itself.

The van begins to slow at the touch of his bare foot on the pedal, the lane he is looking for is somewhere near. He sees the ridge of washed pebbles that marks its entrance, the reminder of past rains sluicing down a narrow bore. He swings in, changing down smoothly. His speed makes the van buck over the ruts and potholes, but its rhythm is stretched like that of a fairground hobbyhorse, long and undulating.

The brown and blue moorland begins to sweep in and then away from him as the ascent steepens. On the slopes ahead fire-breaks slice the afforestation into dark green rectangles. He passes a warning sign showing leaping flames. Beneath it lie a bundle of beaters made of poles and rusted tin flaps. They look unused. A smell of gorse enters the car. The air is sharp, wild. He breathes in deeply.

At the crest he looks down to his right. The village is a toy, a lived-in model only by the curls of smoke that merge quickly into the blue sky. He's so high, above all of it, high, high and free and the van soars on straight up Neely's mountain. And at the summit he doesn't pause, but roars over and down, stones spraying from his wheels. A wild drumming on the chassis underneath his bare feet. He's still laughing at the sensation as he drives straight into the heather for as far as the van will take him when the track finally dead-ends. The engine cuts and he sits at the wheel.

The van has tilted forward, the front wheels dropped in a black peat hole. Curlews cry and the wind patterns the surface of the bog water in the flooded trenches.

When he climbs out the breeze makes him gasp. Then he begins to run, bounding across the heather, leaping turf rows in his path. He feels blank inside, scoured. He flaps his arms in the air as he runs, feeling the sun on his bare shoulders. Run and swim, float and run. His jumps become higher, wilder, and he calls out to the sky and the moorland – a cry like the wild-fowl flying distressed far above his head. He mimics the curlews and a solitary lark like a palpitating dot high in the heavens. Three crows flap up clumsily from a rabbit carcase they've been feeding on by the

179

lough's edge. He hears their cry and shouts in delight. As the water rises up his legs he echoes, "Yarr ... Yarr ... Yarr ... Yarr." The brown obliterating depths rush to welcome him. Yarr yarr yarr ...

He didn't come home last night. But to be expected. The apogee of all these recent frenzies. Fireworks burst at the top of his long climb. Now the slow fall back to earth and sanity. Good for him. Good for me. A time for new beginnings. For both of us. And a time for burning books. This one. I don't even write this final chapter. The words sound in my head once, are born, die. No more tell-tale tale-telling.

Work. The "idea". So simple, so obvious – and staring me in the face all along. Why must it always be like this? So . . . A DAY IN THE LIFE OF YARR – one day in the life of *Albert* Yarr. That revelation discovered in an old kid's hymn book in my room upstairs.

"Albert," I'll say, when he returns – watching his face, "I have a proposition for you. How would you like to star" – no, an insult to his intelligence, an insult – "how would you like to be the main character in *our* film – one day in your life here in Ballyboe?" Of course then he'll say why me etc.? and I'll say – what will I say? what will I say? *Because there can be no one else.*

Yes. That obvious truth that has avoided me – both of us, so energetically, up to now. The final click of the safe combination when the cops' siren begins its scream. A day in the life of . . . the oldest, mossiest idea in the book, true, but the best. My mistake – also the oldest – to try too hard for something new and different. But all's well . . .

Priority is the treatment now. So that when he returns I can brief him right away. Then the crew will arrive at the week-end and we can begin shooting. The light is perfect now, perfect.

Yarr – the *new* Yarr will hold it all together. Every strand threaded through his eyes and ears. Simple, neat, perfect. And his jitters a thing of the past – like mine. A partnership at last. When he returns to find he's a papa all will be well. A son and heir to smooth out the worries. Yes, it's going to be good, it's going to be good – from now on.

A Selected List of Titles Available from Minerva

While every effort is made to keep prices low, it is sometimes necessary to increase prices at short notice. Mandarin Paperbacks reserves the right to show new retail prices on covers which may differ from those previously advertised in the text or elsewhere.

The prices shown below were correct at the time of going to press.

All these books are available at your bookshop or newsagent, or can be ordered direct from the address below. Just tick the titles you want and fill in the form below.

Cash Sales Department, PO Box 5, Rushden, Northants NN10 6YX.
Fax: 0933 410321   Phone: 0933 410511.

Please send cheque, payable to 'Reed Book Services Ltd.', or postal order for purchase price quoted and allow the following for postage and packing:

£1.00 for the first book, 50p for the second; **FREE POSTAGE AND PACKING FOR THREE BOOKS OR MORE PER ORDER.**

NAME (Block letters) ....

ADDRESS ....

....

☐ I enclose my remittance for ....

☐ I wish to pay by Access/Visa Card Number

Expiry Date

Signature ....

Please quote our reference: MAND